**Also in the *Wild* series
by Sasha Lord**

BEYOND THE WILD WIND

SASHA LORD

A SIGNET ECLIPSE BOOK

SIGNET ECLIPSE
Published by New American Library, a division of
Penguin Group (USA) Inc., 375 Hudson Street,
New York, New York 10014, USA
Penguin Group (Canada), 90 Eglinton Avenue East, Suite 700, Toronto,
Ontario M4P 2Y3, Canada (a division of Pearson Penguin Canada Inc.)
Penguin Books Ltd., 80 Strand, London WC2R 0RL, England
Penguin Ireland, 25 St. Stephen's Green, Dublin 2,
Ireland (a division of Penguin Books Ltd.)
Penguin Group (Australia), 250 Camberwell Road, Camberwell, Victoria 3124,
Australia (a division of Pearson Australia Group Pty. Ltd.)
Penguin Books India Pvt. Ltd., 11 Community Centre, Panchsheel Park,
New Delhi - 110 017, India
Penguin Group (NZ), cnr Airborne and Rosedale Roads, Albany,
Auckland 1310, New Zealand (a division of Pearson New Zealand Ltd.)
Penguin Books (South Africa) (Pty.) Ltd., 24 Sturdee Avenue,
Rosebank, Johannesburg 2196, South Africa

Penguin Books Ltd., Registered Offices:
80 Strand, London WC2R 0RL, England

First published by Signet Eclipse, an imprint of New American Library,
a division of Penguin Group (USA) Inc.

First Printing, February 2006
10 9 8 7 6 5 4 3 2 1

PUBLISHER'S NOTE
This is a work of fiction. Names, characters, places, and incidents either are
the product of the author's imagination or are used fictitiously, and any resem-
blance to actual persons, living or dead, business establishments, events, or
locales is entirely coincidental.
    The publisher does not have any control over and does not assume any
responsibility for author or third-party Web sites or their content.

To the brave people out there who stand by their ideals, accept others without judgment and embrace love in their lives. And especially to the strong few who survive and surmount hardships in life—physical, emotional, or simply day-to-day. You all inspire the rest of us.

To my family, who are the bravest of them all.

Acknowledgments

My thanks for the continual support and assistance of my agent, Bob Mecoy, and my editor, Ellen Edwards. While one pushes and prods, the other supports and comforts— together you make a great team!

Prologue

Istabelle O'Bannon crouched in a fighting stance, with her skirts tucked into her waistband. Her dark russet hair snapped in the high winds as her silver eyes flared with fury. She held a dagger with dangerous familiarity and pointed it at the sea warrior who dared attack her.

"You will rue this day, Horik!" she screamed as her hair whipped around her face. The deck of the warship tilted as the ocean rolled, but Istabelle braced herself with the ease of experience. She darted forward and feinted with the blade, slicing Horik's thigh.

He roared with fury and leapt back as blood poured from the wound, drenching his breeches. "It is you who will forevermore regret that the sun rose on this morn, and that the gods laughed at your fate!" He clutched his wound and glared at her, his hatred shimmering in the air between them. "You have been the bane of my existence for three years," he screamed. "What made you into such an unholy female? You should fall to your knees and beg for my mercy!"

Istabelle laughed as she brushed her hair back with the same hand that held the dagger, leaving a bloody streak across her cheek. "I beg favor of no one, least of all from someone like you. You are the lowliest of the low! You prey on those too helpless to fend for themselves. What kind of man are you? A coward?"

Horik swung his axe, intending to smash the dagger from Istabelle's fingers, but she scrambled sideways, narrowly avoiding his assault. The other sailors jumped out of their way, cheering. "Is she too much for you, Horik?" one shouted. "Is the woman going to best you once again?"

Horik stumbled against the railing, his wound weakening him. He swept his maddened gaze toward his crew. They were as evil as he, each cast off from his home because of murder, rape or some equally heinous crime. If the woman won, they would swarm his body and tear it to shreds like vultures ripping into a dead carcass. He must not lose. She was tiring, too. After hours of holding him at bay, she was as exhausted as he. Her eyes were red and she blinked frequently, trying to stay alert. Horik grinned with anticipation as he pushed away from the railing and stalked her again.

"I have plans for you," Horik murmured.

"If you meant to kill me, I would already be dead," she hissed back as she lifted her blade.

"I'm not going to kill you," he replied. "What I have in mind is far worse. After I am done with you, there will not be a waking moment when you will not think about me. From sunrise to sunset I will be in your thoughts, in your mind, embedded in your soul. There will be no escape."

"Why?" Istabelle demanded. "Why are you so angry with me? I am only a woman who sails the seas, assisting others. You are a mighty sea warrior. How could you be threatened by me?"

Horik's hand shot out and grabbed Istabelle's throat. "I am threatened by no one!" he roared. "You should not sail these seas. Go home and breed babes like a woman should!"

Istabelle drove her knee into Horik's groin.

He yowled and released Istabelle as he clutched his nether regions. "You fiend!"

Istabelle staggered back and coughed. She wove in place as she gulped several deep breaths of salty air. Pointing her dagger at him, she foolishly continued. "My mission is to protect those who need my help. I will never marry and have children, for I have seen too many instances of the mighty destroying the weak. I will not stand by and allow someone like you to prey upon those with no resources. You are worse than a pestilence! You eat the heart and soul of the peasantry and leave them destitute. You raid the peaceful and the godly. You do not fight for honor, pride or your county. You are a despicable locust!"

Her words echoed across the deck as the sailors shorted the sail and pulled on the oars that kept the warship stabilized. High winds whistled around the ship, wailing with the mournful sound of a storm about to explode in fury. The ship sank into a trough, then rose to a new height as the waves grew in size and strength.

Suddenly, the screech of a falcon pierced the air and a tingle of energy whispered along the deck, making the men shuffle uncomfortably.

As the warship rode the crest, a sailing vessel loomed to her left amid cries of warning from the oarsmen. "The woman's ship, *The Adventuress*!" the men shouted. "She found us! Her enchanted falcon led the ship to us!"

Horik spun around. "It is only a bird. It has no power!" he shouted, but he shivered as the gray form of the powerful animal gained upon them.

"Throw her overboard!" a sailor screamed, pointing at Istabelle. "She will be the cause of our demise! Get rid of her! Kill her!"

"No!" Horik shouted in reply. "If we kill her, her family will swear vengeance upon us that will never cease. They are too powerful, too well connected in Scotland. I cannot kill her. We will do as I planned. Bring her down to my cabin. Now! We have no more time for games!"

The falcon circled above the warship, her impressive wingspan casting a frightening shadow over the men below. Horik cringed as superstitious fear raced through him. "Raise the second sail!" he commanded his men. "We can outrun her. I need more time!"

"You will never outrun *The Adventuress*," Istabelle taunted as she advanced once again, holding her jew-

4

eled dagger in her hand. The nearness of her friend the falcon gave her courage. "My ship is faster than any vessel on the sea. Don't you remember? I caught you thrice before. I stole your goods—the same gold and treasure you stole from others. It is not my family you should fear, but me and my men!"

As Horik's crew scurried over the deck, raising the square sail, Horik shook with rage. "You are foolish to remind me of why I hate you, Istabelle. You are an unnatural daemon mistress of the ocean. Your thievery brought me shame. My ancestors will rise from their graves and haunt you!"

"Shame can only be brought against those with honor. You are nothing! You are a disgusting man from the north who can't be bothered to bathe and only fights those who can't fight back! Your people have abandoned you. You live on the fringes of society. You are an outlaw!"

Horik roared and ran straight toward her, his axe raised over his head. He swung at her neck, the blade swishing through the air. The falcon dove, talons extended, and struck at Horik's forehead, then rose into the sky and screeched. Horik ducked, but four bloody streaks marred his face. The eerie sound and lightning speed of the gray bird made the others freeze in terror, but Horik could not be stopped. He continued his murderous attack, his gaze fixed upon Istabelle.

She dropped to the deck and rolled. Barely avoiding his blade, she scrambled to her feet and glared at Horik as he yanked the axe out of the boards where she had been standing. She breathed rapidly, her muscles shaking with fatigue.

Horik glanced at several of his men who watched from the crossbeams, or *bites,* and the line of planks that joined together from stem to stern to form the *meginhufr* of the old-style warship. The men sat low in the hull, next to the oar ports that lined the second strake, and were thus well protected from attack. Their eyes glittered with avid interest as they watched Istabelle stumble with exhaustion.

One sailor, an older man, pointed to a pile of netting. "Chasing her with an axe will do nothing for either of you," he said with a hint of disgust. "If you cannot kill her, then capture her like a fish." He glanced at Istabelle's intent face and admiration briefly flickered over his face. She reminded him of his own daughter—his daughter who had been murdered many years ago. Because of that terrible day, he was now an outlaw, forced to join company with Horik and his men. The memories were too painful and he yanked his gaze away. This was not his concern. He sailed with Horik because he had no choice; Istabelle had taunted Horik with reckless disregard for the consequences. She was foolish and irresponsible and must be prepared to take her punishment with the same courage she showed in battle.

Unaware of the older man's turbulent thoughts, Istabelle glanced at *The Adventuress* as her shadowy figure swept down upon the warship. Soon it would reach them. She needed only to stall for a few minutes more. . . .

Horik grinned and picked up a net that was bundled next to the railing. He slowly unfurled it as he advanced upon her. Istabelle watched him warily, stepping around the mast in order to keep it between them. Blood dripped down Horik's face and thigh, but he did not seem to notice it. "If you bind me and throw me out to sea, my men will kill every last one of you for revenge," she warned him.

"There are other ways to get revenge and I intend to enjoy them!" Horik replied.

Istabelle trembled inside, but she did not show her fear. She gripped her dagger more firmly and waved it in front of her face. "Touch me and you will regret it," she threatened.

Horik laughed, tossing his head back, and joined the wind with his lusty voice. "I don't think so, daemon sea-mistress."

"My ship approaches!"

"What I intend to do will only take seconds." He swung the net over his head. It whirled in the air, the sound muted by the moaning wind. "After I finish with you, you will never forget that I made you call me master!"

He flung the net as Istabelle jumped down from her place and sprinted aft, but the net tangled in her feet and she crashed to the deck. Horik clambered toward her as she struggled to free herself.

"No!" she screamed as he gripped her arm and yanked her upright. She twisted and plunged her dagger into his chest, but his massive muscles prevented a fatal thrust.

He howled with pain and grabbed her other hand. "You witch!" he shouted just as the stormy sky erupted into sheeting, sideways rain. The wind and rain ripped through the first sail, shredding it, and the ship suddenly listed. Ropes whipped loose, cracking overhead.

Horik fell, crushing Istabelle beneath him and knocking the breath from her. She went limp. Horik lumbered to his feet and dragged her behind him as he headed for the hold. "Keep ahead of *The Adventuress*!" he shouted to his men. He pulled Istabelle below, her head bouncing down the ladder steps as the sailors struggled with the torn sail, battling the vicious winds.

"The boat . . ." Istabelle gasped. "Your men . . . we will all perish."

Horik ignored her, bent on achieving his revenge. He shoved her into his cabin and stumbled in behind her. The warship crashed against a wave and the momentum swung the cabin door shut with echoing finality.

"You have never known defeat, have you?" he questioned. "You have lived in a precious, sheltered world of love and kindness and now dare to meddle in the affairs of men! Well, that peace will never be yours again!" He shoved her against the cabin wall, on which metal bands were bolted. He shoved her neck into one and snapped it closed, then yanked each wrist into smaller bands on either side.

Istabelle screamed. She flailed against the bonds, but the metal bands held firm.

Horik stepped back and chuckled. "I will always remember you just like this," he taunted. "Bound, helpless and at my mercy. For as long as we both live, I will have this image burned into my memory, and you will know that a man sails these seas who made you weak and helpless. You will have nightmares of this day forevermore." He slowly untied his breeches, his hand becoming drenched with blood from his thigh wound.

Istabelle shuddered as she saw Horik yank his manhood out of his clothing. Fear paralyzed her. She was brave but still only a young, innocent woman. She had faced ocean storms and focused on ensuring the peasants' safety, but suddenly she was at his mercy. After years of stealing from the rich and the evil and giving to the poor and needy, she was the helpless one. Shock and horror poured through her. She raised her terrified gaze to Horik's.

"You will be mine," he told her, his voice worming into her soul and lodging in her heart. "Everything about you. Your soul, your fortune . . . your name. I will own you!"

Chapter 1

Mangan placed the letter, unread, on the table and sat down on his cot. Matins had gone longer than normal, and dawn had already crept over the horizon. He had a few moments to rest before the service of prime. He rubbed his hands against the coarse clothing of his habit and glanced at the letter again. It had taken a month for it to reach him in this secluded place, especially since the author had not known to send it here. Few knew that he was living at the monastery. Only last year he had been fighting on the battlefields with his peers, proudly waving his family banner over his vanquished foes.

But much had changed in the last year and he was reluctant to explain his choices. Of all his family, Cousin Istabelle was the least likely to understand his sudden need for a cloistered life or comprehend the desire for a steady, predictable routine. Mangan stared out the small window and watched thin strands of light streak across the sky. Vibrant colors waxed and waned, yet Mangan remained still and silent, letting the predawn drift into day.

The brother on duty walked the halls, intoning the call to rise. Startled out of his meditation, Mangan hurried to the basin to wash, then went to the chapel for service. It wasn't until much later that day, after the sermons, the meetings and the high Mass, that Mangan returned to his room and the letter once again.

Sighing, he picked it up and broke the seal.

Dearest cousin, it read.

> *I am in desperate need of your assistance. Well, perhaps "desperate" is too strong a word, although I think not.*

Mangan smiled and read on.

Yes, I think that no other word can quite describe my need. I have heard great tales of your prowess in battle, and I am duly impressed, as I still remember you as five years old when we last lived under the same roof. Although we have written to each other over the years, I find it impossible to think of you as a mature man. But you must be if the tales are true. It is, in fact, your battle skills that prompt me to write this letter. I find that I have become embroiled in a difficult situation and need someone like you to help me resolve my problem. I do not want to involve anyone in the family, but I have concluded that I have no other choice. It is a delicate matter and requires the assistance of someone whom I can trust implicitly. Someone like you.

I do not want to unfairly urge you, but nonetheless I remind you of your solemn vow to me the last time we saw each other well over ten years ago. I understand that we were but children, but regardless, the words are binding. But I do not need to remind you. You have always been the honorable one. I am the wayward child who "respects no authority," as you are wont to say.

The matter that needs to be resolved is somewhat personal, and I hesitate to mention it in a letter, so beg my indulgence and let me tell you the details later. Suffice it to say, I need your sword and your tactical ingenuity. Please come to Port Canna immediately upon receiving this missive, as I do not have much time.

Yours lovingly and respectfully,
Cousin Istabelle

Mangan dropped the letter. It fluttered a short distance from his feet until it rested on the floor. He glanced at his cot, knowing that his sword lay beneath it, where he had vowed to leave it for one year. Two months of that year remained.

Mangan walked the four steps to the window of his cell and stared at the gardens. A few monks were weeding while another was tilling the soil with a wooden prong. The church rose behind the gardens, its stone walls bathed in the afternoon sun. Mangan kneeled, and prayed for an answer.

Ruark Haagen swung his sword, slaying one man and maiming the next. The meadow was littered with bodies, its tall grasses trampled and its fresh greenery stained with blood. Ruark yanked his sword free and plunged it into the chest of another, then stepped back to protect the younger man who huddled near his feet.

"Get up, Sven," Ruark snapped. "We will not get paid unless we are standing at the end of the battle." Ruark lunged forward and attacked still another warrior. Seconds later, Sven joined him and feebly thrust his own sword with his left hand. His right arm hung uselessly at his side, blood dripping.

A horn sounded at the far end of the meadow, and the men paused, waiting for the signal. Ruark and his opponent stared at each other, frozen. The horn sounded again, two long blasts in succession. Ruark straightened as his remaining opponent lowered his sword.

"Go," Ruark commanded. "I will respect your laird's surrender."

"My thanks," the man answered. "You are an honorable man." They both looked down at the bodies on the field. Some of the slain were family members and vassals of the clans they represented. Many were serfs with no fighting experience. A few of them were, like Ruark, paid warriors hired to fight in a nameless feudal war.

Ruark flicked his sword at the man, who backed away, then turned and ran. "I have no more honor than a donkey," Ruark grumbled. "I fight for gold, nothing else." He wiped his sword on the cloak of a dead man, then put a hand under his brother's good arm. "How much damage did that peasant do?" Ruark asked him.

Sven blinked as his vision blurred. "I think I should sit back down," he whispered.

"Walk," Ruark commanded and roughly dragged him forward as he wrapped a bandage around Sven's wound. "Hold the bandage tight to stop the bleeding. I will tend it after we are paid."

Sven nodded, trying to stay upright. He noted the splatters of blood that decorated Ruark's tunic, and the irregular cuts that indicated where swords had breached his defenses. "You have been injured as well," Sven chided.

"It matters not. Collect your trophies." Ruark bent down and cut a swath of cloth from the tartans of the six men he had slain. When he stood upright, Sven was weaving in place, a single swath in his hand. Ruark frowned but said nothing. He motioned to the edge of the clearing, where the other victorious men had gathered.

"Good work, Ruark," the McEnri laird commented. Then, for politeness he added, "And you, too, Sven."

Ruark grunted and handed McEnri the swaths. "Ten coin apiece," he reminded him.

"You are an exceptional warrior, Ruark, but there will be a time when you grow older and slower and look for finer pleasures than bloodlust and war. There are many bold and reckless warriors for hire, but no old and reckless ones alive. You have earned countless coins from my coffers alone. You must be a rich man now. Stop while you still have your arms and legs."

"I have no clan," Ruark answered. "I belong to no family. Gold is the only commodity I can own. Until I have enough, I have no desire to saddle myself with a wife."

"You are known far and wide as one of the best fighters in Scotland, but war is only one part of life. You must eventually make a hearth and call it home. Money alone will not give you happiness. Come and live in a cottage on McEnri land. I willingly offer you a home in exchange for your loyalty."

Ruark shook his head. "Perhaps when I am ready, I will remember your advice and ask to till some land. Until then, I will continue to earn my living the way I know best. When I am assured of full coffers, I will rest."

"One day you will wonder where your life went while you fought and plundered. But remember my offer and think of me when you sit beside a fire in the bleak winter. I could even find you a woman to warm your sheets."

Smiling coldly, Ruark replied, "My thanks, but I am not ready yet."

McEnri nodded with resignation. "Here is your fee. And a smaller amount for your brother." McEnri looked at Sven with concern. "There is a monastery nearby. Perhaps you should bring Sven there so that he can recuperate."

"I will tend him. We need no outside assistance."

The McEnri laird shrugged. "So be it. I will raise a flag in the village should I require your services again."

"As always," Ruark answered. He strode toward his horse and mounted without using the stirrups. He motioned to Sven. "Come," he commanded irritably. "Do not show weakness in front of the others, or they will take advantage of you, as I have told you time and again. In our world, might is right. If you act helpless, the vultures will devour you."

Sven staggered to his horse and mounted with difficulty. The bandage around his arm was already soaked with blood. "Ruark," he murmured, "I need to rest . . ."

Ruark swung his steed around and set him cantering away from the battlefield, leaving Sven to follow as best he could.

By nightfall, Sven was burning with fever. The bleeding had finally stopped, but the amount of blood he had lost made his skin gleam palely in the firelight. The wound was swelling and an angry flush was rapidly spreading up his shoulder and onto his neck. Every breath was tight and labored.

Ruark washed the wound once again, placing cool cloths over it. Sven was the only person he cared about, had ever cared about, for as long as he could remember. Forced to fend for himself in the village of Haagen from which he had claimed his name, Ruark had little memory of the violent murder of his mother and father, which had left him alone at a very young age. Although he had been barely four years old, he had fought and scrambled with the other orphans to find food and clothes. He had rapidly developed skills in stealth and resourcefulness and then, as he grew stronger, expertise in combat. There were few who did not know—and fear—his name.

Like Ruark's, Sven's parents were dead, but they had died in a tragic wagon accident. When Ruark had come upon the wreckage, Sven had been a toddler and Ruark a mere youth. Seeing the frightened child had brought forth Ruark's long-smothered compassion, and his deep loneliness had prompted him to tend the boy. Since then, Ruark had become fiercely protective of his new "little brother." Sven was the only person he had ever let himself care about, for no other had ever evoked any deep emotions, which suited Ruark well. He did not want attachments to hinder his quest for fortune.

Sven was weaker than Ruark, and while Ruark thrived on hardship, Sven had difficulties. He chilled easily and became nauseated when he went without food. Ruark learned early on that Sven needed the best piece of meat, the warmest cloak, the softest bed, and Ruark gave him everything he could. In return, Sven gave him companionship and complete devotion.

Ruark pulled out his coin bag and counted his money, even though he knew the amount by heart. "Another year, maybe two," he promised Sven. "We will settle on some land, build a cabin and buy you the bees you talk about. Then we will be beholden to no one. You will have a trade and a way to survive should I fall under an enemy's broadsword."

Sven tried to fix his bleary gaze on Ruark. "I will make honey," he whispered.

"Aye, and sell the wax."

"And you will make mead . . ."

Ruark smiled. The conversation was a familiar one. Because the trades were regulated by guilds, and the two of them lacked any family, Sven could not apprentice to any of the village merchants. Ruark could fight, but Sven had never developed the bloodlust necessary to excel in war. By chance, five years ago they had happened upon a hermit who raised bees. From that day on, Sven had been obsessed with the idea of contributing to their mutual welfare by keeping bees. "I will try," Ruark finally replied. He touched Sven's forehead again, worried about the boy's rising temperature.

As the night wore on, Sven tossed and turned, his fever escalating. His entire neck was swollen and the pressure was making it difficult for him to breathe. Ruark began to fear for Sven's life. Making a rapid decision, he lifted Sven in his arms and remounted his steed. Despite his aversion to outside assistance, it was time to find the monastery.

Chapter 2

Toiling by the light of a small candle, Mangan carefully copied the words from one book onto the beautifully decorated pages of another. Because he knew how to read and write, he had been asked to undertake the monumental task of transcribing the manuscript. With large flourishes and precise placement, Mangan had slowly created a masterpiece. It had taken him over nine months, but as he finished the last line, he sat back and reviewed his work with a small smile of satisfaction. It was appropriately reverent and the illustrations expressed the spiritual content of the book.

Mangan carefully replaced his writing instruments, sanded the page and blotted it. Then he blew out the candle and prayed in the darkness. He knew he could not ignore Istabelle's plea, but he also felt a strong compulsion to remain at the monastery for the final two months of his self-imposed cloister.

Midnight came, and he rose for matins. The line of solemn monks filed out of their individual cells and entered the church, where many stood in the choir. By the flickering illumination of two torches, the men began to chant.

Mangan let the music move through him, fill him, surround him and soothe him. Slowly, as if a cloak were being drawn from a window by a languid hand, Mangan felt God come to him. Bending his cowled head, he accepted his responsibility. He must find a way to assist his cousin, and he was confident that God would be there for him as he had been every step of the way.

The monks sang three anthems, then several lessons were spoken by one of the older monks. As the hours passed, matins and lauds concluded, and the monks filed back out and returned to the dorter for a few moments of rest before sunrise. Although theirs was not a silent order, most preferred to maintain their personal reverie in quiet solitude.

A sudden banging on the main cloister door some distance away startled everyone.

An early tendril of dawn light snuck over the church spire and speared the monks below, casting its glow upon Mangan.

The other monks shifted back, acknowledging God's request. The older monk who had spoken in lessons lifted his hands and nodded as he gazed at Mangan. Mangan copied his motions, then headed through the walled gardens and into the cloister. The steady knocking echoed in the stone halls as Mangan walked through the corridors to the front door.

"Ho there!" someone shouted. "I seek your hospitality and medical skill!"

Mangan proceeded to the door and contemplated the man through the peephole.

"Men of God!" the man shouted again. "Open your doors to the ill and injured! May you have mercy on my brother, Sven."

Mangan reached the heavy door and slid the bolt back. As if opened by another's hand, a gust of wind flung the door wide just as Mangan pulled it free of the doorjamb.

"Ruark Haagen, warrior of great repute," Mangan said as he recognized the man standing there.

Ruark drew his brows down in a fierce frown as he peered at the shadowy figure. "How is it that a monk knows my name?" he queried.

"You were at my side in many battles," Mangan answered. "Do you not know me?" He pulled back his hood.

"Mangan O'Bannon? Heir to the earldom of Kirkcaldy? Why do I find you in a monk's robe in this undistinguished order atop an unknown mountain?"

"God brought me here, as he has many others. I have taken a year to reflect. It appears that God guided your steps to this threshold as well."

"Aye," Ruark replied uncertainly. "We were involved in a small skirmish for the McEnri, and my brother was injured. At first, the wound did not appear serious, but within hours it festered. I fear for him. I have gold to pay for his care."

Mangan nodded. "My brothers here know much about healing. Bring him inside and we will tend him." Mangan noticed the arsenal of weapons attached

22

to Ruark's body. "You should leave your weapons at the door."

"Surely as you know me, you know that I cannot be without their comfort."

Mangan nodded. "Aye, I was once the same. Come, be welcome into our home as you are."

Mangan led the way as Ruark carried Sven down the dark corridors. They made several turns before finally reaching a central area where the other monks were eating. Mangan walked around the table and touched one of the men on the shoulder. The man rose and the foursome left the eating area and went to an infirmary, located adjacent to the guest chambers.

"This is Brother Stephen. He will look at Sven's wound," Mangan informed Ruark.

Brother Stephen motioned for Ruark to place Sven on the mattress, then slowly peeled the bandage off the wound. Sven moaned, barely conscious. After a few whispered words between the monks, Mangan went to the basin and started to prepare a cleansing powder.

"What are you doing?" Ruark demanded.

"The ill humors filling the wound are severe," Mangan said. "Stephen thinks that a piece of metal is still in the wound. Perhaps it broke off the sword." Mangan stared at Ruark, knowing that his friend understood how serious metal poisoning could be. "Brother Stephen will probe the site and try to remove the piece. I will wash the wound, then place maggots on the area to clean the dead tissue."

"It is too soon for that. He received the wound only yesterday."

Mangan shrugged. "Already the skin is black around the edges. If you prefer, we could amputate the limb."

"No, milord. You know I would never allow that. Unlike men of leisure, we must have our limbs to survive."

Mangan smiled, ignoring the implication. "I am not a lord while under this roof. Call me Mangan, or call me Brother, as I call you. Trust us and let us do our work, and we will help Sven."

"With the help of God," Brother Stephen intoned.

"With the help of God," Mangan repeated, then looked at Ruark expectantly.

"With . . . with God's help," Ruark stuttered, unfamiliar with the phrase.

After much exploring, Stephen located the fragment. Using an oddly shaped instrument, he gripped the piece and yanked it out. As it plunked down on the side table, Mangan looked at the rusted edge with concern. "Sven is in grave danger," he warned. "The rust on the blade may give him lockjaw. He cannot be moved, for we may need to feed him through a straw until the illness runs its course. That is, *if* it runs its course."

"Do not let him die, Mangan."

"We must pray."

"I don't pray."

Brother Stephen looked up. "You must serve God so that he looks upon you favorably."

"I find my solace in action, not mediation," Ruark gruffly replied.

Mangan nodded. "I believe God has brought you here to do just that. Come with me while Brother Stephen tends Sven. I have a letter to show you."

"I think God sent you here to help Istabelle, as I am bound to stay in the monastery for two more months," Mangan explained patiently. He had already shown Istabelle's letter to Ruark and described his plan, but Ruark was still shaking his head. For emphasis, Mangan repeated, "I believe you should go in my place."

"I do not work for free and I do not follow orders from women," Ruark said as he flung the letter on the cot. "She sounds like every other aristocratic wench who thinks a tear in her dress is worth a man's life. I have seen too many men die for the petty grievances of a woman."

"Istabelle is not like the women you speak of. She is as different from them as the sun is from the moon."

"Nonetheless, I will not serve a female. I am paid to fight, but I have always chosen my masters with care."

Mangan glared at Ruark. "All who know you have ignored your rudeness and uncouth manners, excusing you because of your rough beginnings, but you have no right to speak of something you know nothing about. I agree that many women would beg assistance for trivial matters, but Istabelle is not one of them. She is one of the last people I would ever expect to show fear, and I detect a high measure of it in these words."

"Is she not a girl born to wealth and privilege? Is she not a child who has never known the rigors of hunger, cold and loneliness?"

Mangan's eyes glittered with anger. "I repeat, you know nothing of her. She is my cousin and was born only moments after me. In God's eyes, we could be twins. She was the product of hatred and greed, for her mother, Isadora of Dunhaven, was a vicious, conniving woman. In one of his mysterious actions, God relieved this world of Isadora's presence when he lifted her off the high towers of Castle Kirkcaldy and dashed her innards against the hard courtyard stone."

"I heard that your uncle, Xanthier, pushed her," Ruark replied.

"Again, you know nothing. Xanthier was on the walkway, and he saved Istabelle from falling, but it was God's will that Isadora plummet to her death. Yet only hours after he saved his own child, Xanthier abandoned her. Poor Istabelle was left with no parents of her own. *Just like you.*"

"You insult me! No woman's trials could be compared to mine. She had a home. She had a family. She had food."

"Aye, my father and mother made her welcome, but she never felt she belonged. It was God's blessing that she met a woman named Alannah. Alannah is a blind woman of extraordinary perception and compassion who gentled my uncle and took in Istabelle and helped raise her as her own. They live in isolation on a secluded isle off the Scottish coast. Bereft of normal social interactions, Istabelle has few civilized restraints, and her impetuous personality thrives on behaving wildly. She has become a notorious female captain of the seas and she acknowledges no authority other than her own. She has made it her ambition to patrol the seas and protect the waters she has claimed as her home. Believe me, she is unlike anyone you have ever encountered."

"If she is so extraordinary, then why is she seeking aid?"

Mangan stared out the window. In a muffled voice, he answered, "I don't know. That is what worries me." He fell silent as he contemplated the trees. The leaves were several shades of green. Pale green, evergreen, yellow green . . . shadowed and light struck . . . silent or whispering in the wind. Leaves, God's creation, were as complex and varied as the wings of dragonflies. Or as intricate as the aspects of a human character.

"Look at the tree," Mangan suggested. "It must drink the rain and soak in the sun. It needs room to grow and space to take root. It provides shelter and shade. It sings in the wind, laughs in the rain, hums in the dead of night."

"Trees burn," Ruark commented.

Mangan nodded. "As timeless as they appear, trees are subject to the vagaries of life, just like us. They wither in drought, go naked in winter and blacken under the onslaught of the devil's fire." Mangan turned and stared directly into Ruark's eyes. "What would have happened to Sven had you not taken him under your protection?"

"He would have died."

"You saved him once, my friend. Save him again. Save me. Save Istabelle. You were brought to this monastery for a reason. God is calling you and you must heed the call. Go to Istabelle and help her. No matter what she says, no matter how she acts, you must do this for her. It is God's will."

"I do not hear God's call," Ruark said disdainfully. "I listen to the sound of coins rubbing against each other and to the cries of enemies dying at my feet. You cannot pressure me to do your bidding for nothing in return."

Mangan glared at him, his anger peaking. Clenching his fists, he turned away and took several deep breaths. This last year at the monastery had taught him to exercise restraint and patience. Sometimes God had to use other methods of persuasion to convince his sons to embrace the good life. Mangan himself had found the monastery through an unusual path. He was an earl's son who had put aside all his wealth and position to serve a higher power, but perhaps to assist Ruark's journey he needed earthly enticements.

"If you go," he finally said, "we will waive your fee for Sven's recuperation."

Ruark shifted his gaze to his brother, who was

lying fast asleep on the bed. He could not join another battle until Sven recovered anyway. In the meantime, what else was there to do? He would become restless and irritable in the quiet solitude of the monastery. He swung his gaze back and grunted at Mangan. "I suppose I have nothing to entertain me, no fights to join," he mumbled, "and if it will save me some coin . . ."

"Understand that if you accept this mission, you will be bound to complete it. I expect you to honor your word from beginning to end and will insist that you treat Istabelle with the utmost respect."

"Of course," Ruark growled. "If you are implying that I would break a promise, you have greatly underestimated my character."

Mangan nodded. "Very well. Then are we agreed?"

"Will the monastery agree to our arrangement? I will pay nothing for Sven's care?"

"I will tell the monks and they will understand."

"Then we are agreed."

Ruark rode through the dense forest, his brows drawn together in fierce concentration. His eyes gleamed like onyx, so dark that they drank in the light. His dark brown hair hung down his back in a thick braid, crisscrossed by a leather thong. He wore a rough hemp shirt laced with leather and form-fitting breeches tucked into sturdy boots. A purse was slung over his chest and a belt encircled his waist. Every item was utilitarian. No decoration adorned his clothing; he had no use for such. The only deviation from strict simplicity was the scrolled pattern etched on the blade of his broadsword.

Ruark reached behind him and untied the bow from his saddle. Stringing an arrow, he let his horse's reins drop. The horse pricked his ears forward and continued walking at a steady pace while Ruark focused on a pair of rabbits nibbling on some grass. Ruark raised the bow, took quick aim, and let the arrow fly. Before the first had gone half the distance to its target, Ruark had strung and released a second arrow.

Both flew true, and Ruark leaned down and picked up the two dead rabbits as his steed walked past them. He pulled his arrows free, wiped them off, then replaced the set. He tied the two rabbits together by their feet with a short piece of rope and draped them over his horse's withers. The entire process took less than a minute, and Ruark hardly broke his concentration from the task ahead.

He dreaded the next fortnight. Whatever the spoiled girl needed, he would do it as quickly as possible and return to the monastery. If there was any truth to Mangan's assertion that God meant for him to help Istabelle in exchange for saving Sven, he was willing to get the deed done, especially since it had the added benefit of not costing him anything. He mentally calculated the money in his purse again. A year—maybe two—and he would have enough.

The trees thinned and he spotted a village nestled in the next valley. As he drew closer, several smoke plumes caught his eye, and he debated which home to approach. The house in the worst repair was immediately eliminated, for it bespoke a lack of male attention. Women in such a household would likely be frightened by his appearance. Homes with immaculate yards were likewise avoided, for they did not need an extra hand. Through this type of careful strategizing, Ruark selected a home of undistinguished prosperity and dismounted at the outskirts. He walked slowly up the path to the cottage. By the time he was halfway to the door, an older man stepped out.

"Stranger," the man said noncommittally.

"Friend," Ruark replied. "I am traveling to the coast and have need of some bread and cheese." He motioned to the cow in the field. "I hope we can arrange a trade."

The older man scanned Ruark's strong back and broad shoulders as well as the two rabbits across the horse's withers. "My wife left this world several years ago, but my daughter can set an acceptable table. I will pack you some supplies, provide you with a good dinner and put you and your horse in the stable for the night. In return, I ask for the stable to be cleaned and the wood to be chopped."

"Aye, that is a good trade." Ruark led his horse to the stable and ducked his head to enter. The scents of cow manure and moldy hay were familiar to him. After unsaddling his horse and rubbing him down, Ruark found a shovel and commenced working.

Within a few hours, the stable was presentable and

he started on the pile of wood. The axe was dull and after a few unsatisfactory swings, he took it into the stable to sharpen it.

"Hello," a female said from the depths. "My father said you were working here today. I brought you some cool water."

Ruark pulled the sharpening stone from his saddlebag and turned to face the girl. She was comely, with honey blond hair and hazel eyes. "My thanks," he said as he accepted the water cask she offered and took a deep draught.

"My name is Thea."

Ruark finished his swallow and leveled his gaze on her. "Ruark," he replied. "Where is your husband?"

Thea shook her head. "He died from the same ailment that took my mother."

"Then you seek companionship?"

Thea blushed. "Few strangers pass through here, and I have not been to town in many months."

Ruark placed the cask on the stable floor and walked up to her. His onyx eyes held no emotion as he lifted her by the waist and set her on a pile of hay. His hands were brisk but not rough as he pushed up her skirts.

Thea sank back, opened her thighs and placed her hands on his shoulders. She smiled at Ruark when he paused and looked at her. "Are you ready?" he asked.

"Yes," she whispered. She dropped one hand down and stroked him through his breeches. "You are, too," she added breathlessly.

Ruark untied the string on her drawers and pulled them down. Thea's soft thighs were white and plump, and the thatch between her legs was dark blond. Ruark slid a finger between her nether lips, testing her, and found her moist. He stepped back and pulled his breeches down, then moved between her legs.

He nudged against her, his cock hard and full. When she tilted her hips to receive him, he held her waist and sank deeply into her.

She gasped and bit her lip. She gripped his shoulders tightly, clinging to him as he pulled out and sank in again. Her initial discomfort changed rapidly to pleasure as he kept a steady rhythm, and she closed her eyes.

Ruark watched her face, watched when she began to lose control, when she began to climb to her height and when she reached her climax. Her face tightened and she moaned. The pulse fluttered in her throat. She twisted in the hay, her blond hair tangling with the yellow stalks.

As she relaxed, Ruark drove into her harder, focusing on himself, then he, too, shuddered with his release.

She opened her eyes and stared at him as he pulled out of her. He used a horse blanket to wipe himself off, then handed it to her. He pulled his breeches up, then gathered the stone he had discarded earlier and went back outside to sharpen the axe.

Thea left the stable several minutes after Ruark, blinking in the harsh sunlight. It had been a mutual release. Each had received and given what the other wanted. Seeing her caused no emotion in Ruark. Sex was an activity to be indulged in when it was convenient, easy and meaningless. Three to five minutes, and two people could find some physical companionship. Ruark wanted nothing more.

Ruark reached the coast by midday. The sun was unexpectedly warm, and he pulled his shirt and purse off because the rough fabric itched his skin. Even so, a thin sheen of sweat coated his chest and formed a line down his back. He pulled some bread from his bag and chewed it. It was dry and tasteless, but hearty. The port town of Canna, where he was to meet Istabelle, was half an hour south.

Wanting to delay his arrival a few moments longer, Ruark reined his horse off the path and moved toward a clearing in the distance. With luck, it would have a lake and he could wash off. He tied his purse to the saddle, then opened it and extracted the ring Mangan had given him. The ruby was encircled by shards of emeralds and the intricate emblem of Kirkcaldy was carved on each side. Mangan had given it to him so he could produce it for Istabelle. Presumably she would recognize it and thus trust the wearer. Disgusted with the flashing colors, Ruark slipped it on his smallest finger so he would not lose it.

He rode through the trees, ducking under the low branches, until he came upon the open space he had spotted. A large, crystal-clear lake spread out at his feet with barely a ripple upon its surface. It looked refreshingly inviting.

Ruark swung down from his mount and stripped off his remaining clothing. Unlike the gentry, he did not wear linen undergarments. The cost of such items was too high. He placed his boots carefully against a tree and draped his shirt and breeches over a branch where the breeze would air them out. Then, with a small grin, he ran waist high into the lake and finally dove deep under the water. The liquid against his sweaty body was incredibly relaxing, and he swam with long, smooth strokes until he was half-way across the lake.

There he stopped and treaded water. Glancing back, he saw movement at the shoreline. He shook the hair away from his eyes. "*What?*" he panted. He wiped the remaining water from his face and peered back to where he had left his belongings. A woman was systematically rifling through his saddlebags.

"Stop!" he shouted.

The woman stepped away from his horse, holding his prized sword and his heavy purse.

"You dare not!" he shouted as he started powering through the water toward her. The sword was his life, his occupation, his soul, and the purse held all his funds. "So help me, I will kill you!" he shouted as his strong strokes brought him rapidly to shore. He cursed his stupidity in leaving his property unattended. "You will rue this day!"

A falcon shrieked far above him and he felt an odd tingling in his scalp.

The woman spun around and raced toward her horse. She quickly lashed the sword and purse to her saddle and swung up, her skirts flying around her thighs. "The unwary deserve to lose their belongings," she shouted back. "I do not allow predators such as you to threaten the people of this area. Feel lucky that I left you your horse!" She kicked her mount over to his, then slapped his on the rump. It leapt forward and trotted angrily away as she laughed. "We shall see if you are an able climber," she called out as she tossed his breeches up into the high branches of a tree.

She laughed again. Her horse danced, its hooves flashing in the sunlight, and Ruark briefly paused in his swimming to stare at her. He swept his gaze down her form, trying to memorize her face so that he could avenge himself, but she seemed to sparkle as if she were drenched in gold dust. He treaded water for a moment and blinked. Her hair was rich and vibrant, cascading down her back in shimmering russet curls. Her shapely legs were strong and muscled and she sat on her mare as comfortably as any warrior he had ever seen, yet her thighs . . . her waist . . . her tightly encased breasts made him well aware that she was female.

Her horse spun as she stared back at him and the glitter covering her skin dazzled his eyes. "*What are you?*" he whispered.

Istabelle held her mare in check, feeling her anxious energy about to explode, but she couldn't tear her gaze from the warrior who was half immersed in the clear blue water. His long hair was slicked against his head, and his face was sculpted in harsh planes. The sun shone upon his shoulders and his bulging chest muscles glistened with moisture. Short black curls dusted his chest and she had a strange urge to find out what they felt like. She yanked on her mare's reins and the horse half reared in anger. Feeling more daring and alive than she had in months, she nudged her horse toward the shore.

"Can you catch me?" she taunted.

Ruark's breath caught. *Had she really said that? Could she be daring him?* With sudden determination, he surged forward again. As his strong arms cleaved the water, he heard the pounding hooves of her horse racing away.

He burst out of the lake, water sluicing off his naked body, and whistled. His steed was well trained, and he had no doubt that it would come to his call; his only concern was how quickly. He strode to the tree where his breeches were dangling. Fury clouded his eyes as he saw how high they were.

"You will pay for this," he vowed as he jumped upward and caught a sturdy branch. He pulled himself up, then swung his leg around the branch, scraping his lower calf. "Augh," he grunted. He reached for a higher branch, tested its strength, then used it to stand up in the tree. His breeches were farther out, swinging on thinner limbs.

He looked around, seeking the woman's form from his vantage point. He could see her horse cantering through the woods to the west. *Good*, he thought. *I'll catch you and you will regret every second you cost me. You don't know me, but I'll make sure you never forget me.*

He broke off a branch from above his head and used it to fish for his breeches. After several tries, he snagged the material and dropped them to the ground. With a growl of satisfaction, he saw his stallion standing nearby, the reins trailing.

He shifted, accidentally dragging his arm across a broken tree stub. Blood welled up and dripped from the injury, but Ruark ignored it. He climbed down to the lower branch, then jumped to the ground. Moving with increasing urgency, he yanked his breeches on, then vaulted up on his horse. With a swift kick, he sent the stallion galloping after the woman.

Istabelle loped through the trees, feeling oddly guilty about her theft. True, the man had left his belongings unguarded, but she could have allowed him a peaceful swim. The water had looked incredible, and the sun was warm. In fact, if she had not come across him first, *she* would have been the one in the water and *he* would have found *her* clothes on a rock.

She glanced behind her, pleased to see that he was not following. She slowed her horse to a trot and motioned for the falcon. The bird swooped lower and rested on a stand that was mounted on her saddle. After praising the falcon, Istabelle glanced at her own arm and rubbed the mica dust that covered her flesh. She really wanted to rinse off. She had spent the morning exploring caves, and tiny particles of the sparkling material clung to her sweaty body. She tried to pick a large flake off with her fingernails, but it stuck to her hand instead. A fly buzzed around her face and she wiped her forehead, but when she returned to looking at her hand, she realized that the mica had transferred yet again. Sighing, she imagined that the glitter was now upon her cheek.

Where was Mangan? Why hadn't he come? As Istabelle thought back over the last several months, wrinkles formed on her brow. Horik had . . . had taken *IT*, and she wanted *IT* back! Of all her treasures, of all the riches she had stolen, the thing Horik had taken from her was the most precious. She would get it back, no matter the cost!

A sound behind her made her turn in the saddle and gasp. The warrior had found her! She saw his stallion thundering through the forest, bearing down on her, his massive shoulders crashing through the underbrush with ease. A thrill raced through Istabelle, and she thrummed her mare's sides with her heels.

"Run!" she shouted. The falcon shrieked and lifted into the sky as Istabelle and the mare shot forward.

Chapter 3

They whipped through the forest, their horses weaving in and out of the trees as the bird swept through the sky above them. Excitement raced through them, a mutual emotion of risk, danger and nameless need that drove them to win, to beat the opponent, to be acknowledged as the most skillful.

Istabelle ducked her head under her arm to assess her pursuer and was stunned to see he was much closer. She leaned to her right, and she and the mare veered south, where a series of stony crags dotted the landscape. Istabelle knew the terrain, had explored it often, and she figured she could confound the warrior by weaving among the obstacles.

Ruark saw her turn and he shifted quickly, closing the gap between them. The luminescent glitter that sparkled on the woman's skin beckoned him forward, and he forgot why he was pursuing her, forgot why his blood was pumping. Suddenly, all that mattered was the chase. His heart thundered and he knew he wanted to catch her, to capture her in his hands and dominate her. He wanted to touch her glittering skin and feel its heat.

Rocks loomed ahead and Ruark was forced to slow. His warhorse stumbled, his agility far less than that of the sleek mare ahead. As the stallion struggled to negotiate the stones, the mare slipped around a crag and was lost to sight.

Istabelle pulled her mare to a quick stop and rapidly searched the area. A cliff dropped off to her right, forming a wall above the lake, and an enormous boulder rose steeply in front of her. Behind her she could hear the blowing of the warrior's horse. Without thinking further, she turned to her left toward a network of deer trails. Selecting one, she and the mare headed downhill.

Suddenly the warrior burst onto their path, blocking their way.

The woman screamed in surprise and hauled on the mare's reins.

"You are very clever, woman, but I have stayed alive by outwitting people like you."

"How did you circle around me?" she demanded.

Not answering her, he moved his stallion closer. He saw the gleam of his broadsword tied to her saddle. "Drop the purse and sword," he commanded. "I have killed for far less than the theft of my possessions."

The woman raised arched eyebrows over silvery eyes. Her russet hair shimmered with silvery blond streaks that bedeviled the eye.

Ruark hesitated, distracted by her unusual beauty.

"I, too, have killed for far less," she said softly, unaware of his thoughts.

The velvet sweetness of her voice wrapped around the grove and swept between them, seducing him. He jerked back and forced his mind to concentrate.

The woman raised a thin sword and pointed it at his chest. "Do not come any closer," she threatened. "I will not hesitate to use my weapon against you."

"You cannot be serious. You are a small female and I am a seasoned warrior. I could smite you in an instant."

"I am deadly serious. And you forget, you were foolish enough to leave your sword unattended. I found it. It is now mine. What will you use to *smite* me?"

Casting around for something with which to arm himself, Ruark spotted a heavy branch nearby. Feigning acceptance, he shrugged. "I must admit defeat. I was unwary and you bested me."

"I doubt you have said that many times in your life, warrior." She deliberately stroked his naked chest with her gaze.

An uncomfortable stirring in his manhood made him narrow his eyes and clench his teeth. "No," he growled, "I have not."

"Perhaps you do not need the services of this blade, for you seem to have another just as strong." She smiled, her full lips curving into a delicious semicircle.

Ruark hardened, despite his rising anger. "Silence," he snapped. "Remember what modesty a lady should possess."

"I am no lady."

"So I have determined." Ruark sent his stallion leaping forward, swiped up the branch and swung it at the woman's hands.

She shrieked and her mare danced backward, almost unseating her. "I warn you! I will not hesitate to use my sword against you!"

Ruark pulled his stallion to a walk, sensing a thread of uncertainty in her voice. Clearly she knew how to hold the weapon, for her grip was firm and well positioned, but he doubted that she would strike him. He stalked forward, forcing her to back up toward the cliff.

The woman glanced back, realizing that the dropoff was close behind her. She frowned as the warrior crept forward. She pulled her horse back again and again until the mare's feet slid on the loose stone.

"Stay back!" she commanded, her voice beginning to shake. "I have no wish to kill over a game. My adversaries are far more important than you. I acknowledge my defeat. You caught me as I did not think you could."

"I think *you* have rarely admitted defeat," he purred, pleased to throw her own words back at her. "Give me my belongings."

The woman fumbled with the saddle ties and finally released the broadsword and the bag of coins. "Back away and I will leave it on yonder granite. After I depart, you can retrieve it."

He nodded and pulled his stallion back several steps, but as she placed the sword and bag on the rock, he moved closer again.

"You promised to let me go on my way!" she cried in dismay as he picked up the blade and turned it in his hand. It felt warm from her grasp, and again he felt his nether regions stir.

"I promised nothing. We still have the matter of your thievery to resolve." He gathered the coin bag and tied it to his horse's saddle.

The woman's mare tossed her head up and down and whinnied nervously.

"Since you now have the objects in question, there was no theft."

"I see it differently." He shifted closer. "It seems fair that you should pay me for my troubles. Give me something I would value and I will let you go." He grinned at her affronted look.

"I think not! I will not give you any of my goods. You are a warrior. Is it not against your code of honor to take from those who are weaker than you?"

He laughed. "You speak of knights. I am a paid warrior with little honor. I fight the weaker clans with pleasure, and get paid for each man I murder. Pleading to my sense of chivalry is useless."

"A man without honor is no man at all!" she shouted. Abruptly angered, he pressed his steed closer and raised his sword. "I am done with this discussion. You have nowhere to go, mistress. Surrender."

She pulled her mare around and peered over the cliff.

"Don't be ridiculous," he snapped. "If you jump, you could die."

She made the mare back away from the edge, then glared at him over her shoulder. "Should I die, 'twill be your fault!" Then, before he could move forward and catch her, she kicked her mare and forced her to leap off the cliff.

Woman and horse flew through the air, the sun striking against her sparkling skin and shimmering hair as if she were a golden nymph floating in the windy currents above the sea, but unlike the faeries, her body plummeted down toward the water below.

Ruark gasped in horror, unprepared for such a reckless and unprecedented action. He sprang off his stallion and scrambled to the cliff edge in time to see her and the horse hit the water. A great splash exploded around them, and then they sank from view.

"God have mercy," he whispered. "What a fool! Isn't your life more precious than your pride?" He stared at the lake, willing them to come to the top. He waited for the wild woman to break the waterline and laugh up at him, to mock him for his refusal to follow her rash act. But she didn't.

Suddenly the mare surfaced, whinnying in fear. She struggled under the weight of the saddle, but managed to keep her head above water as she headed for shore. The woman still did not appear.

"Damn!" Ruark growled. For a few more seconds, he debated. From what he already knew of her, she could be swimming far beneath the water and would emerge under some hidden outcropping. Or she could be drowning. "Damn, damn!" he repeated.

Making a decision, he flung his sword into the grass. He took a deep breath and, without considering the reasons, he dove off the cliff. The long free fall lasted for aeons—his heart stopped and his breath held—until it came to an abrupt, chilling end as his hands and head broke the lake's surface and he plunged into the water.

He kicked, swimming hard as he searched the depths. Blue light filtered around him, shimmering with a magical glow. Deeper and deeper he swam, until the light darkened and he could barely see his own hands. He had to find her! He had to touch her! Then, almost at the lake floor, he felt the soft brush of her hair. He grabbed it and yanked.

Istabelle let herself drift. She did not fight the heavy skirts that pulled her far below the surface. Instead, she accepted the water's embrace and worked quickly at her skirt ties. But rather than release under her deft fingers, the strings knotted and refused to give way.

Panic started to overwhelm her, but she forced it back. She was a sea captain! She could not afford to lose control. She held her breath and worked at the knot, desperately attempting to free herself. The urge to breathe snuck up on her and she bit her lip, de-

46

manding that her body obey her mind. Black spots flickered on the fringes of her vision and she became dizzy. Her fingers slowed.

A burst of pain erupted from her scalp as the warrior gripped her hair and wrestled her heavy weight to the surface. At first she struggled, but her efforts were feeble and she gave up within seconds. The strong upward pull was welcome and she gazed at the man who was rescuing her.

At last they reached the surface and he lifted her up, treading water so she could take a lifegiving breath of fresh air. She gasped with relief, holding his shoulders with white knuckles, but the weight of her skirts started to drag them both down once again. As the warrior slipped under the water, she remembered the dagger strapped to her calf. "My knife," she gasped. "On my leg—"

He slid his hand down her waist and hip, then fought to find her skin beneath the yards of cloth. They both dipped under the water for a moment. He released her in order to swim upward, but her body dropped quickly and he was forced to dive after her again.

Under the crystal blue water they stared at each other. Bits of mica that had covered her body formed a sparkling cloud around her, dancing in her swirling hair. Her silver eyes looked like the shimmering surface of a fish, or the magical scales of a mermaid. Her blouse floated away from her chest, revealing a rounded cleavage, then washed flush against her, enticing him.

She pulled her skirt up and wrapped her legs

around his waist. They sank together, deeper, until the water became cooler. She leaned onto him, pressing her body against his, and he could think of nothing but the feel of heaven in his arms.

Then the cold press of her strapped dagger urged him back into action and he shoved her skirts fully up and ran his hands down her thighs, down her calves, until he located the small weapon. He yanked the blade out of its leather casing. Using his free hand, he held her blouse away from her skin and sliced downward, severing the cloth in two. Then, as the material drifted away, he slid his hand into her waistband and did the same to it. With quick, efficient strokes, he cut the ties and the first several inches of her skirts, until they, too, sank.

Released of the heavy weight, she unwrapped her legs and allowed the final bits of her clothing to slip away, then she swam for the surface.

He followed, and they broke the waterline together. Heaving with relief, he searched her face quickly, assuring himself that she was well. Only a thin barrier of linen covered her body, and the water had turned it translucent. Intense desire surged through him and he reached to enfold her, to kiss her, to taste her.

The stone on his borrowed signet ring flashed red in the sunlight just as a shout reached them from shore.

The woman gasped in shock as she clutched his hand. She stared at the ring in stunned amazement as she treaded water next to him. "Mangan?"

"What?" the warrior asked as he turned to see what was disturbing them from shore. Several ugly-looking men were wading into the water.

"It *is* you! Blessed saints!" she cried.

"Huh?" he said as he pushed her behind him, intent on protecting her from the men.

"Mangan! Cousin Mangan!" Suddenly she swam around him. "Men! Guess who I found! It is Mangan, the cousin I have been waiting for."

The nasty-looking men paused. One shouted out to her. "Is that the truth of it, Captain? We thought you were fighting the man and needed assistance."

"No, no! You have it wrong. I had it wrong. He came to help. In fact, he just saved me from drowning." She spun around and stared back at the warrior's stunned face. " 'Tis lucky for you I figured out who you were before my men reached you. They would have torn you limb from limb had you not been family. Mangan? Don't you realize who I am? I am Istabelle!"

He shook his head. "No, I'm not—"

Istabelle swam into his arms and clasped him in a tight embrace. "I cannot tell you how grateful I am that you came. For weeks, I feared you had abandoned me like everyone else. But I should have known you would come. I trust you like I trust no other. You are the only person I can tell my secrets to, the only person I let know my worries."

He shook his head again. "Miss Istabelle—"

"Don't be ridiculous, Cousin. I have not been called that since I lived under your father's roof. But

I must admit, you are quite different than I pictured. You are much . . . bigger . . . than I remember. But then, I still think of you as five years old. Will you forgive me for stealing your things? I would never have done such a thing had I known it was you."

"Perhaps I could forgive you, but first I must tell you—"

"Shush. My men approach and I do not want them to know anything other than what they must."

She pushed out of his arms and swam toward the men. "Ho there, my friends! This is Mangan, my cousin. Pray, do not slice him to ribbons, for he has come a long way to assist us. His sword arm is experienced and he is a brilliant strategist, aren't you, Mangan?"

"I . . . I *have* come to help you, but—"

The biggest sailor glared at Ruark. "It is lucky he is your cousin, for if I found out he was not, I would gladly stab him in the heart."

"Well, he *is* my cousin, so kindly turn away and get me a cloak. My dress is at the bottom of the lake."

Chapter 4

Ruark trudged out of the lake, his clinging breeches highlighting his state of semi-arousal. He turned, angling his body away from the others. "My things are on the cliff," he mumbled. Then, without waiting for a response, he stalked away toward the shelter of the shadows.

What mess had he inadvertently created? The sailors would not forgive him for compromising their captain if they realized he was not Mangan, and Mangan would damn him to hell if he knew what feelings Istabelle's lithe body had generated in his manhood. After years of perfectly executing whatever military orders he received, he had managed to botch this mission within seconds. She had been all but naked in his arms. Was there any way he could extricate himself from this situation?

Ruark could hear the faint echo of Istabelle's excited voice as she spoke to her crew, and he glanced over his shoulder. She still stood on the shore, but now her figure was concealed within a voluminous cloak of black velvet. A few remaining flecks of glitter sparkled in her hair when the sun glinted down upon her.

She had collected her mare and was soothing her, perhaps even praising her for her obedience.

Ruark shook his head. "The mare is as much a lunatic as you are, Miss Istabelle," he said under his breath. "You would do well to temper your impulsiveness. No doubt, whatever trouble you got yourself into, you deserved it. I will not be led by someone as rash as you."

He turned back and continued up the path. This was not going to work. He could not, in good conscience, take orders from her. He was a warrior and she was merely a spoiled girl with a woman's body. He would tell her in no uncertain terms that he was not her cousin, and because of the circumstances of their meeting, he must be on his way immediately.

Sighing with relief, Ruark reached the large boulder where he had flung his sword before diving into the lake. The stallion was munching on grass, but when Ruark rounded the corner, he lifted his head and snorted.

"I see that you had no intention of leaping after me," Ruark grumbled.

The stallion snorted again, then dropped his head to nibble on more tender shoots.

"Come on, you beast," Ruark replied. "I will tell the wench the truth of it, and she will send us packing." As Ruark mounted up, a twinge of guilt made him grimace. Mangan had hired him to help his cousin. In exchange, he was providing medical solace to Sven. "There will be other ways to repay him," Ruark said aloud, trying to convince himself.

He rode slowly down the hillside, planning how to tell Istabelle that she had mistaken his identity yet also avoid angering the sailors. Although he was willing to battle any who dared attack him, he had no desire to fight unnecessarily. As he approached the group of people, a falcon dove from the sky and swooped past his face.

"Be gone!" he cried as he ducked. The bird struck his uplifted arm, placing three sharp cuts upon his flesh before it climbed quickly to the sky. Infuriated, he pulled his bow from his saddle and rapidly strung an arrow.

"No!" Istabelle commanded as she stepped alongside his stallion. Her velvet cloak swirled around her feet, opening and closing with her strides. Flashes of the wet white linen barely concealing her body made Ruark pause. When he had retrieved his horse and sword only moments ago, he had managed to forget the effect her form had upon him, but now he clenched his fist in reaction and looked away.

"The bird attacked me," he growled as he scanned the sky, noting that the falcon was now out of range.

"She is Péril, *my* falcon, and she attacked because you were wrestling with me earlier. As soon as she gets to know you, she will accept you. After all, you are family."

Ruark looked at her sharply, searching her tone for an underlying nuance, but she merely gazed up at him with her silvery eyes. The black lashes that looked unbelievably long were clumped, forming sharp spikes that cast her eyes in mysterious shadow. "A bird like that should be better trained," he replied. "You should return it to the falconer and exchange it for a more docile specimen."

Istabelle froze and lifted her left brow incredulously. "Mangan, how could you say such a thing? You know I found this bird as a fledgling and raised it by hand. It has never known the indignity of trusses, nor have I ever commanded its obedience. No living creature should ever be subjected to another's will."

The falcon shrieked and spiraled in the sky. It took a quick dive toward Ruark once again and he raised his bow in defense. "Keep the creature away from me, or so help me, I will shoot it down. I have care for my sight and will allow no pet to pluck my eyeballs from their sockets, regardless of your affection for it."

Istabelle gasped, but when it became apparent that the falcon was about to attack again, she briskly waved the creature away. The falcon ceased her attack, but her beady eyes remained trained on the warrior's face.

"Very well," Istabelle replied. "I will ride with you and she will see that you are a friend." Before he could react to her comment, she had gripped his saddle cantle and pulled herself up onto his stallion. She swung her right leg behind him and then sat astride the stallion's rump.

Ruark caught his breath. Her wet body was pressed

against his back and the folds of the cloak were on either side of them. Heat instantly radiated from her flesh to his, and he felt the burning stiffness of her nipples rubbing against him.

"Get down," he said gruffly. "This is not appropriate."

"Don't be ridiculous. The best way to ensure Péril's acceptance is for me to ride with you. The falcon will then see that I trust you and that you have innocent intentions toward me."

He leaned forward in an effort to break contact between them, but Istabelle snuggled close once again. Innocent thoughts were the last thing on his mind, and he glanced up and glared at the bird. Péril shrieked in response, and circled lower.

Whispering, Istabelle breathed into the warrior's ear, "And besides, this will give us an opportunity to talk privately."

"Aye, I wish that as well," he relented and clucked to his horse. "There are things I must explain to you." While the sailors trailed behind them on foot, the pair set out toward the coast. As they ducked underneath branches, the falcon was soon lost to sight.

"I must tell you what is happening, so that you will know how best to help me," Istabelle murmured. "A few weeks before I sent you my missive, my ship was at dock and I was in a tavern, minding my own business."

Ruark twisted around and stared at her in surprise. "You were in a dockside tavern? What did you think you were doing? No lady should frequent such locales."

Istabelle frowned. "I live my life as I see fit. I see no reason why I should not visit a tavern if I wish to do so."

"Things happen to women in places like that. Especially beautiful women."

"Bah," Istabelle replied angrily.

"What happened in the tavern while you were 'minding your own business'?"

Istabelle's forehead dropped against his back and she sighed, her anger leaving as quickly as it had come. "There is an outlaw trader named Horik who has not appreciated my presence on the sea. He raids the coastal villages, and I raid his ships." Istabelle lifted her head and stared at the warrior in front of her. His deep onyx eyes peered into hers, and Istabelle shivered. She did not remember his eyes being so dark, so . . . compelling.

"You raided the ship of an outlaw? Of Horik? I know this man," he said, his voice rising. "He is a vicious raider. One of the few remaining men who follow no rules of combat."

"Yes. I stole from his ship several times."

"That is beyond foolish, even for a woman."

Bristling, Istabelle leaned back and glared at him. "What is that supposed to mean, Cousin? You do not know anything about it! If I were a man, would you say such a thing to me?"

"You are not a man, and thus I will say it."

"I have successfully attacked his ship three times,

and not once has he been able to stop me. Anyone would agree that my methods are admirable."

"Yet this man did get something back from you, correct? He must have bested you in some way or you would not have written."

"That is part of the truth. He did manage to steal something from me, but it was something he had no right to take."

He laughed. "This you say, after telling me that you robbed him three times? I find very little compassion for your plight, Istabelle."

"And I find even less pleasure in your mockery. The thing he took from me was not . . . not acceptable to lose. It was not one of his own treasures, but something uniquely my own."

"Like what?"

"I can't tell you."

"Excuse me? You want my help in retrieving an object you refuse to identify? Are you as insane as I first suspected?"

"Please understand, I cannot tell you the details."

"Can you not at least describe it for me? Is it big or small? Gold or jeweled? Does it have a certain use or is it simply an object of beauty? You must tell me something."

"I cannot reveal any details, but I promise you will understand later."

"I will, will I?" he replied with amusement. "Well, you have made my next statement all the more easy with your dramatics. I, too, must tell you something. I am not going to stay here and help you. I have many important matters to attend to and I would rather spend my time on them than gallivanting across the sea to seek a treasure you cannot describe."

"Please, Mangan!" Istabelle cried as she flung her arms around his waist. "I can trust no other! I need you. Trust me, I would tell you if I could, but I cannot. Not yet. Maybe later. Please, stay and help me. You came all this way, why return now?"

Ruark turned away and squeezed his legs, asking his stallion to walk more quickly. Istabelle's pleading face was too persuasive. The wild, untamed nature of her soul was painted on her cheeks and chin, yet the softness of vulnerability graced her brow.

"It is best this way. You should take it as a lesson to cease your marauding. A woman like you, born to privilege, should be on her knees thanking the gods that you have everything you need. There is no reason for you to steal more."

Silence followed his caustic remarks. When minutes went by with no response, he finally pulled his stallion to a halt and pointed to the ocean, which was visible through the trees. "Here you are. I will spare you what else I should say, so that you will go on your way. Good day."

Istabelle slowly slid off the stallion, her body rubbing Ruark's thigh with clinging wetness. "You would leave me?" she finally said, her voice so faint he had to bend down to hear it.

"Understand that I am doing what is best for you. This was a mistake from the moment your letter touched my hands. I advise you to leave Horik to his treasure and not seek to reclaim it. It will only bring you more misery. In the meantime, enjoy the benefits of your life and live well."

"I don't understand . . . why? Why are you leaving, Mangan?"

He swallowed uncomfortably, embarrassed to tell her that she was still addressing him incorrectly. It would be so easy to ride away and never tell her. She did not need to know that her nearly unclothed body had pressed against the muscles of a stranger. She certainly did not need to know that as she stood below him, he could trace the curves of her bosom from his vantage point. If he left, he would not have to explain anything. Except to Mangan.

Ruark closed his eyes, acknowledging that his action was cowardly, but he was a warrior. He could face any steel, any mace, any weapon of man's destruction, but her silvery eyes disconcerted him. It may be the coward's way out, but he was taking it.

"I do not have time to run around chasing a nameless treasure, and you should leave it alone as well. Don't you want a husband? Shouldn't you concern yourself with finding a man who can protect and honor you? Spend your energies on ladylike activities and you will get yourself in less trouble." Nodding to add emphasis to his words, he reined his stallion away.

"Mangan?" Istabelle said.

Ruark sighed, then answered her as if the name were his. "Yes?"

"You are despicable."

* * *

Istabelle paced her ship's cabin, her heart filled with fury, hurt, confusion and desperation. Mangan was nothing like she remembered. As a child, he had been sweet and caring. He had been her protector. Countless times he had vowed to watch over her, and while the vows had been spoken in a childlike voice, they had been binding nonetheless.

"How could he ride away?" she ranted out loud. "How could he ignore my request and berate me for my life? I cannot believe he would be so callous as to come out here for the sole purpose of telling me that I should alter my ways. How could he have changed so much over the years? He knows that I only seek to help those in need and do not attack anyone who does not deserve it, yet he speaks as if I am as guilty of selfish behavior as Horik himself!"

A knock on the cabin door interrupted her and she snapped at the person to enter.

"Captain," the man replied.

"Boris," Istabelle answered. "What news do you have?" She resumed pacing even before he responded.

"Horik sends a message. He demands that you come to the third island off Canna's northern point. He says you cannot refuse."

"And if I do?"

"He indicates that you will not disobey his summons."

"Well, he is wrong. I will seek him out on my own schedule, not his. Who sends this message?"

"A boy from his settlement. He came to Canna and spread the tale that he needed to give you an important missive."

"Horik let a *boy* deliver his words? How insulting."

"What shall I do to the boy?"

"Bring him here."

"Aye, Captain." Within moments, he returned with a frightened, blond-haired boy who trembled in her presence.

"What is your name?" Istabelle demanded.

"Erik, Madam Captain of the Scottish Sea."

"You delivered a message that displeases me greatly. Why should I not throw you overboard and let you drown?"

"I beg you to have mercy, Madam Captain!"

"Are you related to Horik? His nephew perhaps? Some important person that he would trust with such a risky mission?"

"No, I am merely a slave."

Istabelle's gaze narrowed and she strode in front of the boy and stared down at him. "What do you mean, slave? No one has slaves anymore. Horik has no right to command your life!"

"I was captured one year ago from a northern settlement when he raided our village."

"And your family?"

"Dead, Madam Captain. I was the lucky one."

"You find it lucky to serve someone without choice? I hate any kind of subjugation of one to another. I would rather die than be a slave."

"Am I to die?"

Istabelle glared at him, her silver eyes sparking with anger. "I do not kill helpless boys," she snapped. "I advise you not to return to him. Set yourself free." She spun back around and strode to the port window. The thin wool of her green dress rippled around her boot-clad feet, and her hips were encircled by a simple silver chain. A jeweled dagger hung by another chain from her neck, winking in the swell of her cleavage, while a short sword swung loosely at her side. Many blond strands shimmered in her russet tresses like strands of golden thread. To Erik, she looked like a fighting sea goddess.

"Thank you," he breathed as he fell to his knees.

Glancing over her shoulder irritably, she pointed to the door. "Go on. I must concentrate. Return him to wherever he wants to be and give him some provisions for his journey," she told Boris.

"Yes, Madam Captain of the Scottish Sea. If you would accept it, I would like to stay aboard and serve you."

Istabelle stared out the porthole, her thoughts focused on Mangan. He was so different from what she had expected. He was rough, strong, unrelenting . . . handsome. He stirred uncomfortable feelings in the pit of her stomach.

"Captain?" Erik asked hesitantly. "Where am I to go?"

Startled from her reverie, Istabelle waved her hand briskly. "Wherever you want," she said. "Just be on your way. I have other things to think about."

Erik bowed and followed Boris out of the cabin, softly shutting the door behind him.

Istabelle plopped down in the chair behind a large desk that dominated the room. Charts and instruments littered the surface, and unlike most captain's cabins, the room was in haphazard disarray. Several items of clothing were draped over furniture and the bed was unmade. A rug on the floor was skewed diagonally and Istabelle stared moodily at it.

Her recent encounter with Horik came to mind. He had frightened her. The iron bands had made her helpless and he had torn her self-confidence down to mere shreds. Sweat beaded her brow as she recalled the terrifying moments alone with him in the cabin. Unless she took back some measure of control, she would forever be at the mercy of her memories. She could not slink away and pretend that nothing had happened. She must confront him again.

After years of pledging herself to help others, she needed someone else's help to retrieve her stolen item, for she feared approaching Horik alone. She had to steal it back! If she did not, she would always fear his imminent attack. She would be as helpless as the slave Erik.

"Mangan," she said to the darkening cabin, "you must help me. I will not accept any other answer. For my life and my freedom . . . I cannot."

Chapter 5

Ruark set up camp in a small clearing. He had intended to travel that day, but a strange lassitude had overcome him and he had spent the afternoon lying on his back, staring at the leaves in the trees. At first he had assumed he was suffering from sexual tension, but even after relieving himself by hand, he was unsatisfied. He tried to drag the face of the farmer's daughter to mind, but her features were blurred.

Unfortunately, Istabelle's face was clear and vibrant in his memory, and Ruark groaned when images of her snuck up on him once again. She was certainly different from any other woman he had ever met. Not only her profession—how many female seafarers roamed Scotland's coast?—and her thievery set her apart. There was a fire that lit her from within. She was burning with it, like a bonfire that was almost out of control.

He rolled over and propped his chin in his hands. Too bad she wasn't a man. If she had been, she would have been a fierce fighter to be reckoned with. Images of her breasts, her shoulders and the curve of her cheek made him smile. She definitely was not a man. But he had set her straight, and when he returned to the monastery and told Mangan how he had handled the situation, he would surely get a good pat on the back. Certainly his advice to her was worthwhile and necessary, and Mangan would be pleased that he had been so direct with his cousin. No doubt even now the woman was dropping her sails and looking at invitation lists for prospective husbands. He deliberately pushed her parting words to the recesses of his memory.

Twilight descended and a few stars twinkled in the sky. A cool wind blew the treetops, but he was sheltered from its breath by the bushes surrounding his grove. Even so, he felt goose bumps on the back of his neck. He sat up and looked around, scanning the area. His stallion was grazing peacefully, his tail swishing at occasional insects. His big ears flicked lazily with no indication that he heard anything amiss.

Ruark stood up, walked to the edge of the clearing and urinated. When he finished, he retied his breeches and turned back to the center of the clearing. There, near his stallion, her falcon resting on her shoulder, stood Istabelle.

"How on God's earth did you sneak up on me?" he snapped, infuriated that she had caught him unaware. A faint redness darkened his cheeks.

"I did not mean to surprise you. I thought you would be much farther along and did not expect to find you until tomorrow."

"You were following me?" he asked incredulously. "Why?"

Istabelle smiled, forcing a mild expression on her face. "Because we need to talk before you make a final decision."

"I have already made my decision. What else do we have to discuss?"

"I have a bird that Péril brought to me," Istabelle said, avoiding a direct response. "Would you like some stew?"

He frowned, aware that he had not thought about food all day. His belly rumbled. "You should go back," he said reluctantly.

"The sun is setting, and I would rather not travel by night."

The warrior shrugged. "No," he replied. "It would not be wise for you to travel in the dark."

"Then why don't you collect some wood while I prepare the bird?"

Ruark grumbled under his breath about bossy females, but he fetched wood nonetheless. As Istabelle plucked the bird, he built a small pile of kindling and struck the flint. The two worked silently, each doing the necessary tasks in unspoken harmony, and the pot from Ruark's saddlebags was soon simmering over the fire with delicious smells wafting forth.

Night's promise finally overtook them, and the campfire enclosed them in an intimate circle of orange light. Istabelle glanced up at the warrior, noting the fire's reflection on his eyes. "You have grown into a powerful man," she said hesitantly, averting her eyes before his arrested expression. "No, don't interrupt me for a moment. Please."

He stood up and stepped away from the light. "Very well."

"I have not expressed myself well enough. What I seek from Horik is not merely some trinket I lost. It is something infinitely more valuable, and I need a man like you to help me retrieve it. Mangan," she said sharply when he opened his mouth to talk, "you promised to let me have my say."

Sighing in exasperation, he nodded.

"I have trusted very few people in this world. My life, as you know, began quite harshly. I was almost murdered by my own mother, and although your parents treated me well, I felt the loss of my father when he abandoned me for the first five years of my life. You were the most important person to me. You were kind, loving and, most of all, trustworthy."

"Stop," Ruark interrupted. "I am not the man you think I am."

Pacing in agitation, Istabelle fingered her dagger and dismissed his comments, "Of course I understand that you have changed. How could you stay the same sweet child that you were when you were five? I know you have dealt with many things that would break a weaker man. You are going to be the future earl. You will be responsible for many people. You have lands and politics to worry about and I am only a young woman with a personal problem." Suddenly she dropped to her knee in front of him and looked at him with pleading silver eyes. "You may not approve of my life, but I have done what I can to absolve the evils brought into this world by my mother. I want to erase her memory and replace it with goodness and kindness."

Ruark shook his head. "I don't understand."

"My mother tried to ruin your life, my life, my father's life, my aunt and uncle's lives. She spread nastiness and horror everywhere!"

"That has nothing to do with you, Istabelle," he replied. "I heard that she was a misguided woman and you were but an infant. You have no responsibility."

"Yes, I do! I carry the Dunhaven blood in my heart. I feel it pulsing. The only place where I can control myself is on the sea. Something about the vast expanse calms me and makes me feel cleansed. Can·you understand?"

Frowning, Ruark thought back upon his life as a warrior. Blood had soaked his hands so many times, he was surprised they were not stained red. "When I am fighting, I feel as if my life has purpose. Is that what you mean?"

"In a way, yes. I want to know that I am necessary, and that what I do will make a difference. I want people to remember me for who I am and not for how I came to be."

"Very few are as tortured as you by their early years," he said softly. "Yet you have known love. You have known security. Why do you still feel that you must prove something?"

Istabelle bowed her head. "I don't know, but I

know that the sea was my only solace, and now that has been stripped from me because of Horik. The sea is all-knowing, all-forgiving. It is vast and impersonal. It is safe." Istabelle looked up and tears filled her eyes. They spilled down her cheeks, forming glistening tracks that held the warrior spellbound. "But now, because of Horik, I don't feel safe, and all the fears of my childhood are tumbling after me, building and towering, enveloping me in layers of uncontrollable emotions. I am lost."

"What about your stepmother or your father?" he gruffly questioned. "Ask them for assistance."

Istabelle shook her head. "This is not something I want them to know about. They are happy. They have separated themselves from the world in an effort to avoid these kinds of troubles. I do not want to disturb their idyll."

"I am certain they would want to know. You should go to them."

"No! It is too personal. I want you, now more than ever. When I wrote to you, I hoped that you would be the right person, but I feared that you would not have the qualities I required to fight such an evil man. Recently, in your letters you have sounded more spiritual and peace-loving than battle sharp. Now that I have met you in person after all these years, I know that, indeed, you and you alone are the man I want." She rose and the reflected flames danced against her cheeks, illuminating them. She leaned against his chest and laid her face upon it. "You are strong and wise. I can see it in your eyes, in the way you think about every move you make before you make it. You must help me."

He swallowed, unable to form a response. Her scent overwhelmed him and the softness of her body pressing against him made him tongue-tied. Her pleas pulled him, tugged at the buried kindness in his heart that had responded to Sven's toddler eyes. A wave of protectiveness swept over him and he wrapped his arms around her, pulling her closer. She snuggled into his form, mewing like a kitten.

Perhaps it was meant to be. Perhaps he had been sent in Mangan's stead for a reason. This wild child would not accept a stranger's help. If he revealed his true name, she would leap away from him and deny her need. She would run away, face her problem alone. She would leave his arms and escape once again to the sea, without hope.

He wanted to help her, for the fear in her voice was real. Her vulnerability was palpable. She was not a woman to show weakness, yet she had opened her soul to him. Horik had hurt her by stealing the item she spoke of, and she was close to collapse from the pain. She said it was something personal. Could it be as personal as her virtue? Could this man have harmed her body? If so, what did she mean to do when she spoke of "retrieving" the treasure?

Ruark was a warrior, and while he was not a chivalrous lord, he felt the need to shelter those who needed his protection. If the only way to help her was to pretend to be Mangan, then so be it.

"I will help you," he said at last. "I will help you fight Horik and assist you in recoving your treasure."

"You will?" Istabelle breathed as she leaned back and gazed at his face.

"Aye, but I will have to know what we are searching for. You need to tell me the truth."

"Can I tell you later? I—I cannot just yet. . . . Can you please understand?"

He relented in the face of her pleading gaze. "Very well, but know that there will come a time when you will have to reveal your secret."

Istabelle nodded. "I understand. I trust you, Mangan." She placed a soft kiss upon his cheek.

Ruark flinched and pushed her away before she could remark upon his reaction. Both her kiss and her words made him tremble inside. What was he getting himself into?

After Istabelle had convinced him to stay, they spent a quiet evening eating stew and discussing the sea. Since Ruark knew very little about sailing, he was curious about her ship and crew. Her knowledge impressed him, although he was careful not to express his admiration. She had enough self-confidence and he was not about to add to it. When they spread out their bedrolls to go to sleep, he carefully turned away to avoid staring at her, although he was acutely aware of her presence throughout the night.

In the early morning, they rode toward the coast in single file. Ruark's stallion walked behind Istabelle's mare, tossing his head at each swish of the mare's tail. From her perch on Istabelle's saddle, the falcon peered at the warrior, hissing in anger. Ruark watched her warily, prepared for an attack. "When will that beast accept my presence?" he asked Istabelle.

She stroked the falcon's head, smoothing the feathers, and glanced over her shoulder. Sunlight filtered down upon them, lacing golden streaks across Istabelle's face and shoulders. She shrugged. "I have never seen her take such a dislike to someone before. She usually ignores all humans in favor of me. Perhaps it is a compliment that she notices your presence."

"When I must fear for my safety, I do not call it a blessing. She has lighter coloring than any falcon I have seen, and she is far larger."

"She is a gyrfalcon."

"That is not possible. Gyrfalcons are for kings."

Istabelle laughed. "They may be meant for kings, but this one is mine. Don't you remember me writing to you about her? She was one of seven that were en route to the French king as a gift from some great noble, along with a shipload of other valuables. I did not think one man should be the recipient of so much wealth, so I confiscated some of it."

"That is thievery," the warrior exclaimed. "You should not steal!"

Istabelle stiffened. "As far as I am concerned, the noble stole from the people in order to provide such offerings. I don't believe in such a disparity of riches."

72

"But if the bird was meant to be a gift to the king, you should have returned her."

Istabelle shrugged. "With six others, why should he need this one? I took part of the shipment and distributed the money to people in need, but I kept the falcon for myself."

"What you did was a crime. If you get caught, you will be put in prison."

"I won't get caught," Istabelle replied.

"Besides," the warrior continued, "you should have a kestrel. It would be more your size."

"A kestrel would not be able to navigate the strong winds at sea."

"How do you feed her when you are sailing? The falconers at the castles are involved day and night with tending, exercising and feeding their birds."

"I have only one, and she has adapted. She has developed a taste for seafood, as well as for her normal fare. Do you hawk?"

"No, I have no time for such sport."

Istabelle looked at him curiously. "How odd. I thought, as future earl, you would be an avid austringer. Perhaps you should learn. 'Tis said that the king of Persia kept his falcon at his side and learned how to be a good king via the bird's calming influence."

"She has not had a calming effect upon you, however," he replied, and Istabelle smiled.

"I think you are teasing me, Mangan! Take care, or I will begin to think you are not entirely serious."

Péril lifted from her perch and soared into the sky. Her gray feathers were sprinkled with darker flecks, camouflaging her against the scattered clouds. She rose until she was barely visible and then seemed to drift along with a lazy lack of direction. Without warning, she tucked her wings and dove straight down toward a small flock of sparrows being chased by a black-feathered rook. The smaller birds darted in every direction, desperately trying to avoid the sharp talons of the hunter, but the rook was oblivious. With incredible speed, the gyrfalcon snatched the crowlike animal with her talons, then plummeted to the ground as the rook struggled. The tree branches briefly hid the pair from view, and by the time Istabelle and Ruark turned a corner, Péril was perched on a bare branch, tearing the rook's flesh with her deadly hooked beak.

"Is she not supposed to bring the prey to you and let you reward her?" Ruark asked.

"I do not require her subservience," Istabelle replied. "She brings me food when she wants to, and I thank her for her gifts. She knows that I do not like crows, but I am fond of stew pigeons and small rabbits."

"She is a majestic creature. The color of her wings reminds me of the color of your eyes."

Istabelle shyly dropped her gaze. "I am but an ugly duckling compared to her beauty and grace. But you are kind to say such courtly words, Cousin."

Ruark frowned and looked away. 'Twas good of her to remind him of his deception, even if she did not know what she was doing. He must watch what he said so that she did not become aware of his attraction to her. She did remind him of the bird. She was wild and free, untamed and unpredictable. Yet, for all her fierceness, her talons and her razor-sharp beak, her face was delicate and refined.

As the dawn shifted into day, they rode in silence along the coast toward Istabelle's ship. The crashing waves created a rhythmic cadence to accent the steady clopping of their horses' hooves, and the tang of the salt air complemented the rich smell of drying kelp.

Istabelle looked through her lashes at Mangan. He was so different from what she had expected. Even his voice was surprising. She had expected Mangan's voice to be smooth and polished, but instead it was startlingly brisk. His letters to her had been reserved yet friendly, coming from a man who was comfortable with his station, but in person he seemed edgy and uncomfortable, as if he were greatly troubled by many things. She had not intended to talk so soulfully to him last night, but something about his tight expression and barely held control had made her want to tell him how she felt. It was almost as if she could help him by asking him to help her.

She looked at his powerful thighs gripping his stallion's girth. Her cousin was a supreme specimen of strength. His legs alone were thicker than her waist. His long hair was unusual, and she had an absurd desire to see it loose, blowing in the wind, but she was certain that such spontaneity was not like him. He was not a man who enjoyed sensual moments. She doubted he had ever closed his eyes in appreciation of a delicate peach or let himself luxuriate in the warmth of morning sheets. He was not a man to watch the dawn or stand in the driving rain simply because it felt wonderful against one's bare skin.

He was cold and hard, yet mysterious. He was so unlike the boy she remembered, she was slightly confused. How could he have changed so dramatically? Was it just the transition from child to man that made him intriguing? She felt there was something more. His eyes were hooded, as if he was reluctant to talk about himself, and he appeared constantly on guard.

A flicker of excitement tickled her. She was used to difficult, hardened men. Her crew followed her because they respected her intuitive understanding of the ocean's changing moods as well as the men's rough nature. She was unparalleled in her seafaring abilities and she treated her sailors well. Yet she was still a woman, and the men aboard her ship maintained a certain distance because of her gender. She had their respect, perhaps their friendship, but no one was her confidant.

Mangan would be different. He was her cousin. He was family. She would be able to trust him with her deepest secrets and know that he would protect her. She glanced over her shoulder once again and met his onyx eyes, trying to convince herself. He stared at her unblinkingly until she was forced to turn away.

Recanting silently, Istabelle shook her head. Perhaps she should tread carefully and not tell him too much until she knew him better. There were things about him that made her wary. Until she was certain she could control the situation, she would keep her own council. Besides, she was pleased that she had convinced him to help her, despite his misgivings. After all, she normally got what she wanted, and so far he was doing exactly as she wished.

Chapter 6

By nightfall, Istabelle was not so sure she was pleased. She stood at the helm, guiding the ship out to sea, and had an unobstructed view of her cousin as he sat sharpening his sword. His linen shirt alternately pressed against his chest, then billowed away as the wind flirted with his body. He was brutally handsome—his hard muscles rippled with his repetitive movements. He ran the whetstone down the side of the sword again and again, stroking his blade, rocking with the motion, until Istabelle yanked her gaze away.

"Why is he doing that?" she grumbled at her first mate.

Taber shrugged. "He is a warrior. All warriors think about is their sword. It is like you and the ship."

"I think about more than my ship, and I would not ignore another just to tend to her needs."

"What does it matter that he is not talking to you? Did you expect him to stand at your side and hold polite conversation?"

"No . . . I just thought that he might say something, or do something, other than sharpen his sword. He has done that for well over an hour."

"You should be pleased, Captain. He is respecting your position as leader of the ship and does not want to interfere with your duties."

"Aye, you speak the truth. I do not want him treating me like a stupid lady of the court. I do not know why I am irritable. Take the wheel. I will go below."

Taber nodded and relieved Istabelle of her position, but Istabelle did not immediately depart from the deck. She walked over to the railing and stood in front of her cousin.

Ruark felt her approach and deliberately kept his gaze averted. He was becoming seasick and was loath for her to witness his weakness.

"Is not your blade sharp enough, Mangan?" Istabelle asked.

"Not quite," he responded gruffly, his shoulders tightening at the false name. He turned the sword over and began working on the other side with swift strokes.

"You already did that side," Istabelle chided him.

" 'Tis not finished," he answered.

"If you continue, you will thin the steel and weaken the weapon."

Disgusted that she spoke the truth, he stood up and glared at her. The glorious health that glowed in her cheeks angered him further and he snapped the sword into his belt. "As you command, Captain," he growled.

Istabelle raised her eyebrows. "I did not insist that you stop. I only questioned—"

"I do not have time for your questions. I must prepare to deal with Horik quickly and decisively so that I may return home."

Istabelle stepped back, surprised by his anger. "We will not battle my enemy today. We must learn about his defenses first, then plan our attack."

The warrior flung his arm out, gesturing to the wide ocean. "How do you plan to find him in this heaving mass of blue? 'Tis unnatural to place a bit of wood upon the sea and float around!"

"I did not know you disliked sailing, Cousin," Istabelle said after a pause. "I thought you enjoyed your travels to the south." She peered at his face, noticing the green tinge that darkened his cheeks. "I have a draught that will help you with seasickness if you desire."

"I am not seasick," he raged. "No element can take control of my innards and turn them inside out against my will. I am immune to such illness. I have no fear of thunder, no concern for cold. I have braved the burning sun and have—have—" He gripped the railing and bit his lip.

Istabelle grinned. "I see. Then you would not mind coming below, into the bowels of the ship, where the rocking is more pronounced?"

He vomited. He had no choice. Disgusted, infuriated, embarrassed and weakened, he dropped to his knees and spewed his breakfast over the side of the ship, between the railings. As he heaved, knowledge of his own actions sickened him further, and he vomited again.

"Don't worry, Cousin. Everyone has days when their stomach does not agree with them. There is nothing to be ashamed of."

That made him gag again. Shame was his worst enemy, for it chased him relentlessly. It followed him in his sleep, in battle, in his daily life. He felt the shame of his orphaned existence and his lowly status. Despite anything he could possibly accomplish in this lifetime, the facts could not be erased. He dropped his head to the floorboards and breathed slowly. He did not want to reveal his weak inner soul to anyone, especially not to a woman, not to her.

He glared, anger pulsing through him, and struggled to his feet. "Do not speak to me of shame." He held his sword in front of him and pointed it at her for emphasis.

Istabelle's eyes narrowed and she placed her hand on her own sword in warning. "Are you threatening me, Mangan?" she asked softly.

"I will do whatever I wish," he growled, fighting the bilious urge to vomit again. The anger distracted him and he welcomed it. "May I remind you that you are in need of my help, and thus should take care not to infuriate me?"

Astonished and equally angered, Istabelle pulled her sword free and tapped his. "May I remind you that you are on my ship, and thus are under my command?"

He flicked his wrist, knocking her sword against the ship's railing. "No female commands me!"

She lunged forward with unexpected swiftness, darting her blade underneath his defenses and pressing it against his chest. Her silver eyes sparkled and a rosy flush spread over her cheeks. "I do," she answered menacingly.

Ruark reacted instinctively, forgetting that she was his friend's cousin, forgetting that he was on a ship of her men, forgetting the caution that was a daily part of his existence. He spun away from her blade, swung his sword above his head and sent it crashing against her barely raised defense. Without pausing, he swung again, forcing his opponent to scramble backward. When she ducked to the side, he followed her and smashed his sword against hers once again.

Istabelle gasped. His fury was unlike any she had ever encountered. His strength was greater than Horik's; his agility was superior to that of her own sailors. Fear raced through her and her heart started beating so rapidly that she could hear the blood humming in her ears. A single one of his blows could fell her.

"Mangan!" she shouted as she desperately defended herself. She had only seconds to guard against this enraged beast attacking her. There was no possibility of disarming him—he was so fast and powerful! "Mangan!" she screamed again, terrified. Taking a reckless chance, she sprang forward directly into his arms.

The maddened warrior staggered back, shock freezing his features. Both hands convulsed around her as his sword clattered to the deck. He could feel the length of her body pressed against him and her heat burned through his clothes, singeing his flesh.

"No!" he cried.

Istabelle gripped his face and pulled him down to her. Silver eyes met onyx ones, both equally stunned.

He shook his head. "I did not mean to attack you," he whispered. "I have never lost control like that before." The ship rocked and he paused. His face turned white and he began to tremble. She was so beautiful! Her face was so delicately sculpted—and he had almost killed her without thinking, simply because he did not want her to see him ill! Struggling to form words, he finally gritted out, "I—am—not—seasick."

The crew surrounded them and one sailor yanked Istabelle out of the warrior's arms. Another grabbed the sword from the ground and brandished it at him.

"Stop!" Istabelle shouted. "Leave him be!"

"He attacked you, Captain! He should be killed."

"No," she commanded as she shook off the men restraining her. "He did not mean to hurt me. Bring him to my cabin below and fetch some rum." She held up a hand when the men attempted to argue with her. "I will not hear any dissent! He will be punished, but only after he has recovered. Remember, he is my cousin." She stared at the warrior and silently dared him to disagree. "But I want his sword locked in the weapons room. I do not trust him with it."

Ruark opened his mouth to argue, but the crew's angry faces forced him to remain silent. He swayed in place as the ship dipped into a trough, then rose in a smooth, rolling motion. He clutched his stomach, then leaned over the side again.

Later that evening, the warrior rolled into a ball on Istabelle's bed, clutching his stomach in agony. He braced his foot against a railing, trying to reduce the rocking motion. Beads of sweat decorated his forehead, and his eyes were pressed tightly closed. Istabelle knelt beside him. "Mangan?" she whispered.

The warrior looked up at her with glazed eyes. He shook his head, then groaned at the motion.

She stared down at him, at a loss for what to do. Hours before, he had attacked her with vicious ferocity, yet now he was helpless and weak, unable to lift his head without her assistance. The muscles on his neck were tight and she could see his jaw clench with the effort to quiet his stomach.

She sat at the edge of the mattress and placed her cooling fingertips against his forehead.

"You should leave," he whispered.

"Why?" she asked.

"I do not want anyone to see me thus," he answered, then groaned as the ship rocked.

Istabelle continued to stroke his face. "When I was a little girl, I used to be afraid of spiders."

He blinked and looked up at her. "What are you talking about?"

"Spiders. Creepy, black, spindly creatures that I was certain wanted to crawl into my blankets and bite me."

He smiled involuntarily at the image of a younger Istabelle scanning her blankets for the nighttime beasts. "It is hard for me to imagine you afraid of anything."

She shrugged. "I was terribly afraid, and, if truth be told, still am, yet I have learned to control my fear. It is one of the reasons I like birds so much. They eat spiders."

He chuckled. "You do not need to fear them anymore," he said. "Your gyrfalcon will gobble any that dare trespass upon your bed."

"I never told anyone about my fear," Istabelle continued.

His laugh died as he stared at her serious expression. As the ship rolled through another swell, he concentrated on her, forgetting his seasickness. "Why are you telling me?" he asked.

"I thought you might feel better knowing that everyone has some weakness. Yours is the ocean waves. Mine is spiders."

"How old are you?" he asked after a pause.

Istabelle looked at him quizzically. "Nineteen. You know that. I am only an hour younger than you, though you appear older. Your battles have aged you."

The warrior glanced away. Mangan was nineteen, but he was not. He was almost thirty, close to ten years her senior, yet she had wisdom in her words that few possessed. "How did you overcome your fear of spiders, Istabelle?"

"I imagined squishing them and when that was

not enough, I pretended to make spider soup. Unfortunately, that did not work. The spiders kept reappearing in my imagination as bigger and angrier spiders. Then I tried to cut them up into little pieces, but that failed, too."

"I am having doubts about your sensibilities, Istabelle. Little girls should not pretend to chop up insects."

"I was never a normal child. Eventually, I took a different approach. I learned as much as I could about spiders. I learned what they ate, how they moved, what webs they built. I decided that the more I knew about them, the less they could frighten me."

"Are you saying that I should learn about the ocean?"

"Perhaps. Maybe you should focus on sailing and understanding the sea."

"Perhaps." He rolled on his back and closed his eyes, willing his innards to stop heaving. He thought about what she had said. She was a clever woman. Beautiful, smart and different from anyone he had ever encountered. If he survived this excruciating illness, he would try her approach.

As midnight drew near, Istabelle left her cousin and entered the kitchen once again. It was her third trip, and she was familiar with the routine. In the kitchen, she plucked a ginger root from a latched drawer and pulled a clean cloth from the cabinet. She wrapped the ginger inside the rag and, using a mallet, smashed the ginger. The pounding released the pungent odor of the spice, and the root formed a soft pulp. Satisfied, she replaced the remaining root, collected a basin of water and went back to her cabin.

She closed the door softly and kneeled next to the bed where he lay.

He gazed at her, too exhausted to speak. As she wiped the cloth over his face, he breathed in the ginger and moved closer to her. She represented the hope that he could overcome his illness and walk across the ship deck without the threat of nausea. He leaned against her thigh, breathing in her scent as well. She was clean and fresh. His stomach quieted and he felt safe.

She shifted as if she was going to rise, but he clung to her, needing her stillness, her presence. He felt the bile rise once again as his anxiety peaked, and he groaned aloud.

"Shush," she said. "I am only getting the water."

His sudden worry faded as her soft hands washed his face with the ginger-soaked washcloth once again. She brought peace. Serenity.

"Don't . . . go . . ." he whispered.

"I am here," she replied. She dipped the cloth in the water, and stroked his face. Her actions were awkward, for she was not used to caring for another. In fact, she could not recall having tended a creature other than her gyrfalcon. Her fingers shook, and she glanced down with embarrassment as if she expected him to mock her actions, but instead he leaned against her and placed his head on her lap.

Istabelle held him in the folds of her skirt, and

soon forgot her nervousness. She became absorbed in holding him, stroking him . . . giving him the comfort he needed. He was so powerful and capable, yet he was not indestructible. Like her falcon, he could fight, but he could also ail. An hour passed, then several, and the waves quieted as the wind settled down.

Istabelle stroked his head, smoothing the sweaty hair away from his eyes. His hair was not as soft as hers. It was thick and bordered on being coarse, yet the sheer manliness of it was intoxicating. She ran her fingers through the strands, luxuriating in the closeness the sensation gave her. She gazed out the open porthole and into the black sea, acknowledging her own loneliness. Even though she was surrounded by twenty crewmen, she was separated from them by virtue of her rank, her station and her sex. All she had was her own sense of self. Even the gyrfalcon was separate, held aloof by its innate nature.

But at this moment, holding this warrior in her arms, she felt close to someone. She shut her eyes and leaned back against the headboard. She was tired and wanted to rest. Mangan was sleeping at last, and she hoped that his nausea was cured. Many people felt seasick when they initially sailed, but most were able to overcome it after they grew accustomed to the ship's sway. A breeze snuck through the porthole and she breathed deeply. She would lie here for a moment, then get out of bed and sleep in the chair. Her head nodded and she jerked it upright, but the warmth of the man next to her was seductive, and her eyes drifted closed again. Soon, the night wind covered them with a cool blanket, and Istabelle fell asleep.

Ruark drifted somewhere between sleep and wakefulness. The illness that had felled him was receding, and a sense of peace permeated him. He could not remember where he was or what he was doing here, but he felt relaxed. A woman's hand was buried in his hair and his head was pillowed on her thighs. She smelled like fresh flowers and sweet musk. He turned slightly, burying his nose in her lap. Sea salt and mint . . .

He flung an arm around her hips, pulling her closer. "Ummm . . ." he moaned. "Delicious . . ." His eyes still closed, he stroked her hip, reveling in the swell. Up and down he brushed her, tracing the curve that went from waist to hip and then to thigh. She was soft, luxurious, feminine. He breathed again, soaking in her essence.

His hand drifted to her flat abdomen, touching her lazily. He rubbed circles there, comforted by her presence. There was a brief indentation where her navel was hidden underneath her clothes, then another round curve just above the juncture of her thighs. He rubbed her gently, without any specific thought, feeling her body.

She shifted, sighed and turned toward him.

His hand fell to her hip once again, then moved up to her back. She had a lithe, sinuous back, and he could trace her muscles through her clothes. He kneaded her, finding and smoothing the taut lines with his powerful fingers. For long minutes he rubbed her back, breathed her scent, and drifted in his state of semiwakefulness.

She stretched like a cat that has been stroked, and her leg bent up and over his.

His hand kneaded lower, down to her waist and then to her buttocks. Firm, soft globes that fit his hand perfectly. He rubbed in circles again, feeling the beauty of her feminine body. A soft moan from her made him pull her closer, and he felt the heat of her blaze against his chest, against his leg, against his cock.

He ran his hand lower, seeking the sweetness of her thighs, feeling the strength of her legs, frustrated with the wealth of fabric between them.

More urgent now, he tilted her back, slightly away from him so his hands could reach her front. Moving up her leg, brushing over the curve that tantalized him between her thighs, up her waist, up her abdomen, over her navel and to the symbol of her womanhood. To her breasts. Tentatively, as if even in his half-dazed state he knew that what he touched was sacred, he brushed his hand over the curve of her breast. Full. Swollen. Pebbled with desire.

He wanted her. Now.

Istabelle sighed and arched upward. New sensations rippled through her dream. Erotic, fantastic sensations. She shifted closer to the hot body lying next to her, although her eyes remained closed. "Mmmm . . ." she moaned.

Sweet lassitude overwhelmed her limbs as she lay

pliant and accepting. She wallowed in her dream state, unwilling to wake fully. She felt hands sweeping over her body, touching her in intimate places, and the feelings were so pleasurable, she moaned again.

When he touched her breasts, she gasped. Desire spiraled upward and she welcomed the kneading pressure of his hands and the teasing stroke of his thumbs over her nipples. She panted and tossed her head back and forth. Her breasts quivered.

He felt her body awaking to his touch and his need escalated. With a groan, he rolled on top of her and ground his hips against her pelvis.

Istabelle snapped awake and her silver eyes stared with shock up at the warrior's passionate face. "What are you doing?" she cried as she mentally scrambled to clear her mind and separate dream from reality. "How dare you!"

Ruark froze, caught between desire and surprise. "What do you mean?" His manhood pulsed, still seeking completion.

She shoved his shoulders, wriggling to get out from beneath his weight. "Get off me!" she screamed. When he stared down at her, stupefied, she grabbed the dagger from around her neck and yanked it from its sheath. She pressed it against his side and glared at him. "I said, get off me!"

Ruark's eyes grew cold and hard as passion was instantly replaced by anger. "You were responding. Don't try to deny it. I have never taken a woman against her will." He pushed himself upward with his arms and moved away from her blade. "I warned you before about threatening me. I will not tolerate such behavior."

"And what do you intend to do about it? Where is your sword?"

His eyes narrowed and he pushed his hips against hers, forcing her to acknowledge his hard shaft.

Incensed, Istabelle pushed back and scrambled out of bed, unaware that the bodice of her dress was askew. "What is wrong with you?" she shouted. "You are my cousin! You vowed to protect me! Now you accost me on my own ship and seek to bed me? Perhaps having cousins sleep with each other is acceptable in the royal court, but I find it intensely distasteful. Especially with you!"

Ruark shot out of bed and towered over her. "Believe me, if I had been fully aware, I would never have touched you! You are the last person I would be attracted to." He leapt back as she hissed her displeasure, fearing that she would attack him with her dagger, but to his surprise she backed away. He watched her warily as she moved slowly toward the door.

"Why wouldn't you be attracted to me?" she asked.

He blinked as several thoughts raced through his mind. He *was* attracted to her—in fact, far too much—but he had sworn to treat her with respect. He was supposed to protect and help her, and getting involved with her would compromise his ability to function. He couldn't tell her any of those reasons, however, so he said the only thing that he could think of. "I don't like women who point daggers and swords at me. I prefer mellow, fun-loving females who know their place."

"Ah," Istabelle replied. "That is what my step-mother once told me. She warned me that I would have a hard time finding someone who would accept my unruliness. Thankfully, I do not want to find any-one, so it doesn't matter. I value my freedom above all else, and would never want to get tangled in the spiderweb of emotional attachments."

Ruark stared at her bright silver eyes, noting her reference to the beasts she detested. Something about her vehement statement did not seem right. She was too beautiful, too fascinating, too vibrant to deny her-self male company. It would be like holding gold in your hand and flinging it to the bottom of the ocean. He took a step forward.

Istabelle stumbled back, her nerves still tingling. She was trying to show a brave, unaffected front, but inside she was reeling from the new sensations he had aroused in her. She could still sense his hands on her chest and smell the scent of his lust in the air. She shook her head, trying to dispel the feelings, but they persisted. Her nipples were hard and they chafed against her bodice. She straightened the neck-line and surreptitiously rubbed her breasts, trying to relieve them. When the warrior's gaze immediately dropped to her chest, she whipped around and dashed from the room and into the crew's cabin next door.

Why had she insisted he come along? She didn't want him anywhere near her. His aura of passionate, controlled strength was completely outside her realm of experience. She looked around, assuring herself that no one was in the cabin, and shut the door behind her. She slowly sank against the wall and closed her eyes. A few months ago, everything had seemed so clear. She sailed the seas, protected a few villages, raided a few ships, and enjoyed being the only female captain of the sea. The stigma of the Dunhaven family had seemed to fade, and she rarely heard her late mother's name uttered in her presence.

Now, within a season's time, she was uncertain. Perhaps she was as vile as her mother had been. Maybe that was why her body had responded so quickly to her cousin's touch. Maybe that was why fate had thrust her into Horik's clutches and stripped her of her pride.

She opened her eyes and stared into the darkness. She needed to take action! She needed to prove to everyone—and especially to herself—that she was nothing like Isadora and that she was as fearless as anyone! Spinning around, Istabelle yanked open the cabin door and ran up the hatchway and onto the deck.

"Boris! Taber!" she shouted. "Set course for the eastern channel. I heard that a merchant ship bearing goods for the Scottish nobility is coming through."

Boris frowned. "We have never attacked a ship from our own country before. Toward what end do we change our strategy now?"

Istabelle raised her chin and stared him down until Boris dropped his gaze. "Am I the captain?" she asked softly. When Boris nodded, she continued in a menacingly quiet tone. "Then we set course for the channel."

Boris glanced at Taber. Captain Istabelle had never led them astray. Her instincts had always proved sound, and if she had seemed a bit reckless, she had never taken unnecessary risks.

Taber nodded.

With a shrug, Boris went over to the wheel and rotated it eastward. The situation with Horik had been bad enough, but now they had this new man to deal with. He hoped that the arrival of the warrior was not about to change Captain Istabelle.

Chapter 7

Ruark slumped against the headboard, feeling sick, but this time it was not due to the rocking waves. Instead, his stomach clenched at the memory of disgust on Istabelle's face when she had woken to his amorous advances. As if her body was branded against his, he could feel every curve of her form. He could see the sweep of her cheek and the shadow of her lashes.

Desperately, he tried to shove her memory away and replace it with one of the countless others, but to no avail. No hair had been as soft nor any skin as luxurious. Her soul sparkled with energy and vitality, even when she slept. She was unusually magnetic. And she was completely out of his class.

She was not only the daughter of an earl's brother, but also wealthy and successful. She was uncommonly beautiful and utterly confident. He, on the other hand, was an orphan. His only funds were the coins he carried in his bag, and while he had a well-deserved reputation for being a fierce warrior, he was not going to be awarded a knighthood in the near future. He was a paid sword. If Istabelle had not mistaken him for Mangan, she would never have engaged him in conversation.

Ruark ran his hands through his hair, then rubbed his eyes. He had to keep his mission foremost in his mind. He needed to obtain Istabelle's lost item, return it to her, and defeat Horik the outlaw. Simple. Uncomplicated. His attraction to Istabelle was a hindrance, a distraction, but he had enough strength of will to ignore it.

Sighing, he closed his eyes and lay back down, convinced that he had worked out a practical solution.

By the next day, he knew that ignoring her would not be enough. The ship was tightly confined, and no matter where he went, he could hear her voice or her footsteps. As the day progressed, he began to sweat with the effort of keeping an impassive demeanor.

His attempt to ignore her slowly dissipated, replaced by simmering irritation. Everything about her bothered him. He detested the way she walked, with her hips swaying and her hair swinging. He despised that she ate her lunch with uncommon gusto and obvious pleasure. Most especially he was infuriated that she appeared to have no problem completely ignoring him.

Finally, when he could no longer endure her studied disinterest, she turned to speak to him. "Mangan," she said, "the lookout just spotted a ship. It is rumored to have riches aboard. I suggest you go below and wait out the skirmish."

He stared at her incredulously, his temper rising. "I have fought in three countries, beside two kings and for hundreds of lairds. I have coordinated sieges, trampled superior numbers and saved kingdoms. I will not wait below!"

Istabelle glared back. "I have no intention of giving you back your sword, for I do not trust you with it. Therefore, for your own best interest, I suggest you hide in the crew's cabin." She stood with her feet spread and her arms akimbo, daring him to disagree.

He gripped the railing to keep from hitting her. How could such a petite, sweet-faced woman incite such fury? Throughout his entire life, he had never encountered anyone so obstinate and misguided!

"How have you survived without being murdered in your sleep?" he muttered.

"Excuse me?" Istabelle demanded.

"Nothing," Ruark grumbled as he took a steadying breath. "Whether you give my weapon back or not, I will stay on deck, but I warn you, by keeping me disarmed, you are not taking full advantage of my skills."

"I think I have been the recipient of enough of your 'skillful' actions," she hissed.

"Do you want me to apologize? Would that soothe your wounded pride?"

She blushed and turned away. This was not helping. All day long, she had managed to pretend he did not exist, but within seconds of speaking with him, her blood was rushing and her heart was pounding. She shrugged, attempting to regain control of the conversation. "Do as you wish, but I will not arm you until you promise not to stab me in the back."

He harrumphed. "Then I suppose I will never see the sword again, for I doubt I will ever be able to swear to that."

Twitching her skirts, Istabelle spun around and ascended to the captain's deck, leaving the grinning warrior standing alone. *The wretched man!* she fumed. *The terrible, annoying, wretched man!*

"The ship is portside," Taber announced.

Istabelle looked up at the top of the mast and whistled. Immediately, the gyrfalcon swooped down and perched on the ship's wheel. Istabelle stroked her feathered back and scratched her head. "Péril," she crooned as she pointed to the ship in the distance. "Seek out the enemy and tell me what you see."

With a swift beating of her wings, the falcon rose and headed straight for the other ship.

"What will she be able to tell you?" the warrior asked Istabelle from the lower deck.

Istabelle looked down at him. "I can calculate how far away the ship is by how long it takes Péril to fly there and back, and I will be able to determine if the ship has superior speed by how large an angulation she must make on her return journey. In addition, she will circle my ship and fly away if she senses undue danger, but will fly in front of us if she feels it is safe."

"You place a lot of faith in the judgment of a bird."

"I have never met a man who has proven more clever," she remarked caustically.

"Maybe you've never given anyone a chance."

Istabelle lifted her chin and raised her eyebrows, but forbore to reply.

Within twenty minutes, the falcon returned. She came back at a slight angle, indicating that the merchant ship was traveling slowly, and quickly turned around and started flying ahead of *The Adventuress*.

Istabelle glanced surreptitiously at the warrior. He had taken off his shirt and his muscles rippled under the glaring sun. He had several scars, some appearing serious, but he moved with liquid strength, as if he had never been injured.

The sailors prepared by arming themselves with multiple knives and swords. They laughed and joked, acting as if the upcoming fight was more like a festival than a battle in which death or dismemberment was possible.

Istabelle went below and changed into loose trousers modified from a peasant woman's rough-hewn skirts. She donned a white blouse that tied in a crisscross pattern over her chest, then added two additional ties on her arms to keep the flowing material from interfering in a sword fight. Normally, she would not have given her clothing a second's thought, but today she bit her lip indecisively as she stared at the polished metal that served as her looking glass.

Mangan would surely think her attire immodest and bizarre.

She tugged upward on the neckline, trying to hide the swell of her breasts. When that did not work, she braided her hair and attempted to conceal her cleavage by strategically placing the plait over her chest.

"That will have to do," she mumbled. "If he is offended, he can go below as I suggested."

She adjusted the dagger that hung around her neck and buckled her thin sword low on her waist. As she turned to go back on deck, she noticed that the belt hugged her hips and outlined her curves. Flushing, she started to adjust the strap higher but then stopped. "No!" she said out loud. "I will not let him intimidate me!" She glared at her reflection, daring her image to argue. "I am the captain of this ship, and I will do and wear whatever I want. If he cannot accept that, then he can jump overboard!"

She picked up the polished metal and flung it across the room, where it crashed against the wall and fell clattering to the floorboards. Nodding briskly, she left the room and returned to her crew.

Ruark looked up when she strode onto the deck. His jaw dropped. She looked magnificent! He had never seen a woman dressed in male clothing before, and now he understood why they hid their forms under layers of cloth. The shape of her body encased in the blouse and trousers sent instant heat through his loins. He wanted to drag her into the shadows and fondle her buttocks and taste her exposed throat.

He wanted to press her body against his and grind his pelvis into hers. If she had induced passionate thoughts before, now she inflamed him almost beyond control.

He turned away, attempting to mask his reaction. The other men did not appear to notice her. They were all focused on the merchant ship that was frantically adjusting her sails in an effort to increase speed.

"You can't outrun *The Adventuress*!" one sailor yelled with delight. "She is the fastest ship on the sea!"

Istabelle began shouting orders as they rapidly overtook the slower craft. She grinned as the men aboard the merchant ship shouted obscenities, cursing her and her ship.

"Heave to!" she commanded as *The Adventuress* drew even with the ship. Istabelle pointed her sword at them. With a hiss of steel, all her crew members drew their blades as well, forming an impressive, shining array of sharp steel. "Drop your sails or we will throw grapples over your deck and rip your ship apart!"

"Do you know who I serve?" the merchant's captain shouted back. "I am bringing goods to Scotland for the MacDouglas's new bride!"

"Then there should be plenty for all!" Istabelle replied.

Glaring at Istabelle, Ruark addressed her in a low undertone. "You should not anger the MacDouglas. He will not forgive your trespass. He will seek revenge upon all the O'Bannons and you will start a new feud."

Taber and Boris looked between themselves nervously. It was one thing to infuriate foreign nobles. It was quite another to incur the wrath of their own countrymen. "Perhaps we should let them go," Taber said softly.

Istabelle shook her head. The emotions rolling in her stomach since her cousin's arrival made it difficult to focus and she needed the fury of a battle to clear her head. "Attack!" she shouted.

The Adventuress's crew yelled and shook their weapons as several started swinging large metal hooks over their heads.

"Surrender! This is your final warning," Istabelle commanded.

With a fulsome oath, the merchant's captain motioned to his sailors to drop the sails. Within moments, the large ship lost momentum and began drifting to a stop. The experienced crew aboard *The Adventuress* mimicked her movements in order to stay bow to bow with her.

Istabelle did not wait. She ordered planks flung across the gap and sprinted with admirable agility over to the other ship while both were still moving. Her braided hair bounced along her back and the ocean breeze fluttered against her unusual attire, molding it to her frame.

"What is she doing?" Boris exclaimed. "She never boards first. What has made her so reckless?" He glanced at the warrior accusingly.

Ruark ignored the pointed look and climbed up on the plank, crossing it quickly as well. The ships were moving at slightly different speeds, and the board would soon be unable to span the distance between them. A rope was tied to the plank's end nearest to *The Adventuress* so the crew would be able to pull it back aboard once it fell, but Ruark did not want to leave Istabelle alone on the enemy's ship while it was repositioned.

Just as he reached the far side, the board splashed into the sea, isolating Istabelle and the warrior on the merchant's ship.

The merchant's captain glowered at them. "You insult me. A female and an unarmed man."

A nervous thrill raced through Istabelle as she realized the precariousness of her situation. She raised her sword and pointed to the sky, where the falcon hovered, drawing strength from her protective presence. "I will only take a third of your goods," she replied arrogantly. "The rest I will leave with you."

Bellowing his fury, the captain ran at her, swinging his sword.

Istabelle raised hers in defense, accurately deflecting his murderous attack. Grinning, she leapt backward, but suddenly the rest of the merchant's crew drew their weapons and began to advance.

"Fight with honor!" Ruark shouted. "One on one! Tell your crew to back away from her!"

The merchant captain shook his head. "A woman does not deserve the same battle honor as a man.

She will be dead long before her comrades come to her aid."

He lunged again, engaging Istabelle's sword.

Istabelle's grin faded as she saw the men ranged against her. Why had she come across without Taber, Boris and the others? Why had she boarded the enemy's ship before it was secured? Was her inner turmoil so turbulent? Thoughts flickered through her mind. Horik . . . the chains . . . the humiliation of losing control, losing her pride. Mangan. Loneliness. A pressing need for something she couldn't define.

She backed up against the warrior's solid frame, sensing his strength behind her.

"We only need to hold them for a few moments," he whispered to her. "Your crew is throwing ropes as quickly as they can."

She nodded, although she knew that holding off a dozen men for even a short while would be nearly impossible, especially since her cousin was weaponless.

The merchant men attacked.

As the falcon screeched her fury and swooped through the throng, Istabelle swung her blade. Behind her, bare-handed and bare-chested, Ruark used only his fists.

He feinted right, then swung left, smashing his fist against the first man's temple. As that man collapsed to the deck with a stunned expression on his face, Ruark ducked, narrowly avoiding another attacker. Using his long legs, Ruark kicked the man's knee, crippling him, but as Ruark reached to claim the sword that clattered from the man's hand, two others swarmed toward Istabelle.

Istabelle parried the captain's thrust, then lunged forward, striking first blood. She sensed the others attacking from the side and swiftly swiped her blade toward them. The men scrambled backward, wary of her excellent swordsmanship.

One drew a small dagger. He took aim as Istabelle returned her attention to the captain. A slow smile spread across his face.

Ruark thrust another sailor over the side, then smashed his hand against the arm of still another, temporarily paralyzing the sailor's sword arm. From the corner of his eye, he saw the man with the dagger. Rapidly calculating the man's aim, he drew his breath in with a hiss. Istabelle's back was fully exposed!

Without thinking, he leapt forward, flinging his arm outward to shove her to the ground.

Istabelle spun around as the man released his small blade. Shock, horror—the sudden comprehension of how fragile life could be—rushed through her. Then, just as she expected to feel the burning pain of the dagger plunging into her flesh, instead she felt the warrior's heavy arm crash against her chest.

She screamed and tumbled against the railing.

"Augh!" Ruark yelled as the dagger embedded itself in his bicep. He yanked the blade free and whipped around, assuring himself of Istabelle's safety. For a split second, their eyes met and locked.

At last, *The Adventuress*'s crew swarmed the deck and surrounded Istabelle in an indomitable wall of protection. They waged a fierce battle, slaughtering those who still fought and maiming those who tried to escape.

Within minutes, the few remaining merchant men were subdued and Istabelle took command of the captured vessel. "You should have surrendered peacefully!" she cried. "Look at the havoc you created by your resistance! Admit your foolishness and I will still give you your ship and some of your goods to bring to your master."

The captain shook his head, stubbornly refusing.

"Very well. Then lower the lifeboat and see how well you fare on the ocean in a small craft." She turned away and looked at the warrior, who was being tended by one of her men. Despite his obvious injury, he appeared unaffected. His breathing was measured, and he was calm. On the other hand, she felt breathless and overstimulated. She had nearly died! He had managed to save her without a sword, shield or arrow. His pure power, fighting prowess and muscled body had protected her.

She wanted to thank him. She walked over to him as the merchant's remaining crew climbed down into the lifeboat and her sailors raided the treasure holds. She opened her mouth and attempted to form words of appreciation but nothing came out. Struggling to overcome the lump in her throat, she swallowed and tried a final time.

"Mangan," she started.

He looked up at her, wishing that she knew his true name. She had fought with unbelievable courage. He had seen few men, much less any woman, show such strength of character and fighting superiority. He did not think that he had saved her; rather, he felt that they had worked as a team. "What, Istabelle?" he asked quietly.

She bit her lip. He was so handsome, so capable and strong. She shivered. Her stomach rippled and she felt faint. "Nothing," she mumbled and turned away. It would be too dangerous to establish a rapport with him if her feelings continued to spiral out of control. She had spent her life completely independent. There was no reason to change her course now.

Three days later, Ruark stood at the railing as the sun rose to midday, waiting for the ship to reach port. Since the sea battle, Istabelle had barely spoken to him. Her studied coldness was infuriating, and he could not wait to be away from her for a few hours as they canvassed the taverns for information. She could go wherever she wanted, and he would go in the opposite direction. And perhaps get drunk.

What idiocy had made him undertake this deception? He was not her cousin! His body did not react to her as if she were his cousin. His flesh ached for her as a man longs for his woman. Ruark bowed his head. Their forced proximity on the ship was torture! He would find a tavern girl and wash the smell of

Istabelle's skin from his memory. All he needed was to slake his thirst upon a willing maid.

He stiffened as he heard her footsteps approach.

"Mangan," she said, breaking the silence between them, "we will drop anchor here, then row to shore. First, we will go to the Night's End tavern and ask about Horik's ship while Taber and a few others go to the village market and ask the shopkeepers."

"No. Go with Taber. I prefer to be alone." He did not turn to face her.

Istabelle glared at his back. "Very well. Just remember to return by evening tide. I thought you might want this." She held out his sword.

He glanced at her out of the corner of his eye and then turned to lean against the railing, facing her. "Why do you suddenly trust me with my weapon?" he asked as his gaze swept her form. She had discarded her fighting attire and returned to wearing feminine garb. Today, she wore a black velvet dress shot with silver threads and laced with dark green ribbons. On her hip was her short sword, and around her neck dangled her small dirk in a jeweled scabbard. Her russet hair was drawn back into braids, each pinned to her head in a draping circle. The silver clips that held her hair in place winked in the sunlight, yet were dull against the brilliance of her silvery eyes. He dragged his gaze away, angry that he could not control his reaction to her.

"You should not go into port unarmed," she replied. "Besides, you defended me during the battle. It is only right that I reward you."

Ruark winced. She did not know how true her words were, for the normal fee for saving a leader's life in battle was usually a horse or sword.

Istabelle frowned at his continued reticence in the face of her generosity. "Have you nothing to say?" Feeling hurt when he shook his head, she turned away and addressed Taber as she motioned to Péril. "Is all ready?" Her gyrfalcon swooped down from her usual perch on the mast and landed on Istabelle's gloved arm.

Taber nodded.

Spinning away from the warrior, she stalked over to the break in the railing where the ladder was being positioned. She glanced over her shoulder, noting that the warrior still watched her with a hooded expression. She swung her leg over the side of the ship, inadvertently showing a glimpse of her smooth skin, then swiftly descended the ladder and climbed into the boat. The falcon fluttered to keep her balance until Istabelle settled into her seat. The other sailors followed suit.

After everyone was seated, the warrior climbed down the ladder, his large body surprisingly agile. His sword was belted around his hip. The decorated hilt flashed in the sunlight and he repeatedly touched it as if he were assuring himself of its presence after such a long absence.

Istabelle watched him warily as he pulled his hair back and tied it with a leather thong. Something about his movements seemed too rigid and controlled. He was like a slumbering beast on the verge of exploding and she had no desire to poke or prod him awake. She had never encountered such a powerful personality before, and his palpable anger made her nervous.

There was nowhere to sit other than next to Istabelle, and he sat down grudgingly, turning his head aside. Istabelle shifted as far from him as she was able, but still their thighs occasionally brushed against each other, and each could feel the other's presence acutely. Istabelle flushed while the warrior scowled. Thankfully, they reached shore within a few moments and were able to scramble onto the pier.

Without a word, the warrior set out for town, leaving the others to find their own way. Istabelle and Taber headed for the market and the other sailors arranged themselves in pairs as they, too, went scouting for information.

"What a horrid man!" Istabelle remarked to Taber as she watched Mangan stride away. "How could my childhood memories of him be so wrong? I remember him as so sweet and considerate. Now he is a walking whirlwind of dark emotion. It saddens me."

"Saddens?"

"Aye. I yearned for some solace and I thought he could provide it."

"Men change, especially men who have been in battle. The sweetness you once knew is probably gone, beaten out of him by the horrors of death and destruction."

"Still, I would have thought he would be kinder.

He is so . . . so different. He does not look at me with cousinly love. It is as if he cannot stand the sight of me.''

''No, he does not look at you like you are his cousin,'' Taber replied. *He watches you like a man frustrated by desire. 'Tis strange that a family member would be so taken with his own flesh and blood,* Taber thought to himself. Then, aloud once again, ''Something does not seem right, Captain Istabelle. He doesn't seem to be all one would expect.''

''I would rather ignore him entirely,'' she grumbled in response. ''Come, let's focus on our mission. We must find out about Horik's plans before the winter winds begin, or we will miss him for the season. I cannot afford the delay.''

''Why not just go to the island where he is waiting for you?''

''Because I will never obey his summons like some meek child. I will choose when and where I confront him. I do not intend to sail into an ambush.''

''Aye, I suspect you are correct, Captain.''

After an hour of searching the marketplace, they located a retired captain known to have run the merchant trade routes in the northern seas near Canna.

''Captain Gordon?'' Istabelle called to him when she spied his gray hair in the crowd, near an alley.

The man turned and peered at her through rheumy eyes. The smell of alcohol wafted from his clothing and he stumbled against a vegetable stand as if he still felt the roll of the waves beneath his feet. Struggling upright, he tried to remove a hat on his head.

When he realized he wasn't wearing one, he scratched his scalp in confusion.

"Yes?" he finally replied as Istabelle stood impatiently before him.

"I am seeking information," she informed him briskly.

Captain Gordon smiled. Although drunk, he had kind eyes. "I can't imagine what a lovely miss like you would want with a washed-up captain like me," he replied.

"I am Captain Istabelle of *The Adventuress*. I heard that you often traveled the northern seas."

Rubbing his eyes, Gordon took a moment to answer. "I know of you," he said slowly, trying not to slur his words. "You are the female captain. The one that raids the seas."

"I call no port home and I do as I please," Istabelle answered.

He shook his head. "I am a law-abiding citizen. I'll not help you attack my fellow merchants, no matter how prettily you ask."

Istabelle struggled to hold her temper. "All I want is information about some islands and the surrounding currents. I do not intend to rob an unsuspecting merchant ship and I would never attack someone who could ill afford it. However, I will pay you for your information."

Taber pulled a small pouch of coins from his belt and shook it. Gordon's bleary gaze swung to the bag. He licked his lips.

Leaning closer, Istabelle whispered, "Think how

much rum you could buy. It would procure a cask or two—"

"I used to captain a large ship," Gordon said. "I had a beautiful home and a wife almost as lovely as you. I lost it all to the siren call of rum. Now you tempt me with a pitiful bag of silver so that I can purchase more."

"You delay me," Istabelle cut in. "Either provide the information or I will offer the deal to another." The falcon on her shoulder fluttered her wings and emitted a short, piercing cry of warning.

Gordon tried to jump back but landed on his rump instead as a cloud of dust billowed around him.

Taber glared down at the fallen form. "Perhaps we should find another source," he muttered. "I am not sure we can rely on his memory."

" 'Tis said that he was once a good captain. He will remember," Istabelle replied. "Get him some bread. I doubt he has eaten in days."

As Taber fetched sustenance, Istabelle squatted next to Gordon, ignoring the dirt that coated her velvet skirts. "Tell me what I need to know, old man," she insisted, her silvery eyes boring into his confused ones. Péril leaned forward and hissed, her mouth slightly open and her small tongue just visible.

Gordon shrank back. "The currents are treacherous where the cold northern waters meet the warmer southern flows," he warned. "You must set strong sails."

"I know that much. I want to know about the islands where the outlaws hide after raiding our coasts. The man I seek is a friend to no one, and I wish to right a wrong he has committed."

Gordon shook his head. "Those islands are dangerous. There are hidden sandbars and many sites for ambush. We traders avoid that area and you should, too."

"Do you have any charts?"

"Perhaps." Gordon looked at the bag of silver and eyed the gyrfalcon as it shifted in agitation. "I do know that there is an island named for all its coves. It is the site where most of the raiding ships hide out."

Istabelle smiled. "Where is that island located?"

"Third from the north, adjacent to the mountainous one."

Taber walked up and handed Istabelle a loaf of bread. She broke off a piece, tasted it, then handed the rest to the retired captain. The man took the bread and looked at it curiously.

"Rum is not enough to sustain you," Istabelle said softly. "Eat some food."

Gordon looked at a nearby tavern. His shoulders shook. "I used to have a nice home and a lovely wife," he repeated sorrowfully. "I was a respected merchant . . ."

Istabelle stood up and motioned to Taber. "I learned what we need to know. Take him to his room and see if he does have some charts. I will collect the men. If we hurry, we'll make the tide." She glanced over her shoulder at the drunken man, who still huddled on the ground. She tossed the coin bag in his lap. "So sad," she remarked.

Taber frowned. "Unfortunately, it is all too common."

"What do you mean?" Istabelle asked.

"Most of the men end up the same. You, too, if you aren't careful."

Istabelle scoffed. "I would never let alcohol ruin my life."

"And if you have no reason to live? Gordon had something, but many don't. What if you have no family, no home and no reason to fight the nighttime demons? Can you not understand how easy it would be to let rum become your only solace?"

Istabelle walked away, down the street toward the docks. Fear threaded into her heart. She was just like what Taber described. Was she going to end up like Captain Gordon, lost and alone when she no longer had the sea to claim as her haven?

Ruark ducked into the nearest tavern. Slamming a coin on a table, he motioned for a wench to bring him a full pint of ale. "Bring another," he commanded as he swilled the first in one long swallow, then wiped his mouth.

The girl scampered off to obey and Ruark slouched on the bench and rubbed his head. This assignment was ripping him apart. He would rather brave the highland warriors in the dead of winter than spend more time in the cramped quarters of a ship with that woman. No other maid tortured him as she did, yet she was oblivious to his agony. She snapped back at him when he was disgruntled, then glared at him like he was the one who was being unreasonable. She did not know how her body affected him, and what was worse, she did not seem the least affected by him in return.

"Wench!" he shouted as he waved his empty tankard.

"Whot you trying to forget, warrior?" the woman asked as she slid him another drink.

"Who, not what," he grumbled.

"I can make ya forget any girl. Just half a coin and ya get any place, any where, any way."

Ruark looked at the woman's coarse face, her lank hair and rotting teeth. "Think I would pay for the likes of you?" he snarled. "Bring me something worthy, and I'll give you a pence for your troubles."

The woman shrugged. "Go to the Lord and Lady tavern down th' way. They have girls there that might strike yor fancy. All sorts, but if you find that I'm a bit more to yur likin', come back anytime."

Ruark tossed another coin on the table, finished his ale and rose. "I'll be back if you are telling me false."

"Ach, I don' tell lies. If'n I did, I'd a been finished a long time ago."

Ruark left the Night's End to make his way to the next tavern. On his way out, several sailors brushed past him on the way in. "That she-captain is back in town," one said.

"What I wouldn't do to get her in a dark alley," another replied.

"You'd be a fool, then, for you'd lose your hand if you tried to touch her. She fights as fierce as any man and gives no quarter."

"Well, I heard there is one who bested her."

"I've heard nothing of the sort."

"It was one of the outlaws." He smirked. "The one that shows no mercy to his victims. He brags of it. Snatched her and took her for a ride in his ship."

"Why did he go after her?"

"She stole his plunder two or three times over the last few years, because she detests outlaw captains like Horik, who steal from the peasants. Unfortunately for her, he can't stand to see a female beat him, so he went after her for revenge."

"Can't say as I blame him. I'd as soon never have to admit to her ship overtaking ours."

"Then you'd best stay clear of her, for if she decides that you are plundering the wrong people, she'll attack. Her crew is a loyal bunch. Stay clear of the lot."

Ruark paused and stared after the sailors, but their conversation had switched to other topics and they were just settling in for a night's carousing. Ruark made note of the men's faces, then continued on his way out of the tavern. He had other needs that must be attended to first. Shows no mercy to his victims? Istabelle had definitely antagonized the wrong man.

The Lord and Lady was devoted to serving a man's needs. Its windows were blackened, and torches cast flickering shadows over the patrons. Ale flowed like water, and cups of mead dotted the tables, along with stronger drinks. A stage was set at the back of the room, and a woman dressed in a tight bodice and thin tights was just stepping from behind a curtain.

Ruark closed the door and entered the torchlit area. Within moments, a small, dwarflike woman approached him and touched his thigh.

"Does a big man like you want a little girl like me?" she asked as she fluttered her artificially thickened lashes at him.

Ruark recoiled and pushed the woman's hand away. A burst of drumbeats from the stage captured his attention and he swung his gaze back to the show. A fat, dark-skinned man sat on the corner, drumming on a hollow log covered in animal skin, while the woman onstage began moving to the music, her hips gyrating in an obscene rhythm.

As the woman bent over backward, arching her body in an unnatural position, Ruark found a seat in a corner. The smell of sex permeated the air, and grunts could be heard coming from several darkened areas. A tankard was placed before him, and he gulped it down, feeling the effects of the tankards he'd had before.

The woman onstage changed positions, spreading her legs and bending down so that one could see her face between her legs. She turned her head and kissed her own thigh, then licked it suggestively. A few coins flew from the crowd and landed on the stage, encouraging her to go further.

Ruark gazed about the room, noting that many of

the serving wenches were topless and did not seem to mind the pinches they received from the patrons, as long as they were accompanied by the appropriate coin. A brothel of indecent behavior—a house of purchased pleasure. Usually such places were located well off the regular path, but in this sailing port of rough seafarers, they were on the main street. Frustrated and unusually anxious, Ruark motioned to a woman who stirred his interest.

After sending Taber to follow Captain Gordon and obtain the charts, Istabelle had located most of the crew and sent them to the ship. She found Boris walking down the main street. "I need everyone aboard within the hour," she told him. "Have you seen Mangan?"

"He went into the Lord and Lady," Boris replied.

Istabelle stared at the door of the infamous tavern. "He is in that place?" she repeated furiously. "How could he?"

The sailor lifted his brows. "Why shouldn't he? A man has needs."

"Bah. A man should learn to control them."

"Sometimes control is not possible."

Shaking her head, Istabelle replied, "That is patently false. Anyone can control their reactions."

"Istabelle, you are still young and barely a woman. Until you understand such things, you should not speak about them."

"I know more than you think I do," she said softly.

Then, more firmly, "Come. Let me show you. Let's go in."

"Never," Boris replied. "You should not enter such a place."

"Why? Because it will harm my reputation? Don't be ridiculous. I have no reputation. I sail with men. Whatever I am not supposed to do, I have already done. I want to go in."

"No."

Istabelle swung around and fixed Boris with her silver eyes. She pulled her sword from her belt and pointed it at his throat. "Should you question me again, I will ban you from my presence forever. I will do as I wish and no one will gainsay me."

"What happened on Horik's ship, Captain?" Boris asked. "What made you go from merely reckless and free to feckless and destructive? It is as if you want something to happen to you. You act as if you are on a cliff and can't wait for someone to push you over the edge. First you have us attack a Scottish ship, now you want to enter a brothel. If you continue this way, you will die an early death."

"Then I will die, and welcome the arms that enfold me in black comfort. Be gone, Boris. Go to the ship. Do not dare speak to me like that again." She lowered her sword and stalked away from him. Tumultuous emotions sparked in her soul. It was true that the experience with Horik had affected her deeply, but her cousin's presence was equally unnerving.

She doubted anyone could understand her confusion, her uncontrollable passions, her fears. Her father, for all his strength, was older and had mellowed. Her stepmother was wise and peaceful, and did not comprehend the wildness in her spirit. She was alone in a vast morass of emotional complications.

It wasn't right! She wanted to lash out and prove her strength. She wanted to show everyone that she was capable of handling anything! She snapped her sword back into its sheath and took a deep breath. It was time to take a chance, and the hidden secrets behind the brothel door were exactly what she needed to explore. A slow smile spread across her face as she thought of what Mangan would say when he spotted her in the house of ill repute. She throbbed with strange excitement as she lifted her hands to her braids and carefully undid them, then shook her tresses free.

The falcon shrieked in her ear, but Istabelle ignored her. She began walking again, fixated upon the door of the Lord and Lady, and the bird took off, flapping her wings in an effortless climb to the sky. Unaware of the bird's desertion, Istabelle began walking faster, almost running. She would enter the door and see what Mangan was doing behind those blackened windows.

Chapter 8

Immediately she felt the heat. Waves of warmth reached out and surrounded her, enveloping her in the aromas of sweat, burning torches, stout ale . . . and something else. Something musky and different.

She slipped inside, her black velvet dress making her almost invisible against the near wall. The door swung back in place, closing out the last rays of sunshine and shutting her inside the shadowed room. Drumbeats echoed against the rafters. The hum of voices was punctuated by several high-pitched laughs and many low grunts. A flash of movement drew her attention to the stage, and she opened her mouth in awe at the woman contorting herself into bizarre positions. She had managed to wrap her leg around the back of her head and was in the process of doing the same with the other leg. Every curve of her body was revealed by her attire, and a dark area between her thighs hinted at the thatch of hair there. Her position made her incredibly open and vulnerable, a fact that many patrons apparently appreciated, given the coins decorating the stage floor.

Istabelle dragged her gaze from the show and searched the room for the warrior. She saw him sitting at a table across the room, swaying slightly as he motioned to a barmaid. How could she reach him? Istabelle looked around quickly, trying to devise a way to get his attention, when she saw a pretty black-haired woman approach him.

The woman leaned down, revealing that half her bodice had been removed in order to show her nipples. Istabelle gasped and covered her mouth. She had seen a great many things to do with fighting, battle and blood, but such a sexual display was beyond her experience.

Mangan reached for the woman, stroked her breast, then squeezed it. The woman laughed, tossed her head back and sat down on his lap. She held her hand out, then quickly pocketed the coins Mangan gave her. Hiking up her skirts, she twisted and sat astraddle, facing him. She leaned close, presenting her breasts. He kissed them, then gripped her waist and began rocking her. The woman held on to the back of his chair and assisted, moving her hips and grinding against his lap.

A rush of heat raced up to Istabelle's cheeks, and she felt faint. Her heart started to flutter and her breathing quickened. Such . . . such actions! Such a display! She had seen the harlots on the dock, even heard the grunting men in the alleyways, but she had never felt any reaction to them. She gasped, unable to tear her gaze away from the intense sexual scene. She forgot about feeling angry. She forgot that he was her cousin. His unbridled masculinity reached across the room and overwhelmed her. All she could feel was a desire to be the woman on his lap, to feel his waist between her legs as she cradled his head between her own breasts.

Ruark tilted his head forward and encouraged the woman to move her pelvis faster. Although drunk and nearing satisfaction, he was suddenly distracted by the sense that someone was staring at him. He scanned the brothel for the source.

There, deep in the shadows, was the faint outline of a face. A feminine face with long hair that shimmered in the dark. Ruark narrowed his gaze and tried to pierce the shadows with his vision, but he could not make out any more details. The figure shifted and his pulse raced. It was a woman in a dark dress. A beautiful woman who did not belong in this tavern. That she was hiding herself in a brothel of sumptuous display struck a discordant note. Who was she?

"Warrior," the woman whispered. "Am I not doin' whot you need? Yur looking aside."

"Who is that in the corner?"

"Nobody." The woman shifted her position, lifting her feet up to prop them against his chair back. "Look at me, big man. I will make you happy." She stroked her inner thighs, indicating the lack of linens to shield her womanhood.

Ruark swung his attention back to the woman, the shadowy figure forgotten. He pushed up the woman's skirts, bunching them around her waist. The woman leaned her head back, her black hair trailing. Ruark shoved her onto the table, then pushed her thighs wide. Ignoring the others in the tavern, he unlaced his breeches.

Istabelle could not stop staring at him, his shirt damp with sweat, his hair rumpled by the woman's hands, his breeches half undone. He had glanced at her, but now he had returned his attention to the woman. Jealousy snaked through her heart, and she started moving toward them. She pulled the dagger from her neck. She was not going to let that harlot mate with him!

Two chairs blocked her path and she angrily tossed them aside. Several patrons scrambled out of her way, wary of the passionate rage on her face and the glittering dagger in her hand.

Reaching the warrior, Istabelle leapt on the table and stood towering over the couple. She stepped on the woman's black hair, then kicked the warrior's chest, sending him careening backward against the wall.

The woman screamed and tried to rise, but her trapped hair held her captive.

Istabelle squatted down and pointed the dagger at the woman. "Listen well," she hissed. "You may think your obscene clothing and explicit motions have attracted him, but it is me he wants to kiss. It is me he wants to touch!"

The woman struggled to get away. She shrieked louder and gripped Istabelle's ankles, yanking them with surprising force. Istabelle was flung off balance and tumbled to her knees. The woman whipped around and flew at Istabelle with her nails. "You bitch!" she screamed. "Get out! He wouldn't be here if you'd given him what every man needs!"

Istabelle rolled, avoiding the woman's attack, and kicked, slamming her booted foot in the prostitute's stomach. The men in the tavern shouted with glee and moved back, granting the two women more room to fight. The contortionist onstage paused and all the other barmaids scrambled out of the way.

"Augh!" the black-haired woman grunted as she bent over, heaving with pain. She stumbled back and snarled, "I'm the prettiest woman in port. Who do you think you are! No man would take you over me!"

Istabelle jumped to her feet, slid off the table and grabbed the woman by the throat. Using her dagger, she sliced off half the woman's hair. "Aren't you the lovely one now," she mocked. "How do you think you will look with a set of scars running down your cheeks?" She raised her dagger, murderous wrath glittering in her silver eyes.

Suddenly she was wrapped from behind in a fierce bear hug. She screamed in fury and tried to twist toward her attacker, but she could not escape his powerful grip.

"Cease!" the warrior shouted.

"No!" Istabelle screamed. "Let me go!" She broke away and lunged toward the woman. "She deserves to die!"

"Stop!" Ruark bellowed again. "She is nobody! She

is only a harlot." He gripped Istabelle's arms and held her tightly despite her frantic struggles. Glancing behind him at the overturned chairs, he located the door and dragged Istabelle through the crowd, kicking and screaming.

Within seconds they burst through the door and he slammed her against the outside planks. "What are you doing?" he shouted at her.

"I was searching for you! What were *you* doing?" she yelled back.

"I was about to relieve my tension on that wench before you threatened to kill her."

"She is not the kind of woman for you," Istabelle fumed as she pulled at her arms, trying to free herself but to no avail.

"Not my kind?" he answered incredulously. "And who, exactly, is the kind of woman I am supposed to prefer?"

"You wanted me, in my cabin. You wanted to touch me!"

"As I recall, you told me to stop."

"That does not matter! What matters is that you wanted me and not a painted woman in a crowded tavern."

"You are right, I did want you, and I want you still." He yanked her away from the wall and tossed her into the alley. As she stumbled, he gripped her wrists and shoved her against the darkened wall. He ground his hips against hers. "Feel this? Is this what you want? Do you want to feel what I feel? Do you want me as much as I want you?"

Istabelle shuddered. His ale-soaked breath was hot upon her neck.

He leaned closer to her and whispered into her ear, "You have taunted and teased me for a week, and now you come in and interrupt me when I could have had some release. You will pay for your interference!" He gripped her wrists with one hand and held them above her head as he leaned her against the wall. With the other hand, he grabbed her right breast and squeezed it. "I am no monk to hold my desires in check. You should know the truth! Do not think to rile me again and then stop us. I will get what I want this time." He ripped her bodice, searching for the beauty of her flesh.

"Stop!" Istabelle cried. "Not like this!"

"Stop? Stop! Why? Why should I let you take me to a feverish peak and then leave me tottering on the precipice? I am done with this charade! You are a woman of the world. Undoubtedly you have felt the power of a man's steel between your thighs many times. I intend to release us both from this cage of frustrated desire."

He swept her skirts up and pulled his breeches down.

"No," she whimpered. "Don't . . ."

Ruark paused, his cock throbbing. "What do you mean, 'don't'?"

"Not like this—please stop. I didn't mean to—this is too much." A great tear spilled from her eye.

"Damn!" He stumbled back, panting with effort. "You dare do this to me again? What kind of witch are you? You came to me! You followed me inside! You stopped me from achieving my well-deserved satisfaction and now you refuse me?" He ground his hips against hers. "Feel how ready I am."

"*I* am not ready," she whimpered. "I do want something, but I'm not sure what it is. I am so terribly confused! I don't know what is happening to me. My life is spinning out of control and I don't know how to harness it back."

He pulled back and gently released her hands, his face drawn with concern. Brutally crushing his passion, he stroked her tear-streaked face. He had forgotten his suspicions about Horik. She might have been brutalized and raped, and here he was shoving her against the alley wall. Disgusted with his insensitivity, he took a deep breath and forced a comforting smile. She looked so vulnerable. "You are very young to be a captain," he said softly. "Your strong spirit has led you to success, but wisdom is what will lead you to fulfillment."

"You speak as if you know the way."

He shook his head sadly. "No. I am as lost as you are, little Istabelle. Come, forget what has happened here. I apologize. I would not want your sad tears on my conscience, no matter how much you inflame me."

She sniffed and lay her head against his chest. "I'm sorry," she whispered.

"Believe me," he answered wryly, "so am I."

They sailed out with the tide. Neither said anything more about what had occurred between them.

They both felt guilty, though for different reasons. Ruark was disgusted by his lack of command over himself, for he had never lost control with a woman before. Istabelle was plagued by the sexual feelings the man she knew as her cousin evoked. His rough touch and powerful grip had created an unfulfilled desire that she was vainly trying to suppress.

He was her cousin! Her own flesh and blood! She directed the raising of the anchor and the unfurling of the sails while her mind spun on the inescapable fact that she was drawn to Mangan in a way she had never dreamed possible. Her pleas for him to stop had been as much a cry to herself as to him. Even now, as he bent to coil the ropes, she had visions of his body looming over hers. She flushed and turned aside, seeking to immerse herself in charting the ship's new course.

Ruark straightened from his task and glanced at Istabelle. He was glad that she was looking down at her charts, for surely she would see the need on his face if she were to observe him. He turned and assisted the other sailors, seeking to relieve his physical frustrations in hard work. Thankfully, his seasickness had passed, and the rocking ship no longer made him ill.

Boris knocked against him while securing a barrel. "Watch out," Boris grumbled as he tossed a barrel, almost crushing Ruark's toes.

Ruark pushed the barrel into place and started to tie it.

"Not like that!" Boris exclaimed. "One would

think that the cousin of our captain would know something about sailing. That is, *if* he is our captain's cousin."

"Do you have something to say to me?" Ruark growled.

Boris glanced up at the angry warrior. Few men had such broad shoulders or such muscled arms. Boris shrugged, choosing to cease antagonizing the man. "No," he grumbled. "Not yet."

"Then think about this while you contemplate your choices," Ruark replied in a dangerous undertone. "I did not seek out your captain; she is the one who asked for help. Do you want me to disappoint her?"

Boris shook his head. "Just understand that we will protect her with every drop of our blood, and if you threaten her, we will see that you suffer."

Ruark looked around the ship, noting that several sailors were listening. "She has collected a loyal crew. Such dedication is rare."

"She deserves it," Boris replied. "She treats us well, she provides for our families and she knows the sea."

"What, exactly, do you do?"

Boris averted his gaze, but Taber stepped forward and answered his question. "We steal from those that have wealth in abundance, and give to those in need. It started with one mission, but now we sail six months of the year."

"What mission began your enterprise?"

"Most of us came from Dunhaven land," Taber replied.

"Dunhaven," Ruark mused. "That is the name of Istabelle's mother, Isadora."

"Yes. Many of our families have tilled the Dunhaven fields for generations, but now we cannot even feed our children. The current Dunhavens have raped the land and stripped it bare. They have crippled us with tithes we cannot possibly pay, and then have murdered the few who begged for lesser fees. We did not know what to do."

Boris nodded. "Then Taber decided to go to other Dunhaven relatives and ask for assistance. All refused even to hear our concerns. All except Istabelle. She was incensed to learn that we were being starved to death."

"What did she do?"

"She tried to reason with them, but the Dunhavens despise her because she was raised by the man accused of killing Isadora Dunhaven. After her attempt to interfere, the tithes doubled. That was when she devised the plan to supplement our incomes by skimming a bit from those who have extra."

"Then none of you were sailors in the beginning."

"No one from Dunhaven. Everything we learned, we learned from Captain Istabelle. She taught us how to raise the sails, how to man the oars, how to do everything aboard the ship. Her father, Xanthier O'Bannon, was one of the best commodores of the sea. When she was young, he spent hours every day on the water, teaching her about the ocean and how to navigate its capricious ways. After we banded together with Istabelle, others joined us and we started capturing bigger prizes. We went from a small, single-sail ship to this magnificent vessel after a particularly successful battle. We gained a well-deserved reputation and Istabelle became infamous."

"Surely you have collected enough funds to tide your families over for the next several winters. Why do you still sail the seas and steal from unwary merchants?"

"Once Istabelle realized how much her assistance had done for the Dunhaven people, she wanted to help others. We decided to stay with her, and we will stand by her side until she chooses another path."

Ruark looked up at the captain's deck. Istabelle had pinned a chart to a sheltered pedestal and was poring over it with intense concentration. Her brows were drawn together and she was nibbling on a finger. Glancing up, she scanned the horizon with a looking glass. She stood strong and capable upon the deck, swaying with the ship's movements as if she had been born to them. Powerful. Invincible.

"She is very young to have undertaken the task of saving the oppressed people of our country," Ruark remarked. "It is too heavy a burden to bear."

"She wants to right the wrongs of her family. It is her decision."

"Sometimes infamy brings tragedy," Ruark replied softly. "And loneliness."

Emotion swept through him and he squeezed the ship's railing. She was beautiful, but it wasn't only her physical features that made her special. She was unique. She had depths that were far greater than he had ever imagined. How would it be to hold such a woman in his arms? How would it feel? He could imagine her silver eyes daring him, challenging him . . . wanting him as much as he wanted her. She would demand his response, take it as her own and then . . . then what? What would happen? Would she be able to give anything back? Would they fight like wolves in the sheets or would they flounder like wounded birds?

He had slept with countless women. He had made them scream with ecstasy and moan with satisfaction. He had always been the dominant partner, choosing when and how the act would be done. With Istabelle, it would be different. She would never be content to simply submit. She would want to be an equal.

Later that evening, Istabelle sat at her desk re-reading Mangan's letters. She had kept them all, for his serene voice had always soothed her. So different from the turmoil he evoked in person! He wrote of Kirkcaldy, his ancestral home, and the beauty of the sun-kissed castle walls. He talked of the peasants and how he wanted to improve their lives, inspiring her to do the same. He talked of religion and of being drawn to God.

Istabelle put the letters down and stared at the wall. It did not seem right. The man she knew as Mangan never spoke of those things. His words were not poetic, nor did he seem serene and tranquil. A dark suspicion snuck upon her and she rose from her desk. Could he be someone else? Could he have killed Mangan and stolen the ring?

She paced her cabin, her heart beating wildly. No! He knew too much. He knew of her letter requesting help. He had to be Mangan. Why would she have such thoughts? Was it because she secretly hoped he was not her cousin? Was it because her welling desire for him was bubbling out of control and she wanted to believe anything in order to absolve herself of the guilt of being attracted to her own cousin?

She would prove it to herself. She would demand some answers, and if he could not supply them, she would throw him overboard. If he could supply them, she would shove her emotions under the ocean waves and drown them.

Chapter 9

"Mangan," she interrupted sharply. "Tell me about your home."

Ruark straightened slowly from fixing the hasp on the hatch door. His heart began beating faster just from hearing her voice. "My home?"

"Yes. Why not? Tell me about where you grew up."

"You know all about that," he answered carefully, trying to decipher her mood. "What do you want me to say?"

"What was the name of your castle? I seem to have forgotten." She stared at him with her chin lifted, daring him to answer.

A million thoughts raced through his mind. She suspected. She knew. She wanted something from him and he was not sure what it was. "How could you forget the place where you were born, Istabelle? It is Castle Kirkcaldy."

"Oh yes, how could I be so silly?" she said as she turned partly away from him.

"Indeed. I have never known you to act stupid."

He waited, knowing that she was not done. Should he confess?

She trembled. If he was not Mangan, she would have no choice but to kill him. She bit her lip. She had to know. "Tell me about your childhood."

He took a deep breath and thought about his time with the true Mangan. They had fought together in several battles, and he respected the man immensely. He had a sense of purpose that was at odds with that of a privileged lord, and that accounted for his affinity for the Church. How much did Istabelle know about the true Mangan? How much should he lie? "Why do you want to know?"

Istabelle faced him squarely, her silver eyes round with a hint of fear. "I want to know something about you. Please, tell me the truth. Tell me something about what made you who you are."

He could not lie. But he could not tell her the truth. She suspected but she did not want to know. Averting his gaze, he was silent.

"Please, I need to know something," she whispered.

Wading through the truth of his life and what he suspected of Mangan's, Ruark finally answered. "I had no brothers or sisters, and that made for a lonely childhood. I spent most of my time acting like an adult."

"The heir to an earldom must grow up very quickly."

He smiled crookedly. "Many must grow up too quickly or not survive the rigors of youth."

"At least you had the love of your parents."

He bent his head. *No parents. No love. Only Sven.*
"There were those who made living worthwhile."

"What do you want now?"

You. "To make sure my existence has not been a wasted exercise of survival. To know that my birth was not an accident and my life is not unnecessary."

"You once spoke of entering the monastery."

He grinned. "Do you think I would make a good monk?"

She flushed. "I just meant that it would be a way of doing something important."

"Yes, it would," he answered evasively. "And what about you? What do you want to do when you grow up?"

"I am grown up. This is who I am."

"No, there is more to you."

"We were not talking about me," Istabelle replied.

"Why not? You are a more interesting subject."

"I am a ship captain. I have no friends other than my crew and only my cause to pursue and protect. You are the son of an earl. What does that mean to you?"

The warrior turned away. How could he answer her? "The title means nothing next to the character of the man. One must be willing—nay, desirous—of setting one's needs aside for the good of the people. Few men are able to do that. I have known only a handful. Your uncle—"

"You mean your father," Istabelle interrupted.

"Brogan O'Bannon," he emphasized, "is one of the few men who deserves to hold that respect and is worthy of being called earl."

"And do you think you will ever be worthy of that level of honor?"

He dropped his head. The lies made his chest hurt. He couldn't take a deep breath. Lifting his haunted onyx gaze, he stared into her perceptive silver one. Slowly, he shook his head. "I am the last person on earth who should handle such responsibility," he murmured. "My needs are much more selfish than yours. I could not set aside my desires for the greater good. I have never done anything that did not, in some way, benefit myself."

Istabelle stared at him in shock. His words echoed around her as the pain of their meaning wedged into her heart and made it bleed for him. She stepped closer and placed a comforting hand on his chest. "I do not believe that," she whispered. "Perhaps you have not tested yourself yet and do not know your limitations. I see something in you that is still untouched."

He shivered at the feel of her hand, and an intense longing to bury his face in her hair almost overwhelmed him. "You are imagining something that is not true. I am not what you think," he answered as he gripped the railing to keep from enfolding her.

"I don't know what to think anymore," she answered. "I need your help to face Horik. I want you, but you frighten me. I must ask, are you truly my cousin? Are you Mangan?"

As the question hung in the air, Ruark struggled to find an answer. He trembled, more terrified of this moment than any he had faced in battle. If he told the truth, she would be deprived of his help, which was the sole reason he had undertaken this deception in the first place. If he told a lie, he would be sacrificing his soul and misleading a woman who deserved better than a falsehood. What would the real Mangan do?

"I am someone who has come to care for you more deeply than any stranger could. Your heart beats like mine, and your spirit seeks the same escape mine longs to find. How could we not be family?"

Istabelle stared at him. "Answer me directly, warrior. Are you Mangan? For if you are not, I will slit your throat."

He had no choice. As the heir to an earldom would place his subjects before himself, he must put Istabelle before his desire to admit the truth. If he was going to pretend to be Mangan, he should act like him as well. Ruark smiled and lifted the signet ring that sparkled on his finger. "I am the man come to rescue you from the consequences of your actions. Your questions are foolish and ill founded. Your imagination is running wild and does not befit a captain of the sea."

Istabelle dropped her hand and shielded her eyes. She knew instantly that it was not the answer she wanted. He was right: her imagination was controlling her thoughts. For a moment, a secret desire had wormed its way to her mouth and made her ask the insane question. Of course he was Mangan. Who else could he be? Just because he generated strange emotions in her belly and made her heart flutter with excitement did not mean he had to be someone else. He was her cousin, and such feelings should be squashed under the heel of her boot before they made her say anything else ridiculous.

"We will say no more on the subject," she said after clearing her throat. " 'Tis only that you are different than I expected. Meet me at dinner and we will discuss our plans with the crew."

And you are vastly different from what I expected, he thought to himself as he nodded acceptance of her invitation. "I am looking forward to confronting Horik and seeking an end to the conflict."

Later that night, Istabelle stood over her charts with Taber, Boris and the warrior. "In town, we learned why Horik is hiding in the islands. He thinks that he will have a better chance at ambushing us from hidden coves in the shallower waters."

"And does he?" the warrior asked.

Taber nodded. "His boat is designed with a flatter bottom, which makes her slower but able to navigate shallow depths. We are deep in the keel, making us very fast but not safe in such waters. He will have a great advantage."

"He must be very sure that you will come after him," the warrior commented. "Especially if he has been waiting for you for close to a month."

Istabelle nodded as her lips pressed together grimly.

"Yes, he knows I will come after him. He planned it that way." She picked up her lodestone and rubbed it against a needle, magnetizing it. Using a bowl of water and a straw, she put the needle in the straw and floated it in the water, creating a compass. She placed it near the chart and pointed to a group of islands to the northwest.

"This is where he is waiting. The best way is for us to come from the southeast, follow this deep channel and approach the third island here." She jabbed her finger at a peninsula.

"Shall we do the opposite?" Boris asked.

"No, he will expect me to do that. He is at least that clever. According to Captain Gordon, the sandbars shift and the channels are unpredictable. These charts are several years old. If I only knew how accurate they still were, I could plan our attack more readily. Let us go on deck and meet with the crew. We will discuss the situation and then vote on a plan."

As Boris picked up the compass and Taber gathered the charts, then left the room, Ruark frowned and stepped closer to Istabelle in order to speak to her privately. "You should not let the crew see your indecision," he murmured. "It will instill a lack of confidence and they will be less likely to follow you into battle."

Istabelle grinned. "You come from the land, where authority is based on tyranny. A man is born into leadership and rules by fear." She held up her hand to stop his instant denial. " 'Tis true. Even though some leaders are good, you live by the caste system. We are vastly different. We function as a group. We elect our officers, and all vote on our communal fate. All have an equal voice."

"How can such a system function in battle? It is unnatural. A leader must have unquestioned authority."

"That is why we are so different from the rest of the world. It is not just that we thieve and steal, for many do that. Your merchants and vendors take more from the populace than we ever will. Your kings and lords take what they want as well. Outlaws take everything they can and do not care who they hurt in the process, but all of them exist by dominance. Our governing style sets us apart.

"We—the officers and crew—drink the same water, eat the same food, share our loot equally. We believe that freedom is the driving force of existence. That is what gold can give you."

"I thought gold simply made you rich." He considered his pile of coins and what he planned to do with it. He wanted the same kind of freedom she spoke about, for he had been an unfortunate orphan who had had nothing. Oddly enough, now that he had a decent collection of funds, he was no closer to feeling secure than he had been as a child.

Istabelle laughed. She flung her hands around the cabin, pointing to the unadorned walls. "I have no desire to accumulate useless wealth. I do not need fancy sheets to keep me warm. The goods are to be given to people so that they can live free from worry. I want them to never fear hunger or lack of shelter."

"If becoming wealthy is not your goal, then why are you pursuing Horik for one stolen piece of treasure? Or is the treasure something even more dear, as I have suspected? Tell me, Istabelle. I need you to tell me what he stole."

Istabelle turned away. "It is something special, something that I do not wish for him to have, but of itself, it is not valuable. If I am to give away something of my own, I will do so of my free will."

Ruark stepped forward and turned her to face him. "What did he take, Istabelle? Did he steal a kiss? Did he steal something even more precious?" He dropped his gaze to her mouth.

She licked her lips. "No," she whispered.

"Then what would you do if I stole a kiss?"

Emotions rippled through her body—denial, acceptance, cowardice and excitement. She wanted to feel his lips. She wanted to surrender to his passion. His name did not matter. She wanted to forget her inhibitions and be free of her self-imposed restraints. "You cannot steal that which I give," she whispered.

His eyes darkened to midnight pools and he gently clasped her head in his hands as he tilted her chin upward. Her eyes fluttered closed and she became softly pliant, sweetly submissive. He gazed at her features in awe, transfixed by their symmetry. Her dark lashes cast long shadows on her cheeks and her lips were slightly parted, showing just a hint of the mysteries of her mouth.

Istabelle felt as if she were in another world, as if the rules governing earth were suddenly nonexistent.

She remembered nothing; she thought of nothing but the overwhelming lassitude that was weaving through her blood and the tingling sparks that were tickling her lips. She wanted to feel his body pressed against hers, and she leaned forward, seeking his strength.

As their bodies brushed against each other, they both gasped. Heat blazed between them, but instead of moving apart, they pressed closer, seeking the source of the flames. He bent his head and closed his eyes, joining her in the darkness of sensation. His lips descended until they hovered a breath away from hers. He wanted to kiss her! He wanted to taste her! He shuddered with the force of his desire.

She felt suspended in time, waiting for him. She trembled, knowing that she teetered on some precipice that would fling her into something so uncontrollable, so incredible, that she could not imagine its depth. Her tongue peeked out, seeking his taste. A small moan escaped her.

He heard her and his eyelids slowly lifted as he gazed at her exquisite face. She would hate him if he took advantage of her now. If something had happened to her, she might resent his touch. She might feel guilty that she kissed her cousin, even though he was not Mangan. He couldn't do that to her. He couldn't face the accusation in her eyes. He wanted her, but he wanted all of her and would not be satisfied with less. Perhaps later, when she learned the truth . . . when *he* learned the truth.

He stepped back and forced an easy smile on his face, then placed a soft, tender kiss at the corner of her lips, just missing the succulent fruit of her mouth. "Istabelle, sooner or later you will have to tell me what we seek and why it is so important."

Istabelle's eyes sprang open and she gazed at him in confusion.

Unable to bear her expression, he kissed her on the forehead, desperately clamping down on his desire. When her silver eyes bored into his, mutely asking for more, he swiftly exited the cabin, knowing that if he let her say one word, if he allowed her lips one touch, he would not be able to stop.

Istabelle stood as he had left her, trembling with unfulfilled need. What had just happened? Had she imagined the emotions between them? Had her own desires spun so far out of control that she was left panting while he was completely unaffected? She sank into a chair as her legs collapsed underneath her. Had he kissed her lips, she would have kissed him back like one of the harlots on the street. She would have flung her arms around his shoulders and yielded to his needs in the way a woman surrenders to a man. Not the way a cousin loves a cousin.

She lifted a trembling hand and covered her lips, stifling the moan that threatened to escape once again.

Chapter 10

Taber, as quartermaster, was the counterbalance of Istabelle. While she was the elected captain, respected for her leadership, sailing skills, bravery and cunning, he was in charge of discipline, manning the helm and monitoring and distributing the plunder. They worked as a team, and neither did anything without the other's approval.

Taber was discussing the planned attack when Istabelle finally came out on deck. He glanced at her pale face with concern, but forbore to speak of it in front of the crew. "We were going over the plans," he informed her.

"And has anyone come up with a good one?"

"It appears that we must come from the southeast. Perhaps he will not be expecting a bold attack."

"Aye!" a sailor cried.

"Best approach, Captain. The northern shallows will rip our belly apart," another agreed.

" 'Tis too simple," Istabelle replied. "Horik must be planning something. Why would he sit in the cove, waiting for us to attack?"

"If I may, Captain?" a young voice said from the back of the crowd. "I know something of the outlaw Horik."

Istabelle looked up in curiosity. "Who speaks?"

"Erik," he said as he came forward.

Istabelle frowned. "You were Horik's messenger."

"You gave me the choice, Captain, and I was honored to stay with your crew. I have worked hard, scrubbing the deck and cleaning the dishes. I promise I have not been a burden."

Istabelle raised her eyebrows. "Indeed. What do you know that would interest me?"

"I know Horik's methods. I know what he plans in the islands."

The crew grinned and nodded but waited for Istabelle's final word.

Suddenly Ruark stepped forward. "This boy could be acting as an insider to Horik. He could be offering false information, or even collecting facts for his true master."

Istabelle stared at the warrior over the heads of the other sailors. His black eyes bore into hers and a wave of rebellion rippled through her heart that made her clench her teeth in fury. "You are not part of this crew, Mangan, and thus have no voice in our discussion."

Stepping back in surprise, he shook his head. "Did you not write to me for my tactical advice? It seems inadvisable to ignore some valuable input. This boy could be putting the entire ship at risk."

Istabelle's anger grew greater. His actions only moments ago had confused her, and oddly enough, had made her feel rejected. She put her hand upon the curved blade of her sword and took a step forward. "Do you know anything about life aboard a ship? Do you understand our creed? Do you know anything about *me*? How am I to believe that *you* are offering sound advice since you are not one of us?" Suddenly she wanted to destroy his sense of control. She wanted to see him when he could not dictate his own actions, when the fire of his soul overwhelmed the cold calculation of his mind.

He took another step back and wisely remained silent. This was the unpredictable side of her he was beginning to recognize. Sometimes she was soft and feminine, drawing out his innate protectiveness, but other times she was a wild hellion who might do anything, and he dared not push her further.

"Have them both sworn into the crew," Taber suggested, breaking the searing tension rising between the warrior and the captain.

" 'Twould be best," Boris agreed. "Erik cannot mislead us if he is our brother, or his penalty is death."

"And your cousin can fight beside us if he, too, joins the brotherhood."

"I do not wish to swear any allegiance," the warrior said quickly.

Istabelle pulled her sword free and pointed it at him. "Why not? Do you fear that you could not live up to the articles of agreement?" A thrill raced through her at the flash of animation he suppressed deep in his black eyes.

"I fear nothing," he replied coldly.

"Then join us," she hissed as she swung her blade.

Ruark leapt aside a moment too late, and the sharp steel grazed his shoulder, leaving a thin, bloody streak. In fury, he pulled his broadsword and pointed it at her. "Don't do this again, Istabelle. I've warned you for the final time."

"Why not? What are you going to do now?" she taunted. "Fight me again?"

"I do not enjoy raising my sword against you, but I will do what I must."

He tried to back away, but Istabelle lunged at him again. He lifted his sword and parried her thrust in a smooth, liquid motion. The two swords clashed and the ring of steel against steel reverberated over the ship's deck.

He stared at her between the crossed blades as exhilaration rippled through his blood. Her silver eyes were powerful, intoxicating. No woman had ever dared to attack him, but she did so without hesitation. He had stated that he did not enjoy their fights, but part of him did. She amazed him with her audacity and skill. She excited him. "Beware of what you awaken," he said huskily. "Once aroused, a beast is difficult to tame."

Istabelle flicked her wrist and disengaged their weapons. She waved her blade in the air, searching for an opening. "Are you a coward?" she jeered. "Do you avoid me because you cannot stand up to me? Are you afraid of who I am?"

Shaking his head, he took a step backward. "It is you who is the coward. You are afraid to see what is in front of your eyes. You are the one avoiding the truth . . . the truth about your life, about yourself . . . about me."

She darted forward again, but he was ready for her. He slammed his thick blade against her slim one, intent on knocking the sword from her hands. He raised his eyebrows in surprise when she deftly swept under his attack and pressed the tip of her weapon against his chest.

He froze. "What are you going to do now?" he asked.

She laughed. "You act as if you fear I will kill you." She leaned close to him. "Sometimes I wish I could. You should have stayed home, *Cousin*." She spat on him, her saliva dripping into his fresh wound. Then she stepped back and all the other crew members pressed forward. Before he could deflect their spittle, they spat in his blood as well. As he stared at Istabelle in shock, she swiftly struck Erik with her sword, opening a thin wound on his arm. She spat on it, too. "There! You are now officially one of us. Whether you like it or not, you are now a member of *The Adventuress!*"

"Your customs are barbaric!" he yelled at Istabelle as she smiled with obvious delight at his disgust. "What craziness is in your soul? You are the most—the most—the most *reckless* person I have ever met!"

"And you have no such customs in your land? How about the collecting of trophies on the battle-field? Placing heads on pikes outside a castle wall? Can you tell me that you have done nothing that would make me shudder?"

When he could not answer her, she motioned to the boatswain. "Open the casks! Bring out the instruments! Let us rejoice in the good fortune to have added two such valuable members to our crew."

Ruark gripped Istabelle's arm. "You have no idea what you have done," he whispered. "I told you once before that you did not know who I was, and if you did, you would never have made me one of your crew."

Istabelle stared up at him, her face suddenly serious. "Perhaps I know more than you think."

All around them, the sailors cheered, pleased to have a reason to celebrate. Erik grinned with plea-sure as the crew slapped the two newcomers on the back, congratulating them, then began securing the ship so that their impromptu festival would not be interrupted.

Ruark released Istabelle and rubbed his temples. Too much was happening too fast. He was Ruark, homeless soldier for hire. He had no friends, no brethren except for Sven, no community to call home. He did not deserve unconditional acceptance from this crew, for even now he perpetuated a lie. He was not Mangan. He wiped the wound on his arm and stared at the blood.

"What is done is done," Istabelle murmured. "Stop

fighting. Accept your fate. Enjoy yourself for one night."

Three musicians sat on wooden crates and started to warm up their instruments. One man had a mouth harp, another a lyre and the third, a conch shell horn. As Istabelle walked away and helped Taber fix the ship's wheel, biscuits and salted pork were brought to the deck along with a cask of ale. In a grand gesture appropriate to the occasion, the cook also produced a bucket of gravy for dipping and a large pot of salmagundi. When Ruark peered at the pot with concern, the cook proudly described the contents.

" 'Tis a great dish, thanks be to the captain's falcon. Can't think of a better reason to enjoy a feast! Has a bit of duck, pigeon and seagull in it. I marinate the lot in spiced wine and add it to the fresh provisions we just stocked. Cabbage, onion, eggs, potatoes and leeks are me favorites, but sometimes I put a bit o' carrots or pickled vegetables in as well."

"I smell garlic," Ruark commented.

"Aye! Lots o' garlic. Hot pepper sauce, too, along w' salt, mustard and lard."

"You happened to have this meal ready?" he asked sarcastically. Istabelle's soft words still reverberated in his mind and he was thrown off balance by her unexpected gesture.

The cook smiled. "We always find a reason for a good time before a battle. Don't want to go to yur maker without dancing and drinking aforehand!"

"Before I go to battle, I meditate and focus on honing my skills," Ruark said. "Drinking only makes your reflexes weak and your mind slow."

The cook shrugged. "Far be it for me to tell a great warrior like you what to do, but I'm warning ye, 'twill be a late night, and they'll be expecting ya to say the articles of agreement afore the sun rises."

"What do you mean, articles of agreement? Captain Istabelle mentioned them as well."

Istabelle appeared behind the cook and answered his question. "The articles of agreement are the set of rules we live by. Since you are now accepted as one of the men, you have to understand and accept the rules."

"I thought you lived by no rules. Isn't that the point?" He rubbed his recent injury.

"We only ignore the rules others seek to place upon us, but we gladly embrace our own code of conduct. For instance, we attack merchants primarily to help support those in need, and take only what they can afford to lose."

"The crew on your ship decides what rules it wants? What treasures it will plunder?"

"Aye. 'Tis a fair method, and we find that if everyone is involved with designing the rules, they are more apt to follow them."

"What about the MacDouglas ship? Did everyone agree upon that?"

Istabelle dropped her gaze. "Perhaps I was hasty. I wasn't thinking clearly."

Seeing how uncomfortable his question made her,

he did not pursue the matter. Instead, he asked, "And if someone should disobey a law your crew has designed?"

Istabelle's silver eyes glittered and she lifted her chin. "The punishment is severe. For instance, if you desert your station during battle, you will be set adrift on a small log with no provisions and no paddle."

"I would never leave my station," he replied with disgust.

"Really," Istabelle rejoined quietly as she moved next to him and whispered into his ear. "It seems to me that you have tucked tail and run a few times." She smiled seductively, making sure he understood her connotation. Her eyebrows arched, hinting at a hidden question, and her lips curved with invitation. "Moments ago? In my cabin? You left the battleground with singular haste."

Stunned, Ruark stared down at her, noting the sparkle of challenge that shone in her eyes. She could not be saying what she appeared to be saying! He must have misunderstood her, for verbal sparring was far out of his realm of experience.

He dragged his gaze from hers and looked hungrily at the pints being passed out. Not normally a drinking man, he found he needed some of the soothing brew to deal with the woman before him.

Istabelle placed a hand on his arm, gripping it firmly when he would have jerked away. "Do you need to come with me and have your injury tended?"

Horrified by the prospect of being in close quarters with her once again, he shook his head.

"Are you sure?" Istabelle questioned. "If it is not cleaned, it may leave a scar. See? Mine is scarred." She deliberately pulled the neckline of her dress down and revealed her shoulder.

As if she was the north and he the lodestone, he was helpless to resist staring at her flesh. Sure enough, a thin white scar marred her skin. The crescent traced along her arm and pointed to her chest, where, thankfully, her dress concealed its final destination. He stared at it, transfixed, emotions boiling. Someone had sliced a blade across her body. When had it happened? How had it occurred? Where did the scar end and how much of her had been exposed? He swallowed, unable to tear his gaze away.

"Why?" he finally whispered. "Why do that to yourself?"

Istabelle yanked the dress back up. "It disgusts you so much?" she snarled.

"No, I did not say that."

"I can see it in your eyes. You think it is an aberration. The lily-white ladies of Scotland would never let their bodies be marked, would they?"

Frowning, Ruark thought of the farm girls or the peasants and the rough life they led. Calloused hands, pocked faces and uneven scars were normal; he just had not expected to see evidence of hardship on such a beautiful woman as Istabelle. "When a woman works, she bears the scars of her labor," he finally replied.

"All the fine ladies at court sit at the fire and embroider, but I could not be more different from them. You are appalled by my life and my looks, aren't you?" She lifted her hand when he meant to interrupt. "Don't seek to change my view, for I know yours. You have made it clear."

Ruark clenched his teeth, helpless to explain why her assumptions were wrong. He did not care for the useless women of leisure she referred to. In fact, he felt the same disgust she apparently did, but his forced charade forbade him from reassuring her. As the heir to the earldom, he would associate with only the purest of aristocrats. It was unlikely a true nobleman would appreciate the marks of life upon the hands of a working peasant, and he would, indeed, feel revulsion at the scar on Istabelle's flesh.

"I, too, have scars," he said in an effort to calm her rising fury.

"Is that supposed to make me feel better?" she replied angrily. "Your scars are considered manly, tokens of your leadership and battle strength. Mine is but a sailor's mark of passage."

He looked deep into her eyes, seeing the vulnerability she shielded so well. She glared at him as her hands trembled with fury. Something inside him cracked, and he searched for the right thing to say, suddenly wanting to soothe her insecurity.

"I am proud to have your mark upon my body," he murmured. "Your courage, honesty and sense of freedom are qualities I can only hope to claim one day. I see your mark as a symbol that you have achieved a level of personal independence that few ever can. It is a beautiful scar, Istabelle."

She stared at him, searching his face for the truth. "Thank you," she said softly. "I did not think you felt that way."

He laughed. "I didn't either, but it is true. Everything about you is exquisite, even the things you see as flaws. They are what make up you and to take away even one piece would be to destroy your essence. Don't let anyone, least of all me, change you. Stay as you are, Istabelle. Be proud of your marks of life."

"But what about you? Are you proud of your path?"

He turned away. He was living a lie, pretending to be a titled lord when he was, in truth, the basest of all menial men, a mercenary. Was he proud of his path? "No, Istabelle, I am not. I have had few goals in life other than to gain funds and property. But watching you . . . listening to the passion in your voice has made me wonder what I could do. Maybe one day I will find my destiny."

She gathered his hand in hers and turned him back to face her. "You will," she said fervently. "Everyone needs to achieve something, to define and meet goals. I showed the world that I was not like my mother and I have attained great pleasure in proving myself."

"Have you? Is that your true goal in life? Have you defined yourself in relation to Isadora Dunhaven? Perhaps you should find out who *you* are and follow your *own* path."

Istabelle stared at him, surprised by his words of wisdom. She glanced up at her gyrfalcon, which sat on the tallest mast, staring out over the ocean. She followed the bird's gaze and saw the endless blue. There was no horizon in sight. "I guess we both need to find ourselves," she murmured.

He, too, looked out over the sea and beyond the wind-capped waves and saw the emptiness. "Perhaps we do," he agreed.

Chapter 11

As sunset streaked the sky, the gyrfalcon screamed from where she sat atop the ship's mast. Her voice joined the lilting strains of the lyre and the harsh accents of the horn while the crew gamboled on deck, dancing with gay freedom and drinking with wild abandon.

Istabelle wore a dark burgundy dress with a white undergarment that formed ruffles at its low neckline. Her throat was adorned by a simple chain that suspended her jeweled dirk provocatively in the shadowed recesses of her cleavage. Her russet hair blended with the sunset, although a few golden strands occasionally winked like remembered flashes of sunlight. Her eyes smiled with unfettered joy, twin silver pools that shone with glistening beauty and teasing gaiety.

She drank deeply from her pint of ale, then wiped the foam from her upper lip. She was breathing heavily after a fast reel across the deck, and she rubbed her cheek against her shoulder to wipe away some sweat. On the other side, she located the warrior, who seemed to be relaxing as bit by bit he released the stranglehold on his emotions and let the happiness of the crew envelop him.

He had discarded his shirt, as had many of the other sailors, but he still had a leather thong wrapped around his forearm where he, too, sported a throwing knife. Unlike hers, however, it was simple and unadorned. His hair had slipped from its bond, and most of it was swinging free about his face. It was unreasonably long for a man, but somehow it made him more masculine.

"I want to braid your hair," Istabelle announced as she sauntered over to him and cocked her head sideways. She wanted to touch him and feel his warmth beneath her fingers. As the sun sank behind the horizon, it sent the ocean into shifting twilight highlighted by subtle streaks of orange and red.

He drank, draining his pint, then put it down with careful precision and stared at her without saying a word.

Not waiting for him to deny her, she pulled a burgundy cord from the eyelets on the front of her dress. Her movements were languid, and she ignored the breeze that skated along her skin as her dress opened, revealing more of her white underclothes. She placed the satin string in his hand and he took it automatically, wrapping it between his fingers.

She touched his shoulder and he sat down as if her touch was a command that could not be ignored. Moving to his side, she sank her hands into his hair and ran her fingers from his scalp to the ends, carefully untangling the strands. The hair felt like raw silk.

She repeated the process, scraping her nails from his hairline in front, down around his ears and to his neck, letting her fingers absorb the sensations. His pliant acceptance emboldened her, and she combed his hair with increasing awe. She had never wanted to be this intimate with another, but he did something strange to her, something that made her want him to come closer. As she slid her nails over his scalp, she became completely immersed in her self-appointed task.

He was still, and his stillness made her feel safe. She gathered a small section of hair at his temple and separated it into three strands. Leaning over him, she reached for the burgundy cord that he held clenched in his hand. She felt his breath on her neck, but instead of pulling away, she leaned closer, letting her dress gape open. When she heard his breathing grow harsh, she shivered, sensing the beast that he held caged within.

Gently, handling him as she had handled her falcon that first day, she opened his hand and pulled the cord from his fingers. The cord slid along his roughened hands and finally swung free. Istabelle stood upright once again, but the damage had been done. Neither breathed steadily; both shook internally.

She folded the cord in half and intertwined the

halves with two of the separated sections of hair. She laced one section over the other, slowly braiding his hair along with the cord.

Ruark closed his eyes, caught between agony and ecstasy. Her fragrance surrounded him and he could smell the sweetness of her earlier exertions where her skin was still damp. Along with her sweat was a delicious hint of vanilla and lilac. Such soft scents in such a strong woman. He reeled, his head swimming. He could hear her lick her lips, and the quiet hiss of her indrawn breath.

Every inch of his skin tingled with expectation, with need and desire. She was a siren who wove her spell and beckoned men to the depths of her lair. He wanted to follow her, even if he risked having his heart torn by her talons.

He forgot his deception. He forgot all about Mangan and his promise. Instead, all he thought about was the essence of the woman beside him. He felt her fingers, felt the tug on his scalp as she braided his hair with the token from her dress.

The sunset darkened to night, and the sailors continued to dance to the music, laughing and shouting as they proceeded to drink to the edge of drunkenness. No lanterns illuminated the deck, as they never lit candles after dark. They did not want to announce their presence to any that might be lurking on the sea, so they danced to moonlight and starshine.

He looked up as she knotted the braid, seeing her

eyes shimmer in the darkness. "The articles of agreement," he whispered. "Where are they?"

She returned his gaze, sensing a different question behind his words. A shiver of longing rippled through her, and she took several breaths to steady her voice. Even so, her words trembled in the darkness. "Down below . . . in my cabin."

"Show them to me," he commanded huskily.

She nodded and he rose to stand beside her. His bulk towered over her and she felt overwhelmed by the strength of his presence. The single braid she had placed at his temple hung down to his neck, and she had an urge to kiss the muscled flesh it rested against. Instead, she turned and led him down the hatchway, away from the festival on deck.

The cabin was even darker than the deck. The only illumination came from the moon shining through a porthole. She paused just inside the threshold, waiting for him to join her. As the door swung shut behind him, the strains of the lyre became muted, and they were ensconced in a small, private world.

Fear snaked through her, and she shook her head briefly, unaccustomed to the emotion. Why feel fear? He was standing still, and only his scent and the steady sound of his breathing announced his presence. Her ship was safe. No enemies were in sight. There was no reason to feel frightened, yet she felt waves of that emotion wash over her.

"Over here," she said as she took several steps

deeper into the room. She rummaged on her desk and found a well-worn parchment.

"I cannot read it in the dark," he replied as he moved up behind her. His steps were silent despite his size, and Istabelle jumped.

"I know it by heart," she said as she twisted to face him. His shadow loomed over her, and she half sat on the desk.

"Then tell me what I am getting myself into," he answered. He slowly lifted his hand and touched her face, stroking his finger down her cheekbone to her lips. "What am I doing here?" he repeated.

"The first," she whispered against his fingers, her lips brushing his calluses, "is that every person on ship shall have an equal voice, be he captain or crew."

"Or man or woman?" he asked.

"Or man or woman," she confirmed, then gasped as his hand shifted to her neck.

"Tell me more. I have already learned that one." His fingers rested against her pulse, where the fluttering told more about her state of anxiety than her silver eyes would ever reveal.

"You are entitled to six hundred pieces of eight from the common prize should you lose your right arm in battle."

He dropped his hand from her neck and stroked her arm. She held her breath as he kneaded her upper arm, feeling the muscles she had developed from sword fighting. "You are a strong woman," he whispered. "Yet your body is still so feminine. I like the firmness . . . the strength in your fighting arm. I do not think any monetary prize would be worth losing it."

"Your right arm is bigger and stronger than mine," she replied, then tentatively touched him. Wonderment filled her as she felt his muscles jump at her soft touch and heard him catch his breath. She mirrored his actions, digging her fingers into his flesh and exploring the mountains and valleys of his biceps while he stroked the graceful lines of hers.

"Tell me more," he gruffly reminded her. "What of the left arm?"

"Only five hundred."

He gripped her left hand and raised it to his lips. He rubbed her fingers against his mouth. "It should be a thousand for every scratch, every bruise . . ."

"No, only one hundred for a finger." Shaking, Istabelle shifted her hand and cupped his cheek. It was rough with unshaven stubble, and she could hear the rasp of her nails as she gently scratched him. "How much would I owe you?" she asked, her voice deepening.

"For all the wounds you have cast upon me? Much more than I could count."

"I have not hurt your leg," she answered. " 'Tis five hundred for a leg."

He moved closer, inserting his body between her legs, forcing her to spread open to receive him. "A leg?" he asked. "How could one put a value on that?" He rested both hands on her thighs.

She gripped the edge of her desk. "I don't know

where they came up with the amounts. They are commonly known."

"Perhaps I should check for myself. Do you think so, Istabelle?"

"I—I—"

He knelt down, running his hands down her legs until they reached the hem of her skirt. "A foot? An ankle? Do they have value?" he asked as he unlaced her boots and tugged on her stockings.

"Not that I know of," she gasped as cool air blew between her bare toes. The chilly sensation was immediately replaced by the heat of his breath as he kissed her instep.

She gripped the desk so hard her knuckles turned white and her toes curled. What was he doing? Did she want him to stop or had she known that by bringing him down here something like this would happen? Something she yearned for . . . something wondrous yet mysterious.

"God almighty," he whispered. He pushed her dress up and licked her calf. "I want you." He came across a knife tied to her leg, and he used his teeth to disarm her. "I do not trust you with such a weapon."

Unable to respond, Istabelle concentrated on the feel of his teeth, the moisture of his mouth, the heat of his kisses. The room swirled around her, and shadows danced in the moonlit recesses. She closed her eyes and transferred one hand from its tight hold on the desk to an equally firm hold on his shoulder. It was as if she understood that he alone could support her and that he was her only source of stability in a world of chaos.

"Priceless," he whispered as his lips found the soft inner flesh of her thigh. "Beyond priceless." He licked her again, then gently bit her thigh.

She moaned, her legs opening farther, and his mouth closed around the bite mark as he sucked. Although the darkness hid it, a bright red spot bloomed under his ministrations, marking her. He could smell her arousal and suddenly he could think of nothing but burying himself deep inside her, filling her with his seed, claiming her like he had never claimed another before.

He stood up and roughly undid her belt, then ripped the top of her dress apart so he could see her breasts. Her dagger gleamed in the darkness of her cleavage, but he chose not to remove it. It was part of her.

Her breasts rose from the ruffled edges of her underlinens, swollen, rounded and topped with pebbled nipples that were so perfect he paused and stared. He cupped them in his hands and bent his head to taste them, and her cry of passion goaded him further. As he took one in his mouth, he brushed his hand over the other, feeling her, memorizing her shape, imprinting her body into his mind for eternity.

She trembled with the unfamiliar emotions, sparks of passion shooting through her body like flashes of sunlight on a chest of gold. She held on to him for dear life, not knowing where she was, not knowing where they were going, but trusting him to take her there. Her thighs ached, her breasts tingled and her heart raced. She felt his hands rove over her, felt his lips taste her and yet she could not concentrate on any single touch. Everything melded together in an overwhelming cacophony of sensation that transported her into the world of ecstasy.

He felt her skin flush and heard her panting breath reach a peak, then pause as tiny climaxes swept through her. He leaned back and watched her as her nipples hardened, then softened, and her fingernails dug into his back, then stroked his shoulders like the delicate wings of a bird.

"I have never seen that," he murmured as he lifted her pliant body and carried her to the bed. "Your passion . . . I want to join you in heaven. I want to share your feelings and feel your body as I slide into you. I want everything from you. Do not deny me."

"No," she whispered. "I will not deny you."

He pulled her dress from her, then removed the shreds of her linens. As she rolled her head, still recovering from her experience, he divested himself of his clothes and his weapons. Only her body filled his mind, only her flesh occupied his thoughts.

He lay next to her and gathered her in his arms. She felt so warm against his cool skin. Her breasts rubbed against his chest and her thigh brushed against his rod. He groaned. He dropped his hand to her waist and pushed her onto her back so he could look at her. Her belly was smooth, with just a hint of feminine roundness. The triangle of hair that cloaked the core of her womanhood was as dark as the deepest shadows. He stroked her curls, wanting to explore her body fully, completely.

She cried out and lifted her hips, seeking his touch. He covered her body with his, and the meeting of their flesh caused them both to burst ablaze with searing passion. She wrapped her arms around his shoulders and pulled him closer as he placed his knee between her thighs and opened her legs. Bracing his elbows on either side of her, he rocked, rubbing the tip of his manhood against her pillowed softness. It was no longer his feelings and hers; it was theirs. They felt each motion, they felt each pulse as if they were merged into one soul.

He shifted one hand down to her leg and bent it, then angled his body so that his cock teased her entrance. They both shivered, and he paused to let the waves of emotion sweep them into another world. Then, when he could no longer wait, he nudged inside her.

She gasped, in both pleasure and pain, as he came against her maidenhead. Her eyes sprang open and she scrambled to locate her dagger. "Stop!" she shouted, then shoved his bulk with all her strength.

"Oh my God," he whispered. "I thought Horik . . . when you were kidnapped . . . I didn't know." He tried to pull out of her, but his hips would not obey his mind. He wanted her so much, his body trembled. He slowly shook his head even as her fists pummeled his chest. "We can't stop now," he whispered.

"Get off me! I don't want this!"

He kissed the corner of her mouth as he desperately fought to remain still. Even though every muscle in his body quivered with the need to rhythmically drive inside her, he ruthlessly forced himself to stop moving. "Shush. Trust me. Come back to me. Leave your thoughts behind and join me in pleasure." He nibbled her lips with his. "I will stop if you truly want me to. I don't want to do anything you don't want."

She felt the stretching of her core around his spear. Although his body was motionless, she could feel him twitch and move inside her. Helpless to control her own response, her inner muscles responded by clenching him. She gasped and caught her breath in amazement. "I feel you moving inside," she whispered.

"Yes. I feel you, too. Your body is asking for me. It wants me." He pulled out of her one inch.

"No!" she cried again as she gripped his buttocks. "Don't stop yet."

He grinned in the moonlight as he slowly sank back inside. "I have no intention of stopping, wild woman. I just wonder if you are up to the challenge."

Istabelle stared up at his face, her silver eyes glittering with rebellious passion. "There is no challenge I will not win," she declared.

"Prove it," he answered as he pulled out of her once again.

This time she arched with him. Her hips tilted, forcing his slow withdrawal to rasp against her flesh.

They both moaned at the sensation, but Istabelle swiftly changed to a cry of delight when he plunged back inside. His motion was swifter, firmer, more dominating than before, but still relentlessly controlled. He reached her maidenhead again and paused, taunting both of them.

She lifted both her knees and swept her hands up and down his back, urging him to repeat his actions, to sink in deeper. The shock of his entrance was fading, replaced by shivers of pleasure that made her entire body tingle. She pulled him closer, wanting to feel every inch of his strength surround her as it filled her. It was heady and wildly intoxicating.

He thrust faster, longer, moving his body over hers in a purposeful rhythm that brought him as much pleasure as it brought her. This moment must last forever—for him and for her. He had to pause as his tumescence swelled, and he forced his body to wait. Not yet. He did not want to breach her yet. He wanted to spill his seed deep inside her just as he claimed her completely.

She tossed her head back and forth and lifted her hips to his. "More," she groaned. "I want more."

He plunged into her again, his control intact, and she screamed. Her nails raked his back and she urged him to go faster, to drive into her harder, deeper. "Let go," she commanded him. "Stop being a warrior. Be with me as you asked me to join with you. Trust me!"

He answered her pleas with his body. All his life he had maintained a strict rein on his emotions, but something about this lawless ship, this wild virgin captain, this insane deception, made his control snap. He needed to find his release within her heart. He needed to empty his essence into her core and to open his emotions to her soul. Like a dam breaking, he burst open and screamed with her. "You are mine!"

"Yes!" she cried as her legs wrapped around him. "Take me!"

He grabbed her wrists and slammed them against the pillows, trapping her body. Leaning up, he ground his hips into hers, delving so deeply inside her, she gasped with the power of his actions. Her maidenhead disintegrated under his onslaught with minimal pain.

His buttocks bulging, he pummeled her, his cock sliding in and out of her welcoming channel with increasing friction. Her breasts bounced and her hair tangled as she met him stroke for stroke, urging him on, experiencing ecstasy with every rough, loving motion.

Then suddenly they both tumbled into an unknown universe. Stars exploded around them, and the world tilted, swirled and whipped into a dizzying whirlpool. Their mutual cries were lost within the thunder. He tensed, pulsed, exploded deep within her as she gripped and quivered, wrapping him in the intense heat of her climax.

Chapter 12

The magic swept around them, blanketing them with serenity. The ship rocked gently and small creaks joined the sounds of soft waves as the two slumbered in each other's arms. For Istabelle, the world was reborn. She had never experienced, nor even imagined, such beauty as being held in this man's embrace. The ripples of memory drifted in and out of her dreams, making her smile as she snuggled closer. Nothing would ever be the same. She had discovered a person who brought all her emotions, her needs and her desires into flesh, and for once she felt complete.

Ruark dozed, trying not to let niggling guilt disturb their solitude. He had slept with countless women, from servants or peasants to ladies of high rank, yet nothing had compared to the fantastic explosion they had just created together. He gripped her against his side, feeling the press of her breast against his chest, and although they were both sleepy, he pulled her beneath him and slowly slid inside her once again.

Her body responded sluggishly, yet he was in no hurry. He moved within her in even, easy strokes, luxuriating in the feel of her legs wrapped around his and the heat of her gripping him deep within. He pressed his head against her neck and breathed deeply and she arched upward, baring her throat. He kissed her, sucking gently, and she moaned in appreciation.

The moment was tender. He brushed his lips across hers and she hesitantly responded, unsure how to react to such a simple act. He quivered, remembering how innocent she was despite her wild responses, and softly kissed her again, teaching her how to open her mouth and let him taste her depths.

Istabelle sank into the bed, her limbs weakening. He was moving inside her, creating a swirling center of heat, yet the sweetness of his mouth was overwhelming her. She pulled back and gripped both sides of his face to stare into his eyes. "You are wonderful," she whispered. "This is wonderful."

He smiled and moved faster. "Watch me, watch us," he whispered in return. "Watch what you do to me, and I will watch you."

She nodded, and gazed into his deep onyx eyes as he towered over her, moonlight spilling over his shoulders and illuminating her breasts. Dropping her gaze, she watched her nipples tighten as the steady friction he created began to smolder. The flames of ecstasy flickered closer. Amazed, she jerked her eyes back to his and was captured by the fire in his look.

"Beautiful, aren't they?"

Stunned, Istabelle could not respond. Suddenly the tempo changed, and he reared up, driving his manhood deeper. It rubbed against a new place and Istabelle cried out in surprised pleasure. Instant moisture coated them both. "Now," he commanded. "I can't wait any longer."

"Now," Istabelle agreed breathlessly, her silver eyes glazed with passion.

Yanking her down several inches, he lifted her thighs and draped them over his shoulders. He plunged into her once, twice, three times until she gasped and her eyelids trembled.

"Watch!" he demanded and she forced her eyes open even as soft, subtle waves spread through her body, making her alternately wrap around him and relax beneath him. He ground into her, then the muscles on his neck tightened and his shoulders bulged. He groaned. His body froze yet he held her waist tightly, driving himself as deeply as possible so that every drop of their union would be shared.

She watched him in wonder, astonished that she had made such a powerful man tremble with emotion. His piercing black eyes were suddenly hazy, and his dominating presence was abruptly vulnerable. Without conscious thought, she reached her arms around his back and pulled him down to her, holding him as he shook with the effects of his climax.

"Shush," she whispered as his moist eyes pressed against her breast. "I know. I feel it too."

"You don't understand," he cried softly. "There is something you don't know."

"I don't need to know everything. What we feel right now is all that is important. Don't worry, big warrior. You have joined my crew, which is more meaningful than anything. I will take care of you as I know you will take care of me."

"But—"

"Not now. Talk later. For now, lie here in my arms and let the ocean wind rock us both."

"All right." He did as she bade him, knowing that his words would eventually have to be spoken, but unwilling to ruin the beauty of the moment. This was too precious, too sacred. He relaxed and held her close.

As sunlight peeked through the porthole, Istabelle slipped from between the covers and dressed as quietly as she could. A smile spread across her face as the man in the bed shifted position and kicked off the blanket. He was so powerful when he was awake, it was endearing to see him sleeping like a child. As she laced her blouse and pulled on some breeches, she noted a few red marks where his mouth had suckled. Grinning, she tied her boots and then exited the cabin to check on the ship.

Ruark woke to an empty bed and a cold room. He rolled over and stared at the clothes flung everywhere, recognizing his breeches alongside her discarded velvet gown. Piles of charts cluttered her desk and other nautical items appeared to have no distinct resting place. Neatness was not Istabelle's strongest point.

Odd, really. Mangan, her true cousin, was impeccably neat. On war campaigns, his horse had been perfectly groomed, his tent sparse, and his attire clean. In fact, his simplicity had probably served him well as a monk. The two cousins were so different, it was amazing that they came from the same family. The thought of Istabelle ever considering a life of religious service made Ruark grin.

He, on the other hand, was quite similar to Istabelle. He sought adventure, he welcomed challenges, and he never surrendered—just like her. Her wildness matched his restlessness and he found that he admired and respected her. But there was something that needed to be done to make things clear between them. He needed to explain his deception and tell her his true name. After last night, it felt wrong to let her continue thinking he was someone else.

He rose and found his clothes. He dressed briskly, energized by the knowledge that after today he would not be living a lie. He would hear her whisper his real name in the darkness. He would hold her and tell her the truth about his childhood. She would not flinch from his humble beginnings. She would not care if he was an earl's son or an orphan.

He strode up the walkway and climbed out onto the deck. Looking around, he saw several sailors mending ropes, a few cleaning, and Istabelle standing at the helm. The wind filled the sails and tossed her golden-streaked russet hair back and forth as it pressed the folds of her blouse tightly against her breasts. Upon her shoulder rested the gyrfalcon.

The bird noticed him first. She twisted her neck and stabbed him with her beady gaze. Flapping her wings in agitation, she made several short, piercing sounds.

Turning, Istabelle lifted her lips in a seductive smile. "She signals that an intruder has come aboard."

Stepping fully out of the hatch, he frowned. "She still dislikes me."

"She is very possessive. Does it irritate you that there is one female in this world that does not succumb to your charm?"

Raising his brows, he approached her. "I have never been thought of as charming. And there are many more women than I could count who have had no trouble resisting me."

"Then they are fools," Istabelle whispered as she touched his chest. The falcon screeched and took off.

"I have upset your friend," he said softly, entranced by the welcoming look in Istabelle's silver eyes.

"She needs to seek her breakfast. Are you hungry?"

"Yes, but I doubt that what the cook can supply will satisfy me."

"Could I?"

"I think so."

"Think?"

"Aye. Hope."

"Hope?" She smiled.

"I must talk with you. I must tell you something very important."

"No," Istabelle said firmly as she turned away.

The warrior looked at her back in stunned amazement. "No? What do you mean? I *must* speak with you, *now*."

"I don't want to talk. Let us leave things as they are, and not concern ourselves with petty details."

Frowning in anger, he gripped her shoulder and spun her around to face him. "Sleeping with me is not petty! Are you not concerned with that? Does it mean nothing to you?"

"If you think that I am worried about you being my cousin, I have decided not to be. I am already a female captain and have thrown most social conventions over the bow and let them drift away with the ocean currents. I do as I please, and right now it pleases me to be with you."

Nonplussed by her response, he opened his mouth to argue but she interrupted him before he could form a sentence.

"Let me ask you, did you enjoy last night?" she questioned as she pressed against him.

"Of course. That is not the point, Istabelle."

"Do you want to sleep alone in a hammock tonight?"

He stepped back and saw the pleading in her eyes. She seemed to be afraid of what he was going to say. Did it matter if she called him Mangan when his name was Ruark? As he well knew, happiness was an ephemeral dream that touched one only for fleeting moments. Why upset this moment? Why disturb this dream?

He forced a smile and brushed his thumb across her cheek. "Very well, Istabelle. We won't talk, but one day we will have to. Nothing can be hidden forever." He tilted her head up and peered into her wide eyes. "Do you know how to play Mancala?" he asked, to change the subject.

Istabelle shook her head. "I do not know how to play any games. I did not play much as a child."

"Then let me show you. Mancala comes from the south, from the dark people. It is an ancient game that requires little preparation but much strategy. We need forty-eight colored playing pieces and a piece of chalk. But I warn you, I have added a few rules of my own and I do not like to lose."

"I do not like losing, either," Istabelle replied, but she grinned, her eyes sparkling with anticipation. "What shall we play for?"

"A favor. The winner can ask the other for something and the loser must give it, no matter what it is."

"That seems like a dangerous prize," Istabelle answered.

He leaned closer and whispered in her ear. "Are you afraid you will lose, Istabelle?"

"Absolutely not! I am already thinking about what favor I will demand from you when I win!" She rummaged around and located a pile of pebbles on the top of the rain barrel. "We use these to filter the water," she said. "Will they work?"

He nodded. "They are perfect." Then, using the chalk she produced, he drew six pairs of circles parallel to each other and two large rectangles on either end. "The object is to get as many pebbles into your own rectangle, or Mancala, as possible. You move the pieces by scooping up a pile of stones in a circle on your side and then placing them in the circles, one at a time, in order to the right. When you reach your Mancala, you place a stone in it and it is your point."

"What if I have more stones after I reach my Mancala?"

"You must place them in successive circles on my side and I have access to them for my turn."

"It does not seem that difficult."

"Strategy, rather than strength, will determine the winner." He smiled and motioned to the circles. "We will start with three stones in each circle and end when either one of us has no more stones to move. You go first."

Istabelle bit her lip and stared at the game. If he had suggested a game of fighting or force, she would have felt more confident about her ability to win. She peered up at him through her lashes and found him grinning at her discomfort. She frowned and grabbed a pile of stones and dropped them in circles, ending with one in her Mancala. "Hah!" she exclaimed. "I already have a point!"

"Indeed." He mirrored her actions, ending with a point as well.

She huffed and tried another move, but failed to win a point. Soon, they were immersed in the game, their points quickly adding up as stones filled the rectangular Mancalas. As the end drew near, the warrior's pile grew taller and Istabelle became agitated. " 'Tis not fair! You are better at this than I!"

"I have played it before," he answered, laughing at her disgruntled face.

"I demand a rematch."

"Very well, but I have already earned a favor. You will not break your word, will you?"

"Best two of three," she offered slyly. "Any gentleman would grant a lady some extra time to learn the game."

Ruark leaned closer and whispered in her ear. "I am not a gentleman and you did not act like a lady last night."

She turned her head and breathed on his neck. "Does that mean you do not accept my offer?"

He shivered, her husky voice instantly arousing him. Her lips were so close, he could feel the moisture of her breath settling on his throat. He closed his eyes, imagining her mouth kissing him, her lips stroking him. He forced himself to shake his head. She was already too strong a woman. If she realized how powerful her feminine wiles were, she would be incorrigible.

"A deal is a deal," he replied.

"Bah!" she shouted as she leapt back and scrambled to her feet. She kicked the stones and scattered them across the deck. "You do not play fair! You are taking advantage of my inexperience!"

Ruark opened his eyes and watched her warily, fully expecting her to pull her dagger and attack him.

He rose and faced her with his legs spread, anticipating her assault. "You are the one not playing fair," he chided her gently, glancing pointedly at her mouth.

She sidled up next to him and placed a delicate hand on his chest. Smiling seductively, she licked her lips and ran her tongue over her teeth. "Please," she begged. "One more game?"

He gave in instantly, disarmed by her unexpected choice of weapons. Had she fought him with a blade, he would have been exhilarated but firm. Had she railed at him, he would have remained stoic. But her fervent plea was so unnerving, he was helpless to resist.

"One more," he agreed. And the next game, he lost.

Chapter 13

As night fell, the evening crew took over sailing the ship. Istabelle conferred with them regarding the stars, the wind and the weather, and was soon satisfied that they would reach the islands by morning if all went well.

Ruark listened to her, fascinated by her sailing knowledge and self-assured leadership. She was respected by her crew, and he was rapidly agreeing with them. Few had ever earned his admiration as she had.

Inside the cabin, he pulled her onto his lap and kissed her neck. "You amaze me," he murmured.

"I do? Here I thought you did not approve of me."

"I don't agree with everything you do," he answered honestly, "yet I must acknowledge that you have done quite well being who you are."

She smiled and lay her head against his chest. "Thank you," she whispered, swallowing tears.

"Did I say something wrong?" he asked in concern.

"No. 'Tis just that you might not say that if you

knew everything about me. I have failed to do the very thing I needed to do most. I have not protected my family's people."

"What do you mean? I thought you did. You have dedicated your life to providing for them."

She shook her head. "Never mind. I'd rather not talk about it."

"You have to share your troubles or they will grow larger and haunt you. I know. I have done it."

"No."

He held her face in his hands and angled her to look at him. "If I must, I will use my favor to force you to tell me."

"Then I will use my favor to insist that you do not."

"Istabelle," he said. "Tell me what has made you feel that you have failed."

Her tears fell, wetting his shirt. She sobbed silently, her shoulders shaking with wrenching emotion. She could not tell him. Not before, when she had been embarrassed, and certainly not now, when she was terrified of what he would do when he found out. It was the treasure. If he knew what they were seeking, he would turn her aside and cease his caring attention. It would have been better if the item had simply been a piece of gold. Instead, Horik had stolen her freedom, her self-respect and her meaning in life. She could not admit her failings to Mangan. She did not want him to turn her aside. In a niggling, insidious way, he was beginning to mean something special to her.

He wrapped his arms around her and held her tightly, at a loss. What was causing this strong, confident woman to crumble? What terrible fate had befallen her? What awful act had she done to warrant such self-flagellation? He kissed her head. "Shush," he whispered. "Don't worry. You don't have to say anything."

She snuggled closer and nodded her head in gratitude.

In brooding discontent, he watched her gather some charts the following morning. They had fallen asleep on the chair, and he was stiff and irritable, while she acted as if nothing had happened between them last night. How could she not feel the boiling emotion—the sense of so much left unsaid? How could she act so nonchalant?

"What are you doing?" he asked, his voice expressing his annoyance.

"I am preparing to launch a scouting party. We reach the islands at dawn and I want to evaluate the area. The charts do not appear entirely accurate."

"I will go with you," he stated, expecting an argument.

"Very well," she replied. "I intend to row a boat to the tallest island and then make my way to the top of the high cliffs. From that vantage point, I should be able to scan the surrounding landscape and spot evidence of Horik's ship."

"Wouldn't it be just as easy to sail around the islands and look for him while staying aboard?"

"Aye, but we could sail into an ambush since I do

not know the area well. My charts are incomplete
and Erik told us that Horik knows this area. It makes
sense for us to do some initial scouting. The island
of hidden coves is near and we should be able to see
it from the cliffs."

"I expected you to argue with me about accompa-
nying you," he said as he yanked up his breeches
and relaced them.

"Of course not," Istabelle replied. "Your skills are
on land while mine are at sea. I welcome your
knowledge in tactical observation, and, should he be
lying in wait for me, I want your fighting arm beside
mine. We will make up one party, and I will send
another to the other side of the island to scout the
other direction."

"Do you have anything else to say?" he growled.
"Anything about why you were so upset last night?"

Turning, Istabelle looked directly at him. "No.
Nothing." She shook internally, but willed herself to
remain calm. This was not the time. She would have
one more night with him before she must confront
Horik. After that, he would know everything.

He stared back. Then, with an inaudible snarl, he
left the cabin.

The ship's anchor was lowered, and the clanking
sounds yanked her back to the present. It did no
good to hide in her cabin. She must go on deck and
act tough and brazen. No one must question her authority or her focus, least of all Mangan. She was a
captain and did not have time for emotional up-
heavals.

She glanced at her small bag containing fire-starting materials, a pot for boiling water and two sturdy blankets. Biting her lip, she lifted the lid on her clothing trunk, searching for one more item to add to the satchel. She had to dig down to the bottom until her fingers encountered the soft feel of silk. Why not? She carefully extracted the material and placed it in the bag, between the two blankets. A shiver of excitement went through her. If tonight was the last night she would have with him, she wanted it to be special.

They rowed ashore and together lifted the boat above the high-tide line. Without consulting her, the warrior took the bag and hefted it over his shoulder. Istabelle did not protest.

"Shall we go up the mountainous side, which is easier but longer, or the cliff side, which is shorter but more dangerous?" she asked.

"Scaling the cliff will put us at a disadvantage should the winds pick up, but I would rather finish this quickly. We will take that narrow path up the cliff."

"Péril will enjoy the flight," Istabelle agreed as the falcon circled over their heads.

With a grunt of acknowledgment, Ruark set off on an animal path that appeared to wend its way up the cliff. Many bushes lined the path and several spindly trees had managed to dig their roots into tiny patches of soil. He was still irritated with her but was trying not to start another argument.

Istabelle walked behind him, relishing the view of

his strong backside as he strode up the path, hacking stray branches out of their way with his sword.

"You are angry," she said when he cursed at a prickly bush that scratched his arm.

"No." He contradicted her through clenched teeth.

"Oh. It just seems as if you are rather tense."

"I am thinking, that is all."

"What are you thinking about?" she inquired.

He spun around and glared at her. "I am not thinking about anything," he growled.

She lifted her brows. "A storm is brewing."

"I am not angry!" he shouted.

Grinning, Istabelle shook her head. "I was not talking about you. I was referring to the weather."

Stymied by her abrupt change of subject, he glanced at the sky. A few dark clouds were gathering on the horizon. "They seem far away. Do you think they will come much closer?"

"Aye, it is likely to break by tonight. Undoubtedly we will be forced to stay overnight on the island, as rowing back to the ship will be dangerous."

He looked into her smiling silver eyes. "Did you suspect that a storm was coming before now?" he asked.

"Yes."

"But you still had us come ashore. Together."

"Yes," she repeated softly.

He sighed. "I don't understand one thing about you," he finally replied, his anger fading.

"That is all right. I don't understand much about myself, either."

He held his hand out to her. "Let's make the top as soon as we can so I can build us a shelter. If we are going to spend an evening on a deserted island together, we might as well be dry and comfortable."

She took his hand and followed him as he led them rapidly up the path. It felt good to have his large hand envelop hers, and she walked behind him trustingly. His irritation had disappeared and an aura of comfortable companionship surrounded them. At times, they were forced to release their handhold in order to scramble up the cliff, but as soon as the terrain leveled, they touched fingers again. Once, Istabelle stumbled and he gripped her hand tighter to stabilize her.

"I intend to have you to myself for the night," he teased her. "I am not going to let you hurt yourself."

She laughed. "If I sprained my ankle, would you carry me back to the ship?"

"Of course I would, but you should not tempt the fates by talking that way."

"You are superstitious? You do not seem like a person who thinks anything is ruled by fate."

"On the contrary, I believe the fickle gods dictate almost everything we do and everywhere we go."

"And everyone we meet?"

"Definitely."

"Your family is so Christian. Don't I remember you admiring the monks?" Istabelle questioned.

He shrugged. "Do not try to merge who I am now with who you think I was as a child. For tonight, put aside all your former thoughts and simply learn about the man in front of you." His onyx eyes were intense as he stared at her. "Can you do that? Can you be with *me* tonight? Not Mangan as you knew him, but *me*?"

Istabelle nodded. "Yes. Will you do the same?"

"Yes. Tonight we have no past and no future. We live only in the moment."

Smiling, she pointed over the water to *The Adventuress*. A shimmering blue flame danced on the ship's mast. "The Fire of the Gods. It is a good omen."

"What is that?" he asked in amazement. "The fire is not consuming the wood."

"No, it is a sign from above that a storm approaches, but fortune follows close behind. Have you never seen it before?"

"Never."

"It will disappear in moments, but as the air begins to hum with the power of lightning, more flames may appear. It is a phenomenal sight."

Istabelle's silver eyes reflected the blue flames as she watched them cavort upon her ship's mast. Ruark brushed a stray strand of hair back from her face and placed a gentle kiss on her neck. "Phenomenal," he agreed.

When the blue fire winked out, they finished climbing to the top, where they were greeted by the gyrfalcon. A large rabbit lay at her feet.

"Péril has given us a gift," Istabelle stated as she approached the bird. "Many thanks, my friend."

The falcon screeched in response and fluffed her feathers. "I will skin and gut it while you make a shelter," she suggested when it was clear Péril would not let the warrior take the offering.

"Agreed," he said.

"Horik and his crew are likely anchored in a sheltered cove, waiting out the storm. There will be no battle tonight."

"Let us hope that his common sense outweighs his need for revenge."

Nodding, Istabelle proceeded to dress the rabbit, cutting some pieces for Péril and hand-feeding them to her. The powerful beak of the gyrfalcon could easily have crushed Istabelle's slim fingers, but the bird plucked the morsels out of her hand with delicate precision.

"Here," Istabelle said as she pulled the liver from the rabbit. "Do you want to feed her?"

Ruark looked at the beady eyes of the falcon with suspicion. "She will probably bite my finger off."

"Don't be silly. Your finger is not nearly as delicious as raw liver."

"Thanks," he replied sardonically. Holding the choice piece in his hand, he offered it to the gyrfalcon.

Péril cocked her head and screeched.

"She doesn't like me," Ruark stated, repeating what he had said several times before.

"Take it slowly," Istabelle answered. "She must come to you."

He held out his hand. The bird hopped closer and opened her mouth, emitting a hiss.

"Stay steady," Istabelle cautioned.

Péril fluffed her feathers and hopped once again, putting herself within arm's reach of the warrior. She spread her wings and flapped them, but did not rise off the ground.

"What is she doing?" he asked.

"She wants to show you how big she is."

"Well, her display is impressive." Suddenly, Péril darted her head forward and pecked the liver from his hand. Tilting her head upward, she swallowed the piece whole. "Why didn't she chew it?" Ruark asked as he wiped his hand on his breeches.

"She has no teeth, but she will swallow gravel to grind up the meat and make it easier to digest. She can swallow metal and eventually grind it to nothing. It is the way birds break down food."

"Fascinating."

Thunder rumbled in the distance, causing Péril to burst up into the air. After her abrupt ascent, she landed in the top branches of a pine tree, then hopped down the branch until she was covered by an overhang. From her vantage point she stared at the clouds that were rapidly gathering. The air hummed with expectation of the coming squall and the gyrfalcon, along with all the island's animals, was preparing for its eruption.

"She will stay there until the rain is done," Istabelle stated as she started looking for a place to build a fire.

"Will she be safe?" Ruark asked.

"Aye, probably safer than us, if you don't start building."

"If any other soul had dared insult me like that, I would have run him through with my sword. You are too used to commanding men. Remember that I am not accustomed to taking orders from a woman."

Istabelle smiled sweetly. "Well, then, I apologize. Pray forgive my forthrightness. I will endeavor to dance around the subject next time."

He laughed at her mocking words. "Fortunately, I am beginning to understand you. Don't bother trying to change for me. I know it would be a useless exercise. I am fond of you as you are."

Istabelle dropped her eyes, unnerved by his endearing words. There had been such turmoil between them, she did not know how to respond to his kindness.

"Don't tell me that you are at a loss for words, Istabelle? I find that hard to believe."

"I am simply concentrating on the rabbit," she mumbled.

Laughing again, he turned away from her and began collecting branches to form a shelter. It felt good to laugh, for he had had few opportunities to feel such happiness. It was liberating and made him feel energized. Glancing back at Istabelle, he was pleased to see a smile on her face as well. She deserved to feel as good as she made him feel, for he suspected that she had not laughed much either. A pair of serious fighters, each struggling to ignore the hurts of the past—perhaps for them the future would be filled with a new emotion.

He finished the shelter as the first drops of rain

fell, and Istabelle ducked under the overhang with a bundle of kindling. She quickly built a fire while he spitted the meat.

"I am impressed by your cover," Istabelle commented as he properly angled the rabbit over the small flames.

"I have fought countless battles and have slept out in the forest more nights than I have slept in a bed."

"And I have slept on the ocean waves more times than on solid ground."

Ruark leaned against the tree that formed a portion of the shelter's back wall. The place was composed of three sides and a thick roof, leaving an opening that faced toward the cliffs. The arrangement allowed them to keep watch over the ocean as well as let the smoke draw away from the hut's core. It was practical yet panoramic.

Rain began to fall in earnest. Istabelle snuggled between the warrior's bent legs and leaned back against his chest. They watched the ocean darken as millions of raindrops peppered its surface, its rat-a-tat music falling all around them.

Laying his cheek against her head, Ruark spoke aloud a question they were both thinking. "Is that how you want to live forever? Sleeping alone in a ship's cabin far from civilization?"

"I don't know. My stepmother has no need for anyone but my father. She is content to roam her private island and shuns all society."

"She is blind," he stated, waiting for confirmation.

"Yes, but her blindness is not what makes her

enjoy her solitude. She is, at heart, a peaceful woman who needs no other stimulation."

"You are not like her."

"No, although there are times when I wish I was. I envy her self-assurance and self-sufficiency. For some reason, I am constantly beset by the need to explore. I am compelled to challenge myself and search for the action that will most shock people. It is almost like a compulsion that cannot be controlled, as if I am lost and trying to find my true home. My father left me several days after I was born, and although I now understand why he did, it still hurts."

"Your abandonment still weighs heavily on your mind. Perhaps you will continue to feel misplaced until you are convinced that someone you love will not leave you again."

"Perhaps, but since that miracle is unlikely to occur, I have resigned myself to my fate."

Ruark turned her in his lap and faced her. "Istabelle, you will find someone who will match your strength, understand your needs and fulfill your passions. You are too wonderful to be ignored. Do not fear that you will be lonely forever."

"What about you? Will you find someone who fills your emptiness?"

Pain clouded his eyes. "If I do, I would wish it happens in the clear light of honesty. I am not a good catch, and I doubt that any woman who truly knew who I am would want to spend more than a night in my presence."

"That is not true, Mangan," Istabelle said softly.

Ruark closed his eyes and resettled Istabelle in his lap so that she could not see his face. He was beginning to hate that name. "One day you will understand, but I am like you. I do not want that day to be today." Deliberately distracting her, he ran his hands over her breasts, teasing her nipples.

"What do you mean?" Istabelle asked, but she hardly listened for his answer as her body blazed to life under his experienced hands.

"I mean that I have other thoughts about what to do tonight," he whispered as he kissed her neck.

"I want to see if the Fire of the Gods is flaming again," she gasped.

"It *is* flaming," he growled as he nibbled her ear.

"Wait, I want to change."

"Don't change," he argued softly. "I like you as you are."

"Change clothes," Istabelle clarified as she shifted out of his embrace. "Please," she begged when he would have pulled her back.

Adjusting his breeches, the warrior reluctantly nodded.

"Close your eyes," Istabelle commanded.

"I would rather watch you."

"Close your eyes," she repeated as she stood in the tall section of the shelter and placed her hands on her hips.

"If you insist."

Istabelle tiptoed over to the bag and pulled out the two blankets. After placing them on the ground beside the fire, she extracted the white silk cloth she had carefully hidden between them. Shaking with nervousness, she turned her back on the man and unlaced her dress.

Ruark opened his eyes a slit at the sound of rustling. The fact that she was completely unaware of his spying made it all the more titillating to see her undress. She pushed her hair over her shoulder and proceeded to pull the neckline of her dress down. As she bared her back, she paused and fiddled with her underclothes, doing something to the front of them that he could not see. The anticipation made him squirm.

Istabelle looked over her shoulder. "Are you looking?" she asked suspiciously.

"Absolutely not," he lied shamelessly.

Istabelle returned her attention to her clothing and was finally able to divest herself of the dress as well as the various pieces of linen. A groan made her hesitate. "Are you making noises?"

"No," he answered in a strangled voice. "Pray proceed."

She bent over and picked up the white silk. Stroking it reverently, she held it against her chest and breathed deeply, unaware that her naked derriere was causing the warrior acute agony. "Just a moment," she promised as she unfolded the item and shook it out. Just as Ruark was about to leap up and rip it from her hands, she slipped it over her head.

The white cloud floated around her, falling in soft, subtle layers. He had never seen anything so exquisite.

"You can look now," she whispered.

He opened his eyes fully as she turned and faced him. "What is it?" he asked in awe.

"A night rail from the Far East," she answered. "I—I obtained it when I overtook a merchant about a year ago. I never had an opportunity to wear it before. Do you like it?"

"Oh yes," he replied reverently. "I like it very much. Turn around . . . slowly. I want to see every inch."

She spun around and the silk fluttered around her. A few drops of rain splashed her through the open side of the shelter and darkened the white silk.

"Come here," he commanded huskily. "I want to feel you."

She walked up to him and stood between his legs, resting her hands on his shoulders. "Do I look silly?"

"No, of course not. Why would you say that?"

"I'm not sure. I'm not sure such delicate clothing looks appropriate on me."

"How would you know? Have you always known who you were? How you wanted to be?"

"Yes, at least I thought so. Now I am not so sure . . ." She dropped her gaze as her voice trailed off.

"What do you want from me?" he finally asked when it was clear she would not say more.

"I'm not sure about that, either," she answered honestly.

"You know what I want?"

She shook her head and looked at him.

"I want to hold you in my arms, stroke your lovely, silk-covered skin and watch the rain."

"Is that all?"

He stroked her hips through the flimsy silk garment. "Maybe yes, maybe no," he replied with a grin.

"I love the rain."

And I think I love you, he said silently as he opened his arms.

Chapter 14

When the sun peeked over the cliffside and illuminated their makeshift shelter, both Ruark and Istabelle were sound asleep. One blanket lay underneath them and the other covered their naked bodies. The delicate material Istabelle had been wearing had long since been discarded when the warrior had bared her body to the heat of his gaze. Unlike before, this time they had spent hours touching and stroking, letting their hands explore each other in secret, intimate ways, until they both felt the power of the elements shudder through their souls and the storm rage through their flesh.

It was magical, unforgettable, and as Istabelle blinked awake in the sunlight, memories flooded her mind. His touch had been both sensual and sensitive. He had made her feel cared for in a way that was unique and special. His whispered words had lifted her from mere pleasure to overwhelming ecstasy.

She propped herself up on one elbow and looked out over the calm ocean. The cry of her gyrfalcon came again, and she realized that had been the sound to wake her.

"What, Péril?" she murmured. "Do you need something?" The cry came again and Istabelle sighed. "I hear you," she said grumpily, displeased to leave her warm bed. "I'm coming." She slid out of the covers and carefully tucked them around the man still sleeping before pulling her clothes back on. They were damp from the rain, but she ignored the discomfort.

As she ducked out of the hut, the falcon swooped down and landed on her shoulder. "Augh," Istabelle grunted. "I was not ready for you. Don't grip so hard with your talons. They hurt."

Péril loosened her grip and made a soft noise in the back of her throat. Then she rose into the air and flew toward the west. Several smaller islands dotted the sea and a thin layer of fog still flirted with the island's coast. Péril flew in a circle and cried again. A shaft of sunlight burned through the fog and reflected off the smooth hull of a ship anchored in the protected cove of another island.

"Good falcon!" Istabelle cried as she peered at the vessel. It was located just north of them and would have been completely hidden to her if she had not been on the high cliff. "Mangan!" she shouted as she dashed into the shelter and shook his shoulder. "Péril found Horik's ship!"

The warrior opened his eyes and stared at the woman excitedly packing their things and preparing to dash down the path. After last night's closeness, he detested his false identity more than ever. He rose and pulled his clothes on in silence. This evening he would tell her the truth, no matter what she wanted to hear. He was not willing to spend another night with lies between them.

Istabelle raced up to him and grabbed his hand. "Come, Mangan. We must hurry. Today I want no distractions. By this eve, I will have reclaimed my property and all will be well. I am pleased that you will be beside me. It is a beautiful gift to be able to depend upon another. Thank you."

He forced a smile. Tonight. Tonight he would tell her his real name. "That is what friends . . . and family . . . do for each other."

"Aye." She kissed him on the cheek and then scampered down the steep cliff. Even though stones slid underneath her feet and gravel tumbled around her, she did not slow her steps.

Ruark followed after her more carefully, thinking about the battle ahead. He still did not know what they sought. What item was so important that she had felt it necessary to send for Mangan's assistance?

As they rowed to the ship, he spoke. "Istabelle, are you ready to tell me what treasure we are seeking?"

She flushed. "If you help secure the deck, I will search Horik's cabin."

He frowned. "Anything can happen in battle. You could be injured. If you cannot board Horik's vessel, there must be another person to claim your treasure, or this fight will be all for naught. You said you trusted me."

"Yes, you are right. If anything should happen to me, I want you to search his cabin for a piece of paper."

"Paper?" he asked incredulously. "What is written on the paper?"

"It is a statement of ownership, but he does not have the right to own the property in question. It has to do with Dunhaven."

"Ahhh. Land. I should have known. All major wars have been over power, money or land."

"Or women," Istabelle added teasingly.

"No, not over women. Over love."

"What do you know of love?" she questioned.

He pulled on the oars and bumped the rowboat against the ship. "I believe that a man would lay down his life for someone he loved."

"Then that would be a foolish man, for if he died, he would not be able to enjoy his lover's company."

"I have heard that men in love do many foolish things."

"Bah. I would not wish a lovestruck man to do anything foolish for me."

As he handed her out of the small boat and onto the rope ladder, he leaned over her shoulder. Whispering in her ear, he said, "I think you are the one who knows nothing of love."

Istabelle turned and stared at his serious face. Her stomach fluttered oddly and she felt dizzy. Love. She knew nothing about the emotion, yet the word itself made her feel weak. "I love my ship. I love my freedom."

He shook his head. "No, Istabelle. We are not talking about that kind of love. We are talking about love between a man and a woman."

"You mean what we have done together?"

"Our bodies have touched, but I am talking about our hearts. Do you feel the difference?"

Her eyes dilated as his face filled her vision and his presence dominated her surroundings. The rocking waves and the creaking mast faded. He braced a hand beside her head, holding her swaying body in place. "Feel the difference?" she asked softly as she clung to the ladder.

"Do you feel something else? Did you feel something special in my embrace?"

"Captain!" Boris shouted from above the lovers.

Ruark pressed closer. "Do you?" he asked insistently.

"Captain? Mangan? Did you locate Horik's vessel?"

Istabelle shuddered. "I feel . . . something . . ."

Boris leaned over the rail. "When the falcon came back we thought you'd found him. We are ready to set sail immediately."

"What did you feel?" the warrior asked, trying to ignore Boris.

Istabelle looked up. "Yes," she replied to her crew member. "Péril located Horik and showed him to me."

"Which way?" he asked.

Istabelle glanced back at the warrior's face. It was suddenly shuttered and withdrawn, all the emotion wiped away. "To the north," she called out.

Ruark stepped back. "Never mind the question," he said coldly. "Your priorities are elsewhere." Confused, Istabelle touched his face, but he flinched and pulled away. "Go on up, Istabelle. I will secure the rowboat."

An hour later, *The Adventuress* sailed out of the cove with Istabelle at the helm. After a brief tactical discussion, the men were stationed at the sails, at the oars and along the railing according to their skills. Ruark placed himself at the railing with his sword in hand and several knives strapped to his body. He stood a few feet from Istabelle, in order to protect her as best as he could.

He thought of Sven and his injuries. According to Mangan, he was on this mission because God had placed him here. God had neatly arranged for Sven's injury and subsequent care at the monastery in exchange for his military service to Istabelle, presumably one of his favored children. If Ruark should fail, what would happen to Sven? To Istabelle? To Mangan? If he fell during the battle, the course of many people's lives would be altered. He had faced countless battles, but had never feared the outcome.

Suddenly, he did. If so much rested on retrieving Istabelle's paper, he must succeed, and if it ultimately required his death, he was willing to forfeit his existence for the betterment of all. How much did gold and fortune matter when people like Istabelle were fighting for justice and compassion? For once, his bag of coins was forgotten. She had changed his outlook on life, and he was ready to battle for her cause.

Istabelle felt his presence behind her, though she tried to ignore him. She did not have time to wrestle with the strange emotions he evoked. She had to concentrate on Horik and the conflict ahead. Still, she was well aware of his location at her back, and she heard his steady breathing as if he were standing a scant inch from her side. Did she feel something special for him? Had she felt something different for him, as he had asked her on the ladder? Surely she felt something. She had surrendered her body to his touch, but the physical intimacy did not exactly describe what she felt. It was more intense, more personal than mere fleshy pleasure.

Erik pointed to a place where the fog was divided by a spit of land. "That is the landmark Horik uses to locate his secret hiding place. He comes here after a raid and stashes his loot before raiding again. He does it to keep his vessel light and maneuverable during attacks."

"Then he loads all his goods aboard and heads to his settlement for the winter?" Istabelle asked.

"Aye. He is very familiar with these waters. You should take care to be on the ready."

"We are. You are one of us, Erik. Take a weapon and be prepared to attack."

"A weapon, Captain? You would allow a slave to hold a knife?"

Shaking her head angrily, Istabelle rounded on the

boy. "Have you learned nothing? There are no slaves on this ship. You are a free man and able to participate in all our activities. You will get an equal share of the spoils. You are one of us."

Erik grinned and scampered off to get a short sword as Ruark approached Istabelle. "He is inexperienced. He will get hurt in the battle."

"Probably. Do you think it would be wiser to wound his heart by forcing him to cower below? Would you have done so as a boy?"

Remembering the feel of his first knife wound, when he was only six years old, Ruark shook his head. "I would have fought regardless of the odds against me."

"Just as I thought," she replied. "We will reach the enemy in moments." Turning to the crew, she motioned for silence. The men at the oars placed cloth around the oar ports to muffle the creak of their motions, and the men at the sails waited in tense expectation. If they spotted their adversary at anchor, they would have to drop the sails and roll the canvas so that the oarsmen could maneuver the ship into boarding position. The tactic would spare *The Adventuress* by preventing her from ramming the other vessel, but it required split-second action. If, however, the enemy was sailing, they would have to catch up to the other ship's stern, then exactly match her pace as the rudder men used heavy hammers and metal wedges to destroy the enemy's stern post and subsequently flounder the victim.

Everyone peered through the fog as *The Adventur-*

ess slid silently through the water, seeking Horik's warship. As the morning sun burned off the mist, shapes materialized in the distance. Staring intently, the crew strained to locate Horik. The silence was broken only by the quiet splash of waves against the ship's hull and the subtle snapping of the sails' canvas in the wind. Tension spread through the crew as each member prepared for the fight.

The fog began to lift. It rose from the water and shrouded the mast in a thick white blanket. Although Péril was perched on the mast, her form was completely invisible to the people on deck. Flickers of sunlight broke through the mist and reflected off the sea. Instead of increasing visibility, the light obscured distances and created confusing mirages all around them. The crew squinted or held their hands up to shield their eyes. Anxiety soared.

Suddenly, Péril screamed, her warning sound echoing strangely through the fog.

"She sees him," Istabelle whispered. Then, looking up, she whistled.

An answering cry came and the gyrfalcon burst through the fog as she dove down into the cleared area. Swooping to the right, she flew just under the fog bank and screamed again.

"Tack right," Istabelle commanded. "Pull in the main sheet. Secure the ropes. Prepare."

Just as *The Adventuress* swung to the right, the outlaw's vessel burst out of the mist.

"There she is!" Taber shouted.

"Enemy spotted dead ahead!" Boris cried simultaneously as the crew shouted and brandished their weapons.

An answering cry came from the enemy ship, sending excitement racing through the sailors. It was time!

The outlaws sent a flurry of small spears through the air, raining them on *The Adventuress*. The falcon abruptly flapped her wings and tried to climb above the fog in order to avoid the spears, but one brushed her wing tip. She squawked and faltered, falling.

"Péril!" Istabelle gasped.

The gyrfalcon fluttered her wings, barely managing to level her descent. She cried out once again with a faint reflection of her powerful voice, then painfully flapped her wings and flew out of the fray.

"My bird!" Istabelle exclaimed. "She is injured!" As Istabelle stared after the wounded falcon, another volley of spears fell around her.

"Istabelle!" Ruark shouted. "Forget the falcon. The battle has begun!" He shoved her to the side, protecting her from a sharp spear that embedded itself in the wood where she had been standing.

"She is my friend," Istabelle cried. "I can't leave her!"

Ruark gripped her face and forced her to stare into his black eyes. "I promise that we will find her once the fight is done, but right now you must concentrate or you will die."

"You don't understand," Istabelle argued as she frantically tried to look through the mist. "She is all I have."

"I do understand. I have a brother who means the same, but we cannot let our fears make us weak. It is now or never. Fight!"

Istabelle returned his gaze in surprise. Brother? What was he saying? Mangan did not have a brother.

"Captain," Boris shouted. "We are going to ram her!"

Galvanized into action, Istabelle nodded and jerked away from the warrior's hold. "Drop the other sails. Throw the grappling hooks. Prepare to board her!"

The warship's prow rose in front of them. The carved figurehead was not only decorative, it also served as a battering ram.

"Pull! Pull!" Istabelle commanded, and *The Adventuress* swept ahead and to the left, avoiding the debilitating attack. The right oarsmen yanked their oars in and ducked as others flung pronged hooks over the side. The hooks thudded onto the outlaw's deck, then slid until they either lodged in the wood or dropped into the sea. Both ships shuddered as the ropes snapped taut. The momentum of each ship, along with the left oars on *The Adventuress*, sent the bound pair into a slow spin.

"Bring in the oars and attack!" Istabelle shouted just as Horik raised a chilling battle cry from the enemy ship. Almost instantly, the men on both vessels sprang for the ropes, their weapons flashing with deadly intent.

Chapter 15

Istabelle searched over the railing for her nemesis, her russet hair gleaming in the rising sunshine and her face glowing with strength and purpose. "Horik!" she shouted. "I told you I would come back and take my revenge!"

The outlaw shook his battle-axe over his head and leered back at her. His red hair blew around his head in haphazard disarray, forming a halo of devilish flames around his angry face. Pockmarks marred his cheeks and his nostrils flared with the force of his fury. "I dare you to come over here and bow to your master! I own you!"

"I have no master save myself," Istabelle screamed.

"I say differently, and I have proof, sea-daemon," he cried mockingly. "Don't you remember?"

Snarling with anger, Istabelle scrambled over the ropes, her long knife clenched in her teeth.

Ruark followed her, sensing a tension between Horik and Istabelle that bespoke more than simple adversaries. This fight was not just about deeds or treasure. It was far more personal. Unease snaked through him.

An outlaw sailor attacked them as they were swinging aboard. Istabelle jerked back to avoid the deadly axe and lost her footing. Ruark grabbed her arm to steady her. "Don't focus solely on Horik!" he yelled at her. "Any man, be he hired soldier or king, can kill you with a well-placed blade."

Nodding her understanding, Istabelle thrust her sword at the man attacking her. Her weapon sliced his torso and he screamed in pain. On the other side, another brigand attacked, but Ruark blocked his thrust and deftly relieved him of his weapon. When the man stared at Ruark in surprise, Ruark swung his leg out and kicked the man's knee, toppling him into the water. The man screamed in panic as the two bound ships were rocked on the waves and crashed against each other, smashing the hapless sailor between them.

Ruark immediately returned to fight next to Istabelle. He was a warrior, and this was what he was trained to do. Fight. Maim. Kill. Protect his assigned charge.

It was as bloody and violent as any land battle, except that the slow spinning of the ships and the constant rocking of the waves made the footing perilous. The combatants had to avoid the thrusting daggers and the piercing swords, but they also had to stay on deck or risk drowning in the cold water. Istabelle was familiar with the dangers, and she braced herself as she spotted Horik.

The other *Adventuress* sailors flooded around them, swarming the deck and attacking the outlaws. Within moments, Istabelle and Ruark were surrounded by fighting men who swung and sliced viciously, without mercy. Shouts and screams vied with one another as the deck became slick with blood.

Istabelle leapt back as a sword nicked her side. Infuriated, she snatched her dagger from her neck chain and drove it into the attacker's chest. Impressed, Ruark grinned. "You fight like a true warrior, Istabelle!" he shouted over the melee.

A surge of pride raced through Istabelle's heart and she smiled back. His words emboldened her as she retrieved her dagger and spun around with more ferocity than before, knowing he was at her back. She felt his heat as he swung his broadsword, and she heard the gasps as outlaw after outlaw fell under his onslaught. He was mighty and powerful, and his strength infused her with a sense of victory.

Suddenly Erik stepped in front of her. "No!" Istabelle cried as he faced a black-haired bandit. She tried to shove him aside, but the boy stood his ground and raised his small sword against the man's two-edged blade. Laughing, the outlaw used two hands and swung his weapon at Erik's head.

Out of the corner of his eye, Ruark saw the flashing sword descend upon Erik and Istabelle's frantic movements to save him. Acting on instinct, he shoved Istabelle down and desperately tried to block the man's blade. As Istabelle fell, she bumped into Erik and he was flung forward, into the enemy's arms. The sword whistled through the air as the out-law went flying backward and landed on his back with Erik on top. Erik scrambled up, finding himself covered in blood.

"Get your sword!" Ruark commanded.

"My sword?" Erik answered dumbly.

"You plunged it into the man's chest when you fell. You killed him. Now retrieve your sword."

His quiet voice calmed the boy, and Erik yanked the sword free and turned to face another outlaw, still shaking with disbelief.

As Erik struggled to defend himself, Istabelle yanked on the warrior's arm and pointed to the hatchway. "I think Horik is portside. Keep the other outlaws at bay," she demanded. "I will go below and find the paper while the crew takes all they can from the hold. Once we have what we came for, we will drench the deck with oil and set it ablaze. Keep an eye out for Horik in case he returns aft."

Ruark nodded and motioned for her to proceed as he defended her position. He could not locate Horik, but the deck was seething with men. Bodies lay tangled on the boards, many moaning with fatal injuries. Taber fought to his left, his bare chest crisscrossed with bloody streaks. Boris was still on *The Adventuress*, hacking at the outlaws that tried to board her. Erik was pressed against a railing looking dazed, but he had somehow managed to disable another outlaw.

"Hurry, Istabelle!" Ruark shouted as he swung his sword at another attacker.

Istabelle raced down the ladder and into Horik's

personal cabin. Memories flooded her as she yanked open the door. Here was the site of her worst humiliation. Here she had been forced to acknowledge her inferior strength. This room had witnessed her helpless submission to a man she detested. Istabelle's stomach heaved and she swayed in the doorway. She couldn't go in there! She couldn't make her feet carry her across the threshold once again.

She closed her eyes, trying to block out the sight of the cabin and the implements that decorated the walls, but the details remained clear in her memory. In front of her and slightly to the right was the chain. The chain of enslavement. Istabelle opened her eyes and stared at it. She could remember its smell as it had been wrapped around her neck, a bitter, metallic scent that had reminded her of blood. Unable to stop the memories, Istabelle vomited. Leaning weakly against the side of the door, she wiped her mouth with the back of her hand. She had to go inside! She had to take back what was rightfully hers! She would not fail again!

Istabelle took one trembling step inside, then another. She could do it. She could do it!

"Hello, Istabelle," Horik purred from the shadows.

She screamed.

"Such a frightened sound coming from such a strong woman. I am ashamed of you, sea-daemon. I thought you had more spirit."

Shaking with remembered humiliation, she tried to raise her sword. Her arm was heavy and she stared at it in confusion. Black spots swam in her vision.

"You are going to faint," Horik mocked. "How feminine." He stalked closer. "We have one more piece of unfinished business between us, and it doesn't matter to me if you are awake for it or not."

"No," Istabelle whispered as she stumbled back. "Leave me alone."

"It is time to consummate our new relationship." Horik reached out to grab her by the throat when suddenly his hand met the cold steel of the warrior's blade over Istabelle's shoulder.

"Don't touch her," Ruark warned, his voice low and deadly.

"How dare you interfere!" Horik snarled. "You know nothing of what is between me and Istabelle. She is my wife!"

"What?" Ruark replied, his brows drawn. "You do not know who you are talking about. This is Captain Istabelle!"

Horik glared at him. "I know who she is. She is the woman who has plagued me for far too long. She has stolen the goods I have obtained—"

"Obtained through thievery!" Istabelle interrupted angrily. "You subject the peasants to starvation."

"Don't you dare interrupt me," Horik bellowed. "Learn your place, wife!"

"I will not be your wife for a moment longer. My cousin, as a leader in my family, has the power to disallow the marriage before it is consummated. The marriage certificate you forced me to sign will be voided and the marriage annulled!"

Horik swung his gaze to Ruark. Spittle dribbled

from the corner of his mouth as he ground his teeth together. He raised his battle-axe and shook it. "Upon whose authority do you speak? The Dunhaven dowry should be mine! She stole from me thrice. 'Tis only right that I regain my due."

Ruark was frozen. He couldn't speak or think clearly. Istabelle was wed! The piece of paper she needed to retrieve was a marriage document, not just a property deed. She had sent for Mangan because he was the earl's son. She had not needed his sword as Mangan had assumed. Instead, she needed his blood.

He shook his head. "I have no authority."

"Yes, you do," Istabelle shouted. "You will soon be the head of the O'Bannon family, my father's family. Your voice speaks for all O'Bannons. Forbid the marriage now and I will be free!" She blinked rapidly and clenched her fists against her sides. "I cannot remain married to this monster," she cried, "for upon my marriage, my mother's dowry passes to my husband and the people of Dunhaven's northern coast go under his control. Horik will plunder the land and place the people in an even more terrible situation than they are now under Dunhaven rule. I cannot allow him to murder my people!"

Ruark shook his head again and slumped back against the wall. His head spun. If only she had told him what she needed from the very beginning. She should have revealed her predicament sooner. He was useless to her.

"I am not Mangan," he whispered. "I cannot help you."

"What are you saying?" Istabelle cried. She grabbed his hand and held it up to show the ruby signet ring. "You are heir to the O'Bannon earldom. You are my cousin. Tell Horik nay and all will be put to rights. Don't let him destroy my people!"

Ruark pulled his hand back and twisted the ring off. He held it in his hand. "The ring is not mine. I am not Mangan. Your cousin is at a monastery in Scotland. He sent me in his place."

A low chuckle came from Horik's belly, then escalated into a roaring laugh. "You were fooled, Istabelle, and your plans to annul our marriage are foiled. You are still my wife, and after we consummate our pact, you will have no way to destroy it. I will have you, your fortune *and* my revenge."

"What have you done?" Istabelle whispered to Ruark. "You lied to me? You let me believe you were my cousin. If you are not Mangan, who are you?"

"I am Ruark of Haagen village."

She trembled, her face drained of all color. "No," she denied.

"Yes. I speak the truth. I am Ruark, an orphan who spent his youth growing up in the streets of Haagen. Not only am I not the heir to an earldom, I have no family and no home. I am a hired sword. Mangan could not leave his post and he sent me to help you. I tried to tell you—"

"You did not try hard enough!" she cried as she knocked the ring from his hand. "I trusted you! I believed in you!"

Overwhelming guilt assailed Ruark. All his failures

and inadequacies surged to the forefront of his mind. He felt helpless and useless. All his life, he had fought the stigma of being an orphan. He had battled unknown foes in order to collect gold so that he could prove his worth. Suddenly, his path seemed senseless. Gold would not buy him a family. Riches would not gain him family lands. Without those basic elements, he would never *be* anything and he could not *do* anything worthwhile. He had failed Mangan and Sven, and even worse, he had failed the woman he desperately wanted to help.

"I failed," he murmured, his heart breaking.

Tears flooded Istabelle's eyes. "How could you?" She dropped her sword and let it clatter to the floor. "How could you!" she screamed as tears poured down her face. "I hate you!"

"Don't say that," he pleaded.

"I hate you!" she screamed louder. "Go away! I never want to see you again!"

"Istabelle!" he cried as he stepped forward.

Suddenly Horik snatched Istabelle up against his body and pressed his curved knife to her throat. "Don't come any closer," he warned Ruark as the warrior started to run forward. "She is my property. My wife."

Infuriated, Ruark pointed his sword at Horik and narrowed his gaze threateningly. "Let her go. She is not your wife, for I know you have not consummated your vows."

Horik looked from Istabelle's tear-streaked face to Ruark's thunderous one. A sly grin spread his lips as he pressed the dagger deeper into Istabelle's tender flesh.

"Prove it," he replied. "Is she still a virgin? Can a midwife verify that she is still untouched?" When the warrior did not answer, Horik laughed again. "I thought so. You have sealed her fate by doing my job for me. You have proved to be more my ally than hers. Many thanks, Ruark of Haagen village. Now, if you value her life, leave my ship and return to Scotland with *The Adventuress* and let me enjoy my new wife!"

Ruark leapt forward, but Horik viciously cut into Istabelle's neck as he yanked her backward.

"Stop!" Istabelle cried as blood drenched her blouse. "Go away, *Ruark*! You have done enough already. Must you cause my death as well?"

Ruark trembled. Every instinct cried for him to attack Horik and enfold Istabelle in his arms, but he had ruined everything already. "Is that what you want?" he whispered.

Horik pressed the knife upward, making Istabelle gasp in pain. "Now," she pleaded. "Return Mangan's ring and tell the crew to sail home. There is nothing I can do for them anymore."

Ruark's heart bled at the pain in Istabelle's voice. He had failed her and now all the people who depended upon her were in peril. He leaned down and picked up the signet ring. If he had deserved to wear it, everyone would have been saved, but he did not deserve such recognition. He was an orphan and Istabelle hated him. Turning on his heel, he left the cabin.

Chapter 16

As Ruark stalked out, Horik spun Istabelle around and shoved her against the wall. He gripped her hair and tilted her head back, forcing her to stare into his beady eyes. "You thought you outsmarted me, didn't you?" He leaned forward and breathed in her face. "You are a fool if you think you can outwit a man like me. Do you think I am stupid?"

She jerked her head back and glared at him. "If you think the Dunhavens will recognize this farce of a marriage, then you may be in for a great surprise. Even though the dowry is mine, they will not willingly relinquish it."

Horik slammed his fist against the wall next to her head as he spat on her face. "Who do you think gave me the plan to wed you? Do you think I would want to marry a hellion like you? Your Dunhaven relatives have grown weary of your interference. They sent their blessings several months ago, along with a hefty payment. You were sold, Istabelle. As I said, you are mine."

Horrified, Istabelle cringed away from him. "Even

they would not do that," she whispered, but doubt already clouded her voice. The Dunhavens hated her and despised her father's family. By wedding her to a notorious outlaw, they shamed the O'Bannons and disposed of her at the same time. "No one will believe I married you willingly," she offered desperately.

"That does not matter. Your consent is not necessary. However, you are quite mistaken in your assumption. People will find it easy to believe that a rebellious female sea captain fell in love with another seafarer. No one will think it unusual at all."

"I will tell them!" she shouted. "I will tell them that you kidnapped me and forced me to sign the document under threat of death!"

Horik stepped back and shook his head mockingly. "It will not matter. I am bringing you to my northern settlement. I am obligated only to keep you alive. Other than that, the Dunhavens do not care what I do with you."

"I will kill you!" Istabelle screamed.

"I would expect no less than for you to try," he answered as he picked up the heavy collar that was attached to the wall via a long metal chain. "Therefore, I will make sure you don't have the opportunity to do anything violent. When you are sufficiently cowed, we will revisit the matter of your wifely deportment. Think wisely, Istabelle. I am your husband and my will is law. Your obedience is required. If I am displeased with you, I can punish you."

He grinned as he snapped the collar in place despite Istabelle's frantic struggles. "Have a pleasant evening," he said as he walked away. Just as he reached the cabin threshold, he leaned down and picked up Istabelle's sword and pointed it at her threateningly. "Don't forget. All I am required to do is keep you alive. Other than that, I can do anything with you, or the Dunhaven people, I want."

"How could you?" Taber shouted. "We had Horik's ship! We had control!"

"Horik had a knife to her throat. What was I to do? I could not risk her life."

"You already did that by leaving her there. He will kill her the moment we sail away."

"No," Ruark answered. "He wants her alive and I believe he will keep her safe unless his hand is forced."

"We must force his hand! We have to attack and bring her back."

"Start using your head," Ruark snapped. "We will do her no good if we rush in and cause her death. Furthermore, you need to know that your own families are at risk. Horik married your captain and through her now has control of a section of Dunhaven land bequeathed to her from her mother."

Taber's mouth gaped open. "No," he whispered. "How could that happen?"

"Horik kidnapped her last time in order to marry her and gain her fortune."

"She never told us," he said quietly.

"Of course not. She would not want to worry you

or let you know that she could no longer protect you. That is why she sent for Mangan. She wanted him to denounce the marriage and thus save your people from Horik's rule."

"Did you?" Taber asked.

Pain glazed Ruark's onyx eyes. "I could not. I am not Mangan."

Silence greeted his reply. The crew was stunned, although Boris and Taber exchanged a knowing look.

Boris stepped forward. "You could have continued your impersonation and helped her," he accused Ruark. "Horik would not have known. You fooled Istabelle, why not fool him as well?"

"I would know and I am not willing to lie anymore. I made a mistake in the beginning, but I will not perpetuate it with more lies and half-truths. There is only one thing I can do. I must return and convince Mangan to go back with you and try to get Istabelle. Mangan has the resources to stage a successful attack."

"And what do you intend to do to help her?" Boris questioned.

Ruark glanced at the outlaw ship that was slowly sailing away with Istabelle. He swallowed painfully and closed his eyes. When he opened them, his face was devoid of emotion. "I will stay out of her life and never utter her name again."

Ruark paced the upper deck as the crew unfurled the sails and set *The Adventuress* sailing south toward Scotland. Though he was a man who prided himself on maintaining absolute control, he felt his internal frustration threatening to erupt in a show of senseless violence against any hapless sailor who had the misfortune to cross his path.

Ruark peered moodily across the sea. The outlaw ship was gone, her sails hidden behind the island. Pain knifed through him and he gripped the railing. He had failed everyone, even Sven. He had succeeded in nothing. He had no friends, no family, little money and now, no reputation. Before, he had been known as a harsh but reliable hired sword, but that reputation would fade as people spread the tale of his failure. It would not matter that he had tried to help her. No one would care that he had been placed in an awkward position. The only important fact was that he had been sent to save Istabelle O'Bannon and he had failed.

In the endless blue of the ocean, a small gray mass caught Ruark's eye. The ship moved closer, and the ripple of her passing caused the water around the gray object to rock. Suddenly, the thing flopped and squawked, startling Ruark so much that he jerked back.

"Péril?" he called. The object squawked again and weakly lifted its head. "Péril!" Ruark shouted. "Get a net! She's alive!" He raced to a small pile of netting and grabbed one. It tangled in his hands and he cursed. The horrid falcon had never liked him and had been a constant source of irritation, but suddenly it meant everything to him to rescue the injured beast. He had promised Istabelle that he would find Péril, and he was going to fulfill that promise!

He leaned over the side of the ship while the crew

tried to slow *The Adventuress*. The ship's own momentum carried her forward despite the abrupt drop in sails, and Ruark feared that they would pass the bird. He finally yanked the net open and unwound the long rope that was woven into the netting. He gripped the end of the rope, then leaned as far over the side as he could. Several other sailors joined him, pointing to the struggling bird as they swept by her.

"There she is!"

"I'll be damned! She survived!"

"Watch out, she'll bite you when you reel her in," Taber cautioned as he watched Ruark fling the net over the gyrfalcon. "Her beak will rip through your hand and crunch bone. Perhaps 'tis best to leave her to her natural fate."

Ignoring him, Ruark twisted the net and yanked on the rope, enveloping Péril in its strands. The falcon screamed in fury, flapping her wings and exhausting herself. "Easy, mighty creature," Ruark whispered as he drew her toward the boat. "You'll only hurt yourself more." The weight of the net dragged the falcon under the water as the ship passed her, and she abruptly sank from sight. Ruark yanked, pulling the net free, and swung it upward, but Péril was no longer entangled in it.

"Hell!" Ruark shouted. "Where did she go?"

"Lost to the sea," Taber said. "It is an honorable death. Istabelle will understand."

"No, she won't! I will not fail at rescuing her damn bird!" Ruark shouted as he leapt over the railing and into the frigid water.

"Man overboard, man overboard!"

Ruark gasped as the cold water froze his chest. The ship's wake knocked him sideways and he struggled to keep his head above water. Casting about frantically, he saw a few gray feathers floating limply near where he had last seen Péril. Without hesitating, he dove under the waves and swept his hand around, seeking contact with her body. Flashes of his first meeting with Istabelle flickered in his mind. The golden sparkles, the press of her wet body, the pure strength of her silver gaze—he had rescued her from a watery grave and he fully intended to rescue her feathered companion from this one.

His hand grazed something sharp, and he reflexively grabbed it. It was a talon on Péril's foot. He pulled it closer and kicked, bringing both of them to the surface. As he treaded water, he lifted Péril up. Her head hung lifelessly. The spearhead had passed through her wing and was still partially embedded in her breast.

"Hold position," cried Taber from the lifeboat heading toward them. "Hold position—we are coming."

Ruark gently shook the falcon. "Please, great one, don't die now. I don't know what to do with you. I don't know how to revive or heal you. You must help me to help you."

The small dinghy reached them and two sailors leaned out to haul Ruark and his charge aboard. "Damn foolish," Taber grumbled. "Damn foolish. Strip your clothes and wrap yourself in the blanket."

He shoved the blanket at Ruark as he motioned the men to return to the ship.

Instead of using the blanket for himself, Ruark wrapped it around Péril after carefully wiping the worst of the water from her feathers. "The spear is stuck in her chest, but I think it is resting against her breastbone. When we get aboard, we will need to pull it free."

Taber shook his head. "No bird could survive the trauma," he said sadly. "They stop breathing when you hold them too tightly or their hearts freeze when they get too frightened. I fear you have rescued her for nothing. She will surely die."

Ruark glared at the man. "Have you no compassion? Don't you care that this animal has fought for your captain like a member of the crew? She deserves our efforts, no matter how futile they may seem."

Taber shrugged, but Erik, who was also in the boat, finally spoke up. "I will help you," he said. "It is Captain Istabelle's falcon, and I would not wish it to die for lack of our trying. If anyone can save it, I am sure you can."

Ruark turned away from the young boy's earnest face. "Don't invest too much belief in my abilities. If Péril survives, it will be because she is as strong and brave as any warrior."

Erik opened his eyes wide but nodded, hearing the intense emotion in Ruark's voice.

The boat bumped against *The Adventuress*, which had finally ceased its forward momentum and now bobbed in the sea, awaiting their return. Ropes were cast down and tied to the dinghy as the sailors clambered aboard. Ruark held the bird wrapped in the blanket and rubbed her chest, trying to encourage her to take a breath. She was heavier than he had thought she would be for such a graceful animal. How could her large body soar so effortlessly in the sky?

Boris peered at her and shook his head. "She'll never make it," he said sorrowfully.

"She will," the warrior replied forcefully. "Erik will help me remove the spearhead."

As he entered Istabelle's cabin, he placed the gyrfalcon on the bed and unwrapped her. She did not move. He rubbed her breast and blew on her face. "Don't die," he murmured. "You are a strong beast. Don't let a mere piece of metal fell your courage."

When Erik followed him into the cabin, Ruark turned and explained the procedure. "We can't push it through, or we will kill her for sure. You will have to hold her while I pull it out."

Erik nodded and carefully supported the bird between his hands.

Ruark gripped the spear. "Be ready." Then, he quickly bent the spear back and forth to loosen it, and yanked it out with great force.

The bird burst to life. It flapped and clawed, spinning out of Erik's hand.

Ruark swiftly swept her off the floor but she instinctively attacked. Her beady eyes glazed with pain, she struck out at the person who held her, sink-

ing her sharp beak deep into Ruark's palm and ripping it open.

"Augh!" Ruark shouted, but he managed to resist
the impulse to fling the bird across the room. Péril
reached with her powerful talons and sliced at Ruark's arms, creating deep, bleeding furrows.

"Let her go!" Erik shouted.

"No, she'll fall again and further injure herself,"
Ruark yelled back. "Throw me a towel." Using the
proffered linen, he managed to fold Péril's wings
down and capture her legs in a firm wrap. Her head
was still free and she whipped it forward, striking
Ruark's hand once again.

"You beast!" Ruark shouted. "I'm helping you!
Stop biting me!" A red stain quickly spread from
underneath the white towel covering her breast.
"Stop struggling. You will only tire yourself."

"Is that blood from you or from her?" Erik asked.

"I don't know. Both, I suspect. She has stopped
flopping around. Rip a strip of cloth and I will tie
her wings in place to prevent her from trying to fly."

"We need to tend your wounds as well."

"After we care for the bird," Ruark insisted.

"After," Erik agreed, handing him the tie.

Chapter 17

Istabelle lunged like a wild dog on a leash, snarling with vicious ferocity and forcing Horik to leap back to avoid her outstretched nails. The leash attached to her neck snapped taut as her forward momentum reached the limits of its length, but Istabelle strained forward nonetheless and managed to strike his face.

"You bitch!" Horik screamed as he touched the bloodied tracks on his cheek. "If I had my choice, I would kill you now and be done with it!" He yanked his breeches up over his limp manhood, embarrassed and infuriated. His attempt to humiliate Istabelle by raping her had failed because he could not force his rod to rise. Ever since the day he had fought with her on his boat, the blood flow to his groin had been impeded. His rage escalated and he lifted his hand to strike her.

"But you can't kill me, can you?" she shouted back. "You can't do much of anything! You can't act like a man and you must keep me alive and healthy or you won't receive the reward from the Dunhavens."

Horik glared at her. "Perhaps I will decide that the dower land is not worth the sacrifice," he threatened.

Istabelle laughed harshly. "I doubt that. You are too greedy to let such a fortune slip away."

Horik pulled his belt free and swung it back and forth. He grinned as Istabelle watched his motions warily. "You are wrong," he informed her. "I do not have to keep you healthy. In fact, I am certain your family would be more than pleased to know that you suffered in my care. Press me further and I will rape you and torture you until you beg me to cease!"

"You would have already raped me if you could!" she shouted. "You are nothing! You are less than a man! Our marriage will never be consummated because you can't do it!"

He swung the belt and slashed it against her chest, barely missing her face. "How dare you taunt me," he screamed back at her, his face twisted into an ugly, evil mask. "Your knife severed my manhood. Not only have you caused me humiliation by stealing from me, you have also ruined my future. I will make you suffer for all eternity!"

Istabelle fell backward as she desperately tried to avoid the next strike. Red-hot pain bloomed as he struck her with the belt again and she flung her hands up to protect her eyes. Slash after slash rained down on her huddled body as Horik beat her until he stood over her still form, panting for breath.

"Don't ever doubt me," he warned her. "I despise you and will enjoy taming you. Fight as hard as you want, sea-daemon, for it only makes the punishments more severe. I enjoy making you suffer."

Istabelle looked up, her eyes thin slivers of pure hatred. "You have made a grave mistake," she warned in a soft, menacing tone. "One day you will regret every blow and every strike you laid upon me and you will beg for my mercy."

Fear snaked up Horik's spine. She should be whimpering with fear. She ought to be cringing and cowering, but instead she continued to threaten him. She was not natural!

Something flickered in her eyes. He imagined he saw the outline of a winged beast flying straight at him and he stepped back in terror. Her curved nails seemed to grow into sharp talons, ready to rip his flesh to shreds, and her harsh breathing changed into the subtle hiss of an attacking predator.

He stumbled back and pointed at her. "You are the one who will beg for mercy," he cried, but his voice trembled and he began to sweat.

"Will I?" Istabelle taunted as she rose and stalked closer to him, her chain rattling at her feet.

Terrified, Horik spun around and fled the room.

For three days, Horik denied her food in an attempt to debilitate her, but when Istabelle still railed against him, the three days lengthened into seven. As Horik's ship sailed northward to his outlaw settlement, Istabelle finally staggered to the floor, exhausted and weak.

Why did she fight? Why not surrender and accept

her fate? Everything would be so much easier. There was nothing she could do anymore. She had failed the people and had failed herself. She was not as strong as she had thought. After all her daring words and all her wild ways, she was a humbled and enslaved wife like any other woman.

Yet, she could not surrender. Horik strode in and held a hunk of meat in front of her, daring her to eat the food from his fingers and admit her defeat. Instead, she spat on him, covering his scarred cheek with saliva that oozed down and pooled on his neck.

He kicked her, and even when she felt a rib crack, she would not surrender. Her gaze dared him, taunted him, mocked him until he finally left her alone.

Then the dreams came to her. Her father, her stepmother . . . the island where she was raised . . . the wild horses that roamed there. Seagulls. Her falcon. Her mind skittered, feeling pain at the loss of her friend. No, don't think about the gyrfalcon. Her cousin . . . not her cousin . . . who was he? She forgot his real name . . . The warrior. That was his name.

Pain sliced through her again. Her heart crumbled. Where was he? Why had he left her? What had happened that was so terrible? She forgot. Something teased her memory, something that should rile her, but she couldn't quite remember. Ruark. That was his name. It was a good name. Ruark. Where are you, Ruark?

She slumped down, unconscious, and the shadows enveloped her frail body like a death shroud.

* * *

Ruark trudged through the dense thicket and finally spied the stark outline of the monastery. The sight should have given him joy, but instead he stared at it with dread. The last week and a half had been a living nightmare. He could not escape the image of Istabelle in Horik's hands, her body and soul at his mercy. Her final words echoed in his memory. *Go away! I never want to see you again!*

She did not want his interference. She had made that abundantly clear. She needed a powerful lord, not a penniless soldier for hire. His skills were useless to her. *He* was useless.

The gyrfalcon perched on his shoulder screeched, and Ruark frowned. They still did not like each other, but neither Péril nor he had anyone without Istabelle, which forced them to form an uneasy alliance.

"You should go free and find your own kind," he grumbled to the bird, but he knew that Péril would not leave. Night after night she had returned to him after her hunt, and if he saw loneliness in her eyes, he was surely imagining it.

"That is the monastery where it all started," he told the falcon. "I brought my brother to find a healer, and instead found Mangan O'Bannon. And the letter. If only I had never come to this monastery." He shrugged and started his final trek to the stone building. He did wonder about Sven's recovery. It had been close to a month since he had left here, although it felt so much longer.

Pausing, Ruark stared at the sun as it began to sink

behind the trees. He could not appreciate the beauty. His soul was dead. His heart was wooden. How could he have made such a terrible mistake? How could his judgment have been so misplaced? He prided himself on avoiding personal entanglements, on keeping aloof from all the intrigue that surrounded him, yet he had tumbled down the path of every foolish, inexperienced youth and fallen for a beautiful, unattainable woman. He sighed and the falcon fluffed her feathers in response.

"I must not think about her," he murmured. "After this, I must forget her."

Despite his strong words, he paused when he heard a cry in the wind. It sounded like a woman in pain. Like the woman whose name made him shudder with longing.

Ruark pounded on the door to the monastery, then waited in dread for it to open. The nagging feeling that something was terribly wrong would not leave him, yet he could not determine what made him so anxious. Perhaps Sven was ailing. Perhaps he was worried about Mangan's reaction. Perhaps Istabelle . . .

He could hear chanting in the far reaches of the monastery. It was eventide and the monks were at Mass. Turning with a sigh, Ruark slumped against the door to wait. Péril perched on a nearby branch and cocked her head.

"Why should I disturb them?" he asked the falcon. "I am in no hurry to announce my failure."

Péril shifted and fluffed her feathers, then spread one wing out and stroked the flight feathers with her beak. Small dark gray spots on the feathers' shafts contrasted with the dull pewter of the tips. She changed her balance and stretched the other wing out. Before it was fully extended, Peril flexed it back into place.

"Still hurts on that side?" he asked her. Ever since he had fished the bird out of the ocean he had started the habit of talking to her. Something about the gray color of her feathers reminded him of the silver of Istabelle's eyes, and talking to the gyrfalcon made him feel closer to the woman. "Well, my knee aches in the winter and sometimes I feel a knot in my shoulder."

The bird stopped her preening and focused her beady eyes on him. She hopped along the branch until she was closer, then peered down at him with disconcerting intelligence.

"What are you thinking, wise falcon? What do you know?"

Péril abruptly took flight and the large door of the monastery swung open, knocking Ruark over. Embarrassed and slightly irritated, he rose to his feet and met Mangan's gaze.

"Ruark. Welcome."

"Many thanks," Ruark mumbled as he brushed the dirt off his thighs.

"Come inside. Sven will be pleased to see you."

"He fares well?" Ruark asked as he followed Mangan inside. As the door shut behind him, he heard Péril screech.

"As well as the Lord intends. That is my little cousin's gyrfalcon, is it not?" Mangan questioned as he led the way down the corridor.

"Aye," Ruark replied in a clipped voice.

Mangan turned and faced the warrior. "Then where is Istabelle?"

"Let us discuss everything after I see Sven. It will take some time to explain." He shuddered. He had not heard Istabelle's name spoken aloud for over a week, even though he thought about her constantly. The word was like music.

Mangan leveled a stare at Ruark, noting his unusual reaction to his cousin's name. He turned and continued down the hall. "After dinner, then, when you are rested. I will be interested to hear your tale." Mangan opened the wooden door to the sickroom and waved Ruark inside. "I will send someone to you when the meal is served."

Ruark nodded his thanks, feeling immeasurably guilty. No doubt Mangan would not continue to be so hospitable once he heard Ruark's story.

"Brother!" a young voice called from the window.

"Sven," Ruark replied. "You are up and out of bed."

Sven shrugged and pointed to the chair. "I still cannot walk well and have spent most of my time confined to this piece of furniture." He grimaced. "The blood poison ran deep. It traveled from my arm, down my side and into my leg. The arm has healed, but I almost lost the leg."

Ruark walked over and gazed down at Sven. "How does it feel?"

"It . . . it is fine. Are you ready to leave?" He made to rise.

Ruark placed a restraining hand on Sven's shoulder. "Tell me the truth."

Sven flushed and looked down. "It hurts. It hurts to put pressure on the leg. The monks say that the muscles were damaged by the infection and they must mend before I can walk properly."

"And if you use them too soon?"

"They say they will not heal well."

"How much more time?" Ruark asked as he gazed out the window into the peaceful courtyard. The leaves had fallen and the landscape looked stark but beautiful.

"I am not sure," Sven answered. Ruark nodded and sat down in a chair across from him. When he said nothing, Sven leaned forward. "What is wrong, Brother? You do not seem yourself."

Ruark grunted. "I am not the one we should be concerned with. You are the injured one."

"Yet I *am* concerned about you. My injury is to the flesh and it will heal. What is your ailment?"

To my heart, Ruark replied silently but he forced a smile for Sven's benefit. "I am only tired. Perhaps I could use a rest as well."

Sven frowned. Such lassitude was as foreign to Ruark as the sea was to a rabbit, but before he could comment, the door opened again.

"Supper is ready," Mangan said from the portal. "We have several guests tonight. The king's priest is passing through and has honored us with his presence. He and his entourage are sharing our table along with you."

Sven motioned to Ruark. "Go ahead. They bring me food after everyone is finished. I am not up to company."

Ruark rose wearily. He did not want to speak to strangers either, but he knew he could not avoid Mangan forever. Sooner or later, he had to tell him the truth.

"I met your cousin under . . . unusual circumstances," Ruark started to explain as Mangan sat across from him in the simple front room of the monastery where they had retired in peaceful solitude. Dinner was over after a seemingly endless round of prayers, finishing with soup, bread and mutton. The court priest had remarked upon Ruark's presence, but Mangan had explained that Ruark was visiting Sven, who was recuperating in the sickroom.

Now, several hours and a full belly later, Ruark bowed his head and attempted to explain the past events. He pulled the ruby ring off his finger and held it out to Mangan. As Mangan took the signet piece back, Ruark looked around. Very few items adorned the hall, with the notable exception of a collection of valuable chalices displayed along the wall. The cups were obviously quite old, and many had ancient markings carved into them, whereas others were encrusted with jewels.

"I warned you that Istabelle was an unusual woman. What happened?"

"She introduced herself to me by stealing my belongings. I did not know who she was, and pursued her to retrieve my sword."

Mangan smiled. "Did she escape?"

Ruark shrugged. "She and her horse leapt off a cliff and plunged into the water to avoid my capture. Unfortunately, she appeared to be drowning and I was compelled to jump in after her."

"Indeed? I am told she is an excellent swimmer."

"Forty pounds of wet clothing will hamper any swimmer's chances of survival. I managed to extract her from the clothing and pull her to the surface. It was only then that she recognized the ring and realized I was friend, not foe."

"Good. So then she accepted your assistance?"

Ruark squirmed. "Not exactly. Somehow our communication got bungled and she mistook me for you."

Mangan raised his eyebrows.

"I tried to correct her, but . . . it seemed impossible at the time."

"Impossible to state your name?"

Ruark rose in agitation and walked up to the display case. He fingered a particularly lovely chalice and traced the flowery design on its surface. It was delicate yet strong, and it reminded him of Istabelle. "One thing led to another and I could not. I lied to her."

"Lying is a terrible sin, Ruark. Did you do so for your own gain?"

"No, I did it for her." Ruark replaced the cup and turned to face Mangan. "Perhaps I did it a bit for me as well. She seemed to need me to be you and I could not abandon her."

"As you were abandoned as a child? Did you think you could provide something you never had?"

With a slight grimace, Ruark shrugged. "I do not think as deeply into motives as you do. I only felt her pain and wanted to alleviate it in the only way I could. I offered my sword."

Mangan leaned forward and placed a log on the fire. The meager warmth licked outward, barely stroking the monk's face, but the light provided enough illumination for him to observe Ruark's expressions. Something in the tone of Ruark's voice made Mangan suspicious. The silence stretched between them as Mangan waited for Ruark to continue.

Ruark shifted nervously. "She is a beautiful woman," he finally said by way of explanation.

Mangan leaned back, his keen gaze assessing Ruark. He nodded. "So I have heard."

Sighing, Ruark sat back down. "As the days progressed, it became harder and harder to reveal the truth. I tried, several times, but there always seemed to be a good reason to delay."

"And now? Does she still think you are me?"

"No. We finally came upon the man we were seeking. It was Horik, the outlaw raider."

"What had he done to upset Istabelle so much?"

Ruark bowed his head. "He married her."

"*What?* Why?"

"He married her in order to control her dower lands."

"He could not do that without a family member's

blessing, unless he gained permission from the king himself."

"Apparently, a Dunhaven relative not only agreed to the marriage but arranged it."

Mangan rubbed his jaw and stared at the wall in contemplation. After several long moments, he turned to Ruark with raised eyebrows. "What did she think I could do to help her?"

"She wanted you, as the heir to the O'Bannon earl-dom and future head of her father's family, to de-nounce the union and annul it. As an imposter, I could not do that."

Mangan stared into the flames. A simple iron cross adorned the back of the fire kiln, and it glowed red-hot when flames burned within. Right now, the edges were gleaming but the center was still black. God's message. So much was still unsaid.

"Where is she now?" Mangan asked.

Ruark followed Mangan's gaze and stared at the cross. To him, it seemed to be accusing him of his sins against the Lord, his sins against Istabelle. He clenched his teeth, the pain still making him sick. "She is with him."

Mangan lifted his eyes slowly and pierced Ruark with an incredulous gaze. "You left her with a vi-cious outlaw? A man known to destroy monasteries? Rape women? Kill with no remorse? You left my cousin with such a man?"

"There was nothing I could do," Ruark snapped back. "She demanded that I leave her alone." Ruark pounded his fist against the chair arm. "She told me to go away!"

Mangan rose. "I will have to meditate on this state of affairs. I am not sure what I can do. Go to your brother and rest until morning. Until then, I will pray and ask God for guidance—for all of us."

As Mangan exited the hall and Ruark was left alone, he sank his head into his hands. Despite desperately wishing it were otherwise, he could not avoid admitting that he loved her. The moments in her arms had shown him paradise. Her smiles had given him sunshine. Her very life force had infused him with hope and a belief in the future. What would he do without her? How would he see the sun set or the rain fall without thinking of her?

Moisture filled his eyes and he wiped it away in wonder. He blinked, and yet his eyes continued to fill until tears fell down his cheeks. *God!* he implored as he dropped to his knees in front of the gleaming cross, crying like a child. *Help me!*

Far down the corridor, in a stark and empty cell, Mangan kneeled as well.

Chapter 18

Istabelle knew she could not hold out much longer. She had partially capitulated several weeks ago when Horik's ship had docked at the northern settlement. Tired of fighting, and weak with hunger, she had relented and begun eating. Her cracked rib pained her when she breathed, and her strength waned as her spirit deteriorated. The winter seemed endless, especially as Horik's violence escalated daily. She lived in fear of his rages, managing to survive only by trying to avoid inciting his anger as much as possible. Sometimes she even forgot why she was in this cold northern settlement or what had seemed so important before.

Only one month had passed since her capture, but already she felt hopeless. She lay in the darkness for hours, until the cold air sank into her bones and she felt as if she were part of the earth upon which she lay. She shifted and the clanking chain around her neck chafed a raw site. Istabelle ignored the pain. She was becoming used to it. Snow clouds rolled across the sky, and a chilly wind blew frost through the doorway.

She rolled to her side to face the snowflakes that drifted by. The chain draped across her front and she wrapped her arms around it. The metal was cold and hard. Like her heart.

Horik was hunting, but he had locked her chain to the wall of his abode to prevent her from escaping. Istabelle spread her lips in an ironic smile. Where did he think she would go? Did he think she was so skilled she could commandeer one of the warships and sail it herself, when the winter storms were tossing the ocean to and fro and the currents were shifting with the change in weather?

The clouds sank with the weight of snow. The winds blew stronger until a heavy blanket of snow began to swirl around the structure, sending freezing gusts through the thin walls.

She huddled in a corner, wrapping her arms around herself for warmth. Trying to take her mind off the cold, she thought of warm, comforting things. About the sun on the deck of her ship and the hot wind that whipped through her hair. As she drifted into a half sleep, her thoughts became less focused. A memory of running along the beach . . . a remembrance of a cozy dinner with her father. Then *his* image came to her, and she smiled softly in the dark. The cold wind was replaced by his heated breath and the freezing snow became his passionate caress.

Ruark. She missed him. She was used to his new

name now, and it came to her mind easily. He was not the winter; he was the summer. He was fire and warmth, passion and blazing pleasure. She imagined his hands running down her arms, rubbing them until the goose bumps disappeared. The hands shifted to her neck, and his touch was incredibly sensual, amazingly erotic.

She leaned against the wall and let her imagination drift. Ruark materialized in her mind and she could see the muscles on his arms ripple as he reached for her. She could smell his special scent. Strong . . . powerful . . . commanding. He made her feel something unique when she was near him. What was it? What was that feeling?

His image kissed her neck, teasing her with his tongue. She moaned. She wanted him so much. She longed to feel his touch once again. The fantasy was reality. He was with her, next to her, touching her in the cold darkness and he brought volcanic power to her limbs. She gasped and pressed back against the wall.

"Ruark!" she cried and his name became frozen mist in the air. "Touch me! Come to me! I need you . . ."

His form altered and she felt his body shift against hers. He was strong and hard, his body wanting hers as much as her body wanted his. He moved, and she imagined his thigh wedged between hers, forcing her legs apart. He whispered in her ear, saying something she couldn't quite understand. She shivered with passion.

"Take me," she murmured back. "Love me. Make love to me."

The wind howled a response and she heard him groan. "Yes," he seemed to say. "Yes . . ."

She arched her back, offering her breasts, wanting him to lick and suck them as he had before. Her nipples tingled and she rubbed them, imagining his hands, his fingers. He knew just how to roll the nubs between his thumb and forefinger. He could bring her almost to climax just by touching her.

She gasped, her memories so real she lost control of his motions and the apparition took over. He pushed her back and rocked his hips against hers, using his pelvic bone to stroke her just right. She moaned, not wanting it to stop yet wanting to find that ultimate ecstasy that always foretold the end. "Please . . ." she whispered as his hand dropped between her legs. "I miss you. I want you."

Sparks flickered in her eyes as the emotions spiraled. He towered over her, his face filling her vision as his body moved in a steady, powerful rhythm. Almost . . . almost . . . Istabelle's breath grew short and she tossed her head back and forth. Almost . . . *Ruark! Where are you?*

Later that night as Horik snored in the bed nearby, thoughts spun through her mind. Thoughts of death, of suicide, of giving up. She could relent and her life would be so much easier. She could admit defeat. She could forget the Dunhaven people and stop fantasizing about a man who would never come back for her. She could abandon her memories of Ruark just as Ruark had abandoned her.

If only she had hope—but no one cared about her, least of all Ruark. He would not forgive her angry words.

In utter, hopeless defeat, she stared out the doorway and gazed at the full moon.

Istabelle frowned. It was a full moon already? When had she had her last monthly flow? She shook her head in disbelief. She should have had a flow weeks ago. She was always regular, so why had she missed her monthly course?

She blinked several times as she peered at the luminous body in the sky. Could she be? Could she be carrying a child? Was her belly already harboring the seed of Ruark's passion?

She swept her hand over her abdomen and a tentative smile spread her cracked lips. More than a month had passed since she had lain with Ruark. She gasped. She was! She must be! Soon it would be obvious to all!

Then another related thought whipped through her mind. Through all the beatings and humiliations, Horik had never raped her. His impotence had persisted and he had been unable to consummate their marriage. Unfortunately, that left her with a frightening new concern. What would Horik do to her and the baby when he found out that she was carrying another man's child?

In the morning, Ruark waited impatiently for the lengthy matins to end. He paced back and forth, neither soothed nor lulled by the peaceful chanting. A sense of urgency filled his heart. He needed to get back to her immediately. Every day seemed like a lifetime.

Finally, Mangan and the other monks filed out of the chapel and headed across the cold courtyard. Seeing Ruark, he veered off the path and approached the warrior. "I have spoken with the king's priest," he said. "I explained the dire consequences of Istabelle's marriage to the outlaw, Horik. He is prepared to consider the circumstances of their union and contemplate an annulment, provided that they have not consummated their vows. However, he insists that I bring her to court to tell her tale."

Ruark shook his head angrily. "But what if she cannot prove celibacy? The king won't help her, and we don't have time to negotiate! We must get her now, and solve the problem without his assistance!"

"What do you propose to do?"

"Find and kill Horik. It is the only way."

Mangan stared at the sunrise in silence. After several quiet moments, he addressed Ruark. "The Dunhavens will be infuriated if they discover that their plans have been foiled. They may even declare a feud upon the O'Bannons."

"You are the one who said that we cannot leave her there. You were right. No matter what words she said, nor how risky it is, we must rescue her from Horik."

Mangan turned to face Ruark's impassioned face. He nodded. "Yes, we must do something, but I insist we attempt diplomacy before employing might. Will you agree to my condition?"

Frustrated, Ruark ran his fingers through his hair and ground his teeth. "Horik is not a man to talk, but I will let you try as long as you allow me to use force if it becomes necessary."

Mangan smiled. "How are we to find his settlement?"

"We take Istabelle's ship up north. There is a boy on board who has been to Horik's home. He will guide us."

Ruark's stallion thundered across the meadow several lengths ahead of Mangan. His long hair fanned out behind him and his entire body leaned forward as if he could get to the ship faster by will alone. The horse's neck was lathered with foam and his nostrils were flared with effort, yet Ruark only encouraged him to go faster.

Far above them, as anxious as he, flew the gyrfalcon. Her wings beat rapidly as she battled the cold winds and she periodically swooped downward on the air currents. Her black eyes darted to and fro as she scanned the countryside, searching for the woman both she and the man sought.

As the meadow sloped into a river valley, Ruark was forced to slow his steed. Cursing, he scanned the banks to find a safe place to cross the water. The falcon flew down and landed on his shoulder, but then she saw a flock of sparrows burst from a nearby glade. She rose from Ruark's shoulder and flew after them just as Ruark sent his steed plunging through the stream.

The sun was high in the sky when they reached the coast three days later. Ruark pointed to the ship docked near the small village of Canna. "Over there," he stated. "The crew awaits your arrival." Ruark spurred his horse forward. Every moment made him more and more anxious about Istabelle. How was she faring? Was she in pain? Did she miss him? Did she think about him as much as he thought about her?

The thoughts raced through his mind, along with images that made his heart thunder. *God protect her!* he screamed silently. *Please do not let her suffer at Horik's hand.* Groaning in pain, Ruark galloped along the beach, trying to outrace the dark fears that plagued his soul.

Finally reaching the shore, he reined his horse in and waited for Mangan's mule to reach his side. A rowboat was already en route to them and a trio of young stableboys were racing toward them from the village, ready to take their steeds.

The gyrfalcon swooped overhead, heading for the mast of *The Adventuress.* Her wise eyes peered northward and she screeched anxiously, impatient to find her mistress.

It took ten days to sail to the northern reaches, and then they had to wait for a stiff wind to soften before they could approach the coast and start searching for the outlaw settlement. Once again, Erik guided them.

"I do not know the terrain very well, but I do know that they sailed past that huge set of rocks that jut into the sea."

"How many days past it did they sail?" Ruark asked.

"Two, maybe three," Erik said as he rubbed his forehead. "I was not paying much attention. I wish I had."

"Don't worry. You have already helped us more than we could have expected." Ruark looked up at the top of the mast, where Péril perched. She peered across the sea with deep concentration, seeming to scan the land as intently as the humans below. Both of them felt edgy, evidenced by Péril's ruffled feathers and Ruark's constant pacing. Péril flew from the mast and soared along the coastline ahead of the ship while Ruark leaned against the railing to watch her.

"The bird seems to have accepted you," Taber said as he joined Ruark at the rail.

"We have come to an agreement," Ruark replied with a grin. "She doesn't peck my eyes out and I massage her wing at night."

"Come below, Ruark. You can't make the ship sail faster by will alone. It is time to eat."

Sighing, Ruark assented, but as he climbed down the hatchway, he glanced back. He wished the ship would sail more quickly. He wanted to find Istabelle.

Two days later, Erik pointed to a wide bay. "There!" he shouted. "On the far side of the inlet! That is Horik's settlement! That is where Istabelle is being held!"

Mangan peered calmly over the railing, his simple robes blowing in the wind. Ruark stood beside him with a fierce expression on his face that echoed the threat of the sword swinging at his waist.

"Remember," Mangan admonished him. "I will talk to Horik first."

Ruark nodded grimly.

She had to escape! She could not risk Horik finding out about the baby. For a week she had contemplated her choices, and only one solution presented itself. She could either accept ultimate defeat and chance sacrificing her child or find a way to leave the settlement and head south to safety.

The snow had abated, but freezing conditions still made travel extremely hazardous. She considered taking a boat, but the bay was wide open and she would be spotted immediately. It would be better to escape inland and make her way home overland. If—when—she made it back, she would confront the Dunhavens and threaten to expose their plot if they did not recant their support of the union with Horik. She would tell them that Horik was impotent and the marriage had never been consummated. Of course, that meant that Ruark would have to admit to fathering her growing child.

Istabelle bit her lip. After her harsh last words to him, she did not know if he would be willing to help her. Admitting to bedding her was risky for him, for her familial connections made him an unsuitable companion. Whereas she did not care about the censure, she hesitated to expose him. It was possible that no laird would hire Ruark to fight for him, once he knew, fearing that Ruark would accost a chaste daughter. If that occurred, Ruark would lose his livelihood, and that would destroy him.

Istabelle heard a commotion outside, near the shore. An enemy ship had been spotted and the settlement was rousing to defend itself. If there were a battle, they would not be free to chase after her for hours! There would be no better time than now. She had to steal the key to her chain and collar and escape immediately.

Horik snored in the bed, his hand outflung and his beefy leg exposed from the covers. No one had arrived to wake him, although they would come for him shortly. She had little time to lose. Istabelle glared at Horik, her hatred unabated. He was disgusting! His drool dampened the pillow and the smell of his frequent flatulence permeated the room like the odors from a fetid outhouse. Once she was free and her child safe, she vowed silently, she would avenge every moment of her forced captivity.

Istabelle rose slowly, fighting the urge to race forward and spit in his face. Holding the chain in one hand so that the links did not clank and disturb him, she quietly opened Horik's trunk and rifled through his belongings. He had two shirts, both rank with dried sweat. Neither contained the key. His leggings had no pockets, but she checked the seams nonetheless. Nothing. A few other items cluttered the bottom of the trunk, but she did not find what she was searching for.

Carefully removing the final items, she felt along the trunk base for a drawer or secret compartment but again to no avail. He wasn't that clever! Where would he have hidden the key?

Istabelle replaced the clothes and then looked around the room. The far wall held a cupboard that contained her weapon. She walked over and stared at the sword blade longingly, but she knew from experience that her chain would not reach that far. Horik had placed the sword there to taunt her. She clenched her fists, wishing more than ever before that she could stretch just far enough to grip its familiar handle. It would be so easy to hack off his head. She would swing, sink her steel into his vulnerable neck and watch the blood pour across his pillow. But then what? What if she didn't find the key before the others found his body? She would still be bound in this dank cottage and at the mercy of unscrupulous men.

After carefully searching the room and even testing the floorboards, Istabelle turned to face the snoring man. The people outside were getting more agitated, and she heard that a small boat had been launched. Frowning, she peered out the window to see if she could identify the ship, but it was too far out in the bay. All she could determine was that it was a two-mast fighter, very much like her own ship. Longing stabbed her heart and she almost fooled herself into thinking the ship was, indeed, *The Adventuress*. Shaking her head, she turned away from the window,, scolding herself for her fantasies. This was her best opportunity and she was not about to waste it hoping for the impossible.

Horik had turned to his side and his bare buttocks were visible. Dirt and other brown unmentionable material caked his skin, making Istabelle cover her mouth in revulsion. His belt swung from a peg on the other side of the bed. She had looked everywhere else. If the key was not in the room, it must be on him. The most likely place was his belt, but to reach it, she was going to have to lean across his body.

She knelt on the bed, taking care not to rock the frame. The straw stuffing crinkled underneath her knee and she froze, staring at Horik. He slept on. She bent over Horik's lap and braced herself against the wall. Taking a deep breath, she grasped the belt and tugged. It would not move. Exasperated, Istabelle placed her other knee on the bed and leaned closer, her body brushing against Horik's. She pulled on the belt once again and it fell onto the bed, the key tumbling out of the inner pouch. Gasping with delight, she grabbed the key.

Suddenly Horik snorted and shifted, banging against Istabelle's knees. She slipped and fell fully across him.

"What?" he shouted as he sat up. Istabelle scrambled backward but Horik placed a heavy hand on her arm and held her in place. "What do you think you're doing?" he yelled as the fog cleared from his mind.

Istabelle gripped the belt as a weapon with her free hand as she struggled to get off his naked body. She gagged, Horik's stench making her nauseated.

Horik laughed as he twisted his other hand around her chain and yanked her up toward his face. "You are a single-minded fool," he said, mocking her. "Have you not accepted your fate? You are mine now and you will be punished for rifling through my things."

Istabelle's hand tightened on the belt. "You are the one who will be punished!" she screamed. She swung the leather strap at Horik's head. It smashed across his face, leaving a bright red mark along his cheek.

He roared with fury and leapt from the bed, dragging Istabelle with him. "You daemon!" he shouted. He flung her on the bed and pounced on top of her, pinning her against the mattress. "You will pay for this!" he promised as he crashed his fist against her nose. Blood spurted everywhere as the crunch of broken bones echoed in the room.

Istabelle desperately turned her head, spitting the blood from her mouth so that it would not drown her. She raised her bent leg sharply, intent on driving her knee into his groin, but Horik hit her again, forcing the breath from her body. As she lay limp, struggling to draw air, Horik pulled the belt from her hand and swung it menacingly over her head.

"You wanted this belt?" Horik demanded as he wound the leather strap around his hand. "Do you want to feel it again?" He stood above her, naked and filthy, with the leather belt in his roughened hands. He unwound the strap, then folded it in two. Holding both ends, he snapped the pieces against each other, making a reverberating sound.

Istabelle flinched.

"That makes you afraid?" He chuckled. He snapped the leather again, right next to her ear. "You are breaking down, Istabelle. A week ago you wouldn't have trembled. Now you are fearful. Soon you will be crawling after me, acting like a good little wife."

Istabelle felt tears of fury well up in her eyes. He couldn't be more wrong! She wanted to fight! She wanted to be free! She wanted to escape and save her baby!

Pain burst across her legs as Horik smacked her with the belt. "Hah!" he screamed as she gave an involuntary gasp. He belted her again, this time in the abdomen, then laughed as Istabelle cried out loud.

"No!" she screamed.

Suddenly someone burst through the door. Horik sprang off the bed, snarling with rage. "How dare you enter without my permission, Curtis!" he bellowed. "I was teaching my wife a lesson!"

"Save it for later," the man replied with a quick glance at Istabelle's bleeding face. "An unknown ship has anchored at the mouth of the bay and has sent a boat toward our dock."

"Who is it? What do they want?" Horik demanded, Istabelle forgotten. He yanked his breeches on and quickly tied a leather jacket around his waist. As he pulled his boots on, the man continued.

"So far, they have not seemed hostile, but I cannot imagine why a ship would sail this far north in winter."

"Aye. Ready the men for battle," Horik answered. He grabbed his battle-axe and strapped on two short swords and a throwing dagger. Then, without a backward glance, he left the cabin and joined his men at the shore.

Istabelle rolled on her side, clutching her belly. Pain wracked her abdomen and her face felt like it was going to explode. She lifted her fingers and felt her nose, confirming that it was broken. Tears filled her eyes. She might lose the baby! And Ruark would never want her now, even if she did manage to find him. She was no longer the beautiful, reckless female captain of the sea he had been attracted to. Now she was a woman who had been captured, beaten and disfigured.

As she felt her nose once again, the key fell out of her hand and glimmered in the dirty blankets. She stared at it, blinking rapidly. She had no time to wallow in self-pity. Sitting up, she shook her head to clear the pain and felt along the collar to locate the keyhole. With trembling fingers, she inserted the key into the lock and turned it. As the collar sprang apart, the heavy chain clanked to the floor. Outside, she could hear the outlaws hailing the arriving rowboat. Hoping that everyone was fully occupied, she grabbed one of Horik's coats, bolted out of the cabin and escaped into the woods.

Mangan stood at the helm of the rowboat, fingering his cross. Ruark had refused to join him, still convinced that force would be necessary. The gray falcon stayed behind as well, her anxiety clearly obvious. At least Taber was at his side, along with four other Dunhaven sailors. Mangan hoped that the power of the O'Bannon name would be enough to persuade Horik to release his cousin, but if it was not, he had two other methods of persuasion at his disposal, money and Ruark.

He held up his hands, showing his lack of weaponry to the settlement outlaws as the boat scraped sand and slid to a halt on the shoreline.

"I am Mangan, Lord O'Bannon of Kirkcaldy, and I come on a peaceful mission," he called out.

A filthy red-haired man stepped forward and glared at him. "I am Horik, leader of this settlement. I see no lordly robes or weapons upon you. You are dressed in peasant garb."

"I have recently come from the monastery of St. Ignacio, where I have spent a year meditating. My clothes represent my dedication to God and my lack of defense represents my intention to maintain peace. I have come to talk to you about my cousin, Istabelle."

Horik glared at him and shook his battle-axe. "There is nothing to discuss! The Dunhavens blessed our union. All her holdings are now mine."

264

"The Dunhavens are from her mother's side of the family. I am the son of her father's brother and heir to the Kirkcaldy earldom. My family is much more powerful than the Dunhavens. May I suggest that you reconsider your position. If you relinquish my cousin and accept an annulment, my family will find favor with you."

"What kind of favor?" Horik asked distrustfully.

"For one, we will not name you an enemy. For another, I am prepared to offer you funds from my own treasury."

"A marriage cannot be annulled so easily," Horik reminded him craftily.

Mangan pulled a document from his inner robes and handed it to Horik. "These papers indicate the king's priest's interest in dismantling the vows you spoke with Istabelle. In addition, it questions the validity of the vows themselves, since they were possibly spoken under coercion."

"All brides are reluctant," Horik replied. "She was no different."

"The priest also wonders why the Dunhavens did not ask the king's permission and post banns in the usual manner. Such disregard of convention could be viewed unfavorably by the king himself." Mangan motioned to the other people in the settlement. "I am aware that your villagers have bonded together because of your mutual disregard and distrust of the laws of our country. However, it is one thing to be a thorn and cause irritation and quite another to have the king's anger fully focused upon you. It will only be a matter of time before your settlement is completely destroyed."

The outlaw villagers shuffled uncomfortably. Mangan's voice remained quiet and measured, but the underlying steel enhanced the seriousness of his message. There was no doubt that Horik should carefully consider his proposal.

Horik glanced at the ship, trying to see if an army already swarmed its decks, but it was too far out in the bay. "Is the priest aboard?" Horik asked.

"No."

"Then he has already been to see the king?"

"No. He is waiting at the monastery to hear word of my successful negotiation. Will I be able to tell him that you are a reasonable man?"

"You are leaving me with no choice!" Horik grumbled.

"As you left Istabelle with none," Mangan agreed.

"How much money?" Horik asked, trying to regain control of the conversation.

"We will discuss that after I see Istabelle and assure myself of her kind treatment. The better she appears, the more I will offer."

Horik frowned, remembering the crunch of broken bones heralding her fractured nose only moments ago. Last he had seen, she had been covered in blood. Turning away from Mangan, he whispered to Curtis. "Go to the cabin and clean her up. Tell her that she must inform her cousin that she has been treated fairly or I will hunt her down and punish her, regardless of her family connections. Make sure she understands."

"Aye."

Horik turned back and motioned to Mangan. "Come, share bread with us. Istabelle will be along presently."

Mangan nodded and climbed fully out of the boat. When Taber began to follow him, he subtly shook his head. Horik's capitulation seemed too easy and he still distrusted the man. It would be better to have Taber stay in the boat and be ready to warn the ship if necessary.

Horik and Mangan walked up the beach and entered the village as the other outlaw went to the cabin to fetch Istabelle. Mangan glanced over his shoulder, wary of the men closing around him. He felt cornered, yet everything appeared to be going well and he didn't want to upset the negotiations by appearing untrusting.

Curtis entered Horik's cabin. "Woman!" he shouted. "You had better listen carefully to what I am about to tell you, or you will not live to see another year!"

No one answered and he blinked in the dim light, searching the floor for Istabelle's huddled form. When he did not locate her, his brow furrowed and he glanced at the bed. The chain lay over the blankets, then was hidden from view. Curtis gripped the middle link and yanked hard, expecting to encounter resistance, but the chain snapped backward and sent him stumbling to his knees. He stared at the empty, open collar in disbelief.

He scrambled to his feet and spun around. "Where are you?" he gasped. "Woman? Istabelle?" He ducked under the bed and peered through the dust. When he could not locate her, he paled. He went to the door and looked at the patchy snow. One telltale footprint proved his suspicions. She had escaped!

Curtis raced to the main house, where Horik and Mangan were partaking of bread and ale. As he traveled, he motioned to the other villagers. One man grabbed his shoulder.

"What is wrong? Where is the woman?"

"Gone," Curtis whispered. "She managed to get away! What will happen now? If the priest tells the king that we lost her—"

"I'll stop the men on the rowboat and you blockade the main house. Horik will know what to do with O'Bannon."

Curtis nodded and ran the rest of the way to the meetinghouse. He ducked inside and pulled Horik aside, informing him of the situation.

"How could she escape?" Horik demanded harshly. "She was chained!"

"The collar was open and the key was in the lock."

Stunned, Horik checked his belt. Discovering that the key was missing, he grabbed Curtis by his shirt and pulled him close. "Find her," he snarled. "Find her and drag her back by her hair!" Then he turned and faced Mangan.

Mangan rose, nervous about the sudden rise of anxiety among the men. Horik's flushed face did not bode well. "Where is my cousin?" he asked carefully, trying to maintain a blank expression. Out of the corner of his eye, he saw the outlaws quietly maneuvering in front of the two exits and blocking the single window.

Horik spat on the floor and spoke to his men. "Take him prisoner," he commanded. "Don't tell him anything. For now, we will use him as leverage, but if he has overstated his importance, we will kill him."

Mangan fingered his cross and sat back down. Obviously something had gone wrong with Istabelle. When Taber and the Dunhaven sailors were shoved inside and forced to join him, he swallowed and acknowledged that diplomacy had failed. He closed his eyes and prayed, both for her safety and for Ruark's timely intervention.

Istabelle raced through the trees, leaping from dry patch to dry patch to avoid leaving footprints. Casting a worried glance upward, she saw gathering clouds that signaled another snowfall. She had to get far away from the settlement and find shelter before the snow fell. She touched her abdomen, already attuned to the infant that grew in her womb. She was certain it was safe, for the pain had receded and she was confident that the babe was secure. No matter what, she swore silently, she would continue to protect her child!

But even as she vowed, a wave of loneliness washed over her. She missed Ruark. She missed his frowns, his infrequent smiles and his constant sense of self-assurance. If he were at her side, she would not feel as if she faced the world alone. Losing him and losing her beloved falcon had created a hole in her heart that ached to be filled.

She struggled to fight back tears. Now was not the time to wrestle with her emotions! Even if she longed for his touch and yearned for his presence, she had to function without him. He would expect no less from her.

He, more than anyone, had demanded that she act more like a woman and less like a spoiled child. He had denounced her fecklessness and confronted her passions.

All around her she could hear the creaking tree branches and the whispering wind. A smile spread across her lips as she tilted her face into the breeze. She was free. She was free not only of Horik but also of her own fears. She did not need to show anyone that she was not Isadora Dunhaven, nor did she need to conquer the seas to demonstrate her strength. All her life she had struggled against her worries and tried to prove herself, but this experience had taught her that she had spent all her energy railing against a foe that had no substance.

Ruark was real. Her feelings for him were true. The emotions that swirled between them were more meaningful than anything she had ever felt before. Just before the battle he had asked her what she felt in his embrace, but she had been too confused to answer. Now she knew. She loved him.

She should have answered him then. She should

have touched his face and told him that he made her feel special and precious. Instead, the last words she had spoken to him had been full of anger. He had lied to her about his identity, but she had lied to herself about her needs. Would he forgive her? Would he give her a second chance?

A snowflake floated down, landing on her sore nose, and she shivered. She had to find shelter soon. The snow was only one danger she had to avoid. Horik would soon discover she was missing and would set out to find her, and she feared his wrath should he be successful. Although he had promised to keep her alive, he might decide that punishing her was worth more than her dowry. She had no doubt that he was capable of beating her to death.

As she glanced around, she spotted a bird swooping through the trees. The feathered beast reminded her of Péril. The bird screeched, and Istabelle's heart started to race.

"Don't be a fool," she whispered aloud. "Péril is gone, and even if she did somehow manage to survive, there is no way she could have found me this far north." Despite her words, she peered into the trees. Péril was magical. The ship could sail for miles while Péril hunted, yet the falcon would return to the deck after she was finished feasting. Shaking her head, Istabelle forced the fantasy from her mind, but even as she moved stealthily through the forest, she imagined she could hear the cry of her friend over the treetops.

Chapter 19

Ruark paced the deck. An hour had passed since the dinghy had taken Mangan, Taber and the sailors to Horik's settlement, and still there was no sign of their return. In fact, the boat lay on the beach, completely unattended.

Péril cried out and flew in a circle around the ship. Her agitation was rising quickly. When she perched on the ship's railing, she fluffed her wings and shook her head, then struck the wood with her beak.

Ruark paused in front of her. "What is taking them so long?" he grumbled. "Why haven't they given us some signal?"

The falcon hissed and rose back into the air, circling the ship once again.

Frustrated, Ruark resumed his pacing, but this time he pulled his sword free and swung it while he walked. Another hour passed and clouds darkened the sky. When snowflakes began to fall and none of the men appeared to row back to the ship, Ruark knew something had gone wrong.

He turned to Boris and Erik. "Mangan would not stay this long."

Boris nodded. "Neither would Taber."

"I am going to investigate. If I don't return by nightfall, take the ship south to the village we spotted on our way up here."

"I don't think we should leave you or Istabelle."

"We must protect the ship first and foremost. Without it, even if I manage to get Mangan and Istabelle, we won't be able to escape. Do you understand?"

"I understand."

"Good. Drop the smaller dinghy over the far side as soon as darkness gives us sufficient cover."

"I'll outfit the boat with some supplies."

Ruark agreed and went below to check Istabelle's cabin for additional weapons. He found a second dagger and a small sword that he added to the boat's supplies. Then, as the snow began to fall in earnest and the muted sun disappeared below the horizon, Ruark and the boat were lowered into the bay. Péril immediately flew down and landed on Ruark's shoulder. Boris and the other sailors peered over the ship's railing as Ruark, Péril and the boat slid out of sight.

Ruark rowed in the dark, allowing Péril's piercing night vision to guide them. Heated emotions raced through Ruark's blood as he imagined what had befallen Istabelle and the men. Despite the cold snow, Ruark felt sweat dripping from his brow. If he had caused Istabelle's death by leaving her with Horik, he would never forgive himself.

Soon, the rowboat crunched on gravel and Ruark jumped out to drag it up onto the beach. As he turned toward the settlement, Péril screeched and dove in front of him, striking with her talons.

Ruark leapt back, stunned by the falcon's unprovoked attack, but then she flapped her wings and dove into a bush.

"Damn bird!" a man exclaimed as he was flushed from his concealment, flailing his arms.

Ruark dropped to the ground, silently thanking Péril for her warning.

A second man walked out, laughing. "Curtis!" he said. "I think the falcon is fond of you!"

Curtis glowered at his companion. "If that crazed bird comes near me again, I'll chop it in two."

"While you fight a feathered beast, I'll find the woman and chop *her* in two!"

Ruark gritted his teeth. His impulse was to fight and kill, but he needed to wait and see where the men were going. If they were looking for Istabelle, that meant she had escaped. Perhaps the men knew which direction she had taken.

As the men tramped through the brush at the edge of the coast, Péril perched on a branch and peered disdainfully down at them. After the men disappeared along the coastline, Ruark stood and approached the falcon.

He grinned and pointed to her. "You!" he chuckled. "You are an amazing bird."

Péril twisted her head and looked down at him.

"Find her," Ruark said, his voice deepening with intensity. "Find Istabelle!"

With a piercing cry, Péril rose into the sky.

A noise coming from the left made Istabelle freeze. A flicker of unease ran up her spine and she reached for a branch to use as a weapon. When she had raced out of Horik's cabin, she had neglected to grab her sword, and now she cursed herself for her mistake. Gripping the branch, she listened carefully.

A bush only a stone's throw away trembled as if agitated by a beast and she heard a quick, indrawn breath.

Suddenly fearful, Istabelle began to run. She sped through the brush, ducking branches and leaping over logs, but the sounds behind her only increased. Panic infused her. She had suffered Horik's torture, but she could not survive much more.

"No!" she shouted as she heard someone gain on her. "Leave me alone!" She spied a stream ahead. If she reached it, she would be out of the trees and she could face her attacker. She bent low, running as fast as she could.

A huge weight pummeled her from behind, knocking her to the ground. The breath left her body and black spots danced in front of her eyes. She struggled, but as she lifted her head a thick sack was yanked over her, blinding her. Within seconds, she was flipped over, the sack secured and her hands tied in front of her. Before she could gather

her thoughts, she was flung over a large man's shoulder.

She kicked and pounded her fists against her captor.

"Ugh," the man grunted.

Istabelle frantically wriggled her body and managed to force her captor to drop her onto the hard ground. She gasped as her head smashed against the fallen leaves and her shoulder banged against a rock, but she twisted and kicked out once again.

"Stop," her captor commanded in a rough, muffled voice as he grabbed her flailing legs with his hands. "Or you will fare worse at my hands than at Horik's!" The man yanked her upright and shook her violently. "Are you ready to be still?" he growled.

She could feel the heat of his body through his hands. It vibrated against her skin, making her shiver. When she did not answer right away he shook her again.

"Will you behave?" he demanded.

"Yes," Istabelle replied softly, hanging her head. It was over. She had been recaptured and she would be returned to Horik. She was abruptly shoved against a tree.

The man held her by her throat and squeezed. "You sea-witch," he whispered. "Horik shouldn't be the only one to benefit from your charms." The softer tone should have been soothing, but instead it made her shake more. "He always gets the best prizes. I deserve a bit of my own reward."

He stroked her face through the burlap. A shiver

of something unknown rippled through her and she jerked her head back in response to a new fear. "What are you going to do?" she asked. Horik had been unable to rape her. Had she escaped him only to be taken by someone worse?

"I am going to give you what you deserve," he murmured. "I am going to make you scream like you are about to die."

Istabelle shrank back. "I do not want to die," she whispered.

"Then you had better do what I tell you." He rubbed against her, showing her his unmistakable arousal. He swept his hands down her back, feeling her curves, then squeezed her buttocks. "Then after me, there will be another. What do you think about that? 'Tis just punishment for forcing us to chase after you through the forest."

Istabelle cringed as helplessness surged through her. She was drained of the will to fight. It wouldn't matter. She had no more strength to draw upon.

"You like that?" the man whispered in her ear. "You want this?" He grabbed her blouse and ripped it open.

Istabelle let her mind drift free, disassociating herself from the man attacking her. She went limp and imagined that her soul separated from her lifeless body and soared into the clouds. She stretched her fingers and imagined them as gray feathers stroking the air currents. She swept upward, flying free and leaving the earthbound dangers far behind. She felt snowflakes melt upon her bare breasts, but her imagined downy undercoat protected her and kept her warm.

Then, as if she had conjured her friend, Péril flew beside her, matching her stroke for stroke. The falcon whistled softly, sweetly, comforting her. Istabelle leaned toward her, wanting her embrace, but even as the bird's body heat reached her, she felt herself floating farther away.

She needed other arms to enfold her—solid, human arms that could protect and love her.

Then she was falling, fainting . . . She collapsed on the frozen ground while swords clanged over her head. Three men were shouting and then blood darkened the snow. Péril shrieked and dove in and out of the fight. A man gasped and fell beside her, his gut ripped open. Istabelle closed her eyes, the dream faded and she slipped into unconsciousness.

Ruark panted as he yanked his bloody sword free of the man on the ground. Péril had guided him here, and he had arrived just as the man was about to rape the bound Istabelle. Rage filled him, yet he thanked God that the falcon had helped him save her from more torture.

He recognized the man as the one named Curtis. Furious, Ruark slashed him once again with his large sword, almost decapitating him. Frenzied emotion thrummed through him and he raised his sword, intent on finishing the job, but a new sound distracted him. Glancing up, he saw the second man racing off into the woods, stringing a crossbow.

Ruark spun around and took one step after him,

but he tripped over Istabelle's listless arm. Deciding not to pursue the enemy, he immediately sheathed his sword and swept her into his arms.

"Istabelle? God almighty! Are you all right?" A crossbow arrow twanged into a tree trunk near his head and Ruark swiftly bent down, holding Istabelle close to his chest. Without time to free her from her bonds, he raced through the trees in the other direction, trying to protect her from the remaining outlaw's arrows. Péril flew in front of them, guiding Ruark once again.

After several minutes, Ruark slowed. No more arrows thudded into trees near him, and he suspected that he had outrun the enemy. Nevertheless, he ducked around a stand of trees and paused, listening for pursuit. Trembling with emotion, he clutched Istabelle's still form closer. When she did not stir, he shifted positions and searched for her pulse. To his great relief, he felt it beating steady and strong.

"Lead us back to the beach," he commanded the gyrfalcon, who peered anxiously at them. Then, as the bird rose into the air, Ruark began heading sharply west, toward the coast. "Although the ship will be gone, we need to rescue Mangan and head to the southern rendezvous port."

As he strode quickly through the forest, he kept one hand on Istabelle's shoulder and placed the other on her rump. Thank God she was alive! He had thousands of questions for her—what had happened during her captivity? How had she escaped? Why now, just when they had come for her? And then, the most fearful question: Had they hurt her, as Curtis had been about to do? He closed his eyes briefly in agony. Her wild spirit deserved gentle loving, warm passion and deep consideration. He prayed that the outlaws had not destroyed her spirit. If there was any way to erase her pain, he would do it.

He shifted her from his shoulder and cradled her in his arms. There still was no time to unbind her. As long as the other outlaw roamed the forest, he could not pause to extricate her from the ropes and the burlap bag, but he was able to tear a hole in the bag to aid her breathing. Knowing how unpredictable she was, it might be best to keep her under control when she regained consciousness until he had a chance to explain his presence. Her last words still rang in his ears, and he had no reason to believe she would willingly accept his help.

Istabelle drifted back to consciousness as the falcon in her dreams fluttered down from the clouds and settled back into her soul. She felt its heartbeat infuse her own with strength, and she took several deep breaths.

She was being carried in secure, powerful arms. Her last memory was of Curtis attacking her, but the person carrying her seemed much larger and stronger than Curtis. He also smelled clean and fresh, unlike Horik.

She bit her lip, confused and disoriented. Who held her? Why did her heart race when his arms tightened around her? He carried her as if she weighed nothing and a strange lassitude infused her limbs as she remained unresisting in his arms.

She smelled the sea and knew that they approached the coast. She felt the cool wind that swept over the ocean waves. Where were they going? Where was this man taking her? She shivered and pressed closer to his hot chest.

The man tensed, and Istabelle feared her actions had riled him. Like a dragon's body waking from a deep slumber, the man's muscles rippled with sudden awareness as she shifted position. Istabelle tried to pull back in order to soothe the awakened beast, but he gripped her tighter and her breasts were pressed against him. With each step the man took, her nipples rubbed back and forth and she could sense that he was as aware of her arousal as she was.

Then she felt him place her on the ground. She heard the ocean waves lap at the shoreline and felt the cool sea breeze whisper over her skin. He did not untie her and she dared not move. The sack over her head placed her at his mercy. Sticks cracked and a spark was struck and she heard the welcoming snap and crackle of a newly lit fire, giving her warmth. She followed the man's motions with her ears, straining to hear to his position as he paced back and forth while the fire took hold. She felt his gaze, hotter than the flames, sear into her when he paused in front of her.

He kneeled down and began to untie the rope that held the sack in place over her head.

Istabelle instantly began to flail, as her instinctual

reaction was to fight. She kicked out and twisted sharply, trying to avoid the man's hands.

Instantly, he ceased and was still.

She settled down, too, but when he said nothing, she tilted her head. "What do you want?" she finally asked, unable to bear the quiet.

"You," he answered huskily.

Her breasts tightened with desire at the rough timbre of the muffled voice and she caught her breath in stunned amazement. She scrambled to a sitting position and tossed her head, trying to dislodge the sack.

"If you promise not to attack me, I'll take it off," he told her.

Istabelle swallowed, unsure if she were still dreaming. Could he have entered her cloud-filled sojourn? Could she have conjured him into her thoughts so realistically? She remained frozen as his calloused hands gently untied the rope and pulled the sack off her head.

Ruark handled her as he would a wild beast, aware that her stillness could explode at any moment. He knew how well she could fight and how deadly her intent could be when riled. Unsure about her reactions, he flung the sack away, then rocked back on his heels, leaving her hands bound.

She blinked rapidly, her silver eyes sparkling in the moonlight like large, shining stars. Dried blood discolored one cheek, and her nose was tilted upward and slightly to the right. His heart wrenched at this proof of what she had suffered.

He reached out to brush her face and soothe her injured nose, but Istabelle jerked backward.

"You aren't real!" she accused him. "Go away and stop taunting me!"

Ruark frowned as he stared into her wide eyes. He had never seen her so frightened or disoriented. "Istabelle? Are you all right? You look hurt."

"Go away!" she screamed, kicking. "I don't know who—or what—you are! I'll not let a man from my dreams take my sanity!"

Ruark shuddered at the crazed look on her face. She was like a woman pushed to the edge of control and about to tumble down the far side. He took a steadying breath, trying to figure out how to show her that she was finally safe.

"Istabelle, listen to me. I am Ruark. I am real. I am right here, in front of you."

"No! I don't believe you! You left me and—and I told you not to come back."

He smiled. "I decided to ignore your orders, Captain."

"It cannot be you," she whispered as her hands curled into fists. She braced herself and narrowed her eyes. "Prove it," she demanded. "Prove to me that you are who you say you are." Her long lashes shadowed her gaze and her russet hair glowed in the firelight. Her torn blouse exposed her cleavage down to the nipple.

Ruark felt his groin stir. They were passionate people, physical partners. Words and explanations were not normal for them. They needed something more. Something tactile.

"Will you believe me now?" he answered softly as he gripped the neckline of her dress and pushed her back against a tree. "I want you. I want this." He ripped the bodice the rest of the way, baring her breasts to the firelight, then placed a kiss on the swell of her breast while his dominating eyes captured her frightened ones in a powerful gaze. "You will know I am real by the heat of my hands upon your flesh. My fingers will talk to you, convince you of the truth. Listen to them. Feel them."

Istabelle tried to push him back, but her bound hands hampered her movements. She struggled, afraid of herself and her own reactions.

He leaned back, reached between them and shifted her bound hands over her head. Before she could determine what he was going to do, he lifted her bonds and hung them over a branch. Her breasts rose as her arms were stretched upward, making her nipples point impudently forward. He groaned and licked one of them as Istabelle convulsed in shock.

His breath was searingly hot, yet she shivered. "Stop," she whispered. Then, when he only shifted to the other breast, she screamed. "Stop! I don't believe you! This is a dream. You are a fantasy!"

He bit her, gently but with enough force to show her his touch was not imagined. He sucked the under curve of her left breast, bruising the skin, then licked it gently. He swept his lips up, nibbling the underside of her arm, tickling her in ardent pleasure. "This is what we have together," he murmured. "We have passion. We have love. You cannot deny it any longer. I want to taste your hidden places. I want to make you moan with desire. I want to feel your heat blaze, just like before."

He rubbed her nipples with his hands as he kissed her throat, and she was helpless against his assault. He was using her body to make her betray herself and she couldn't stop her own responses. Stabs of pleasure shot through her core and she felt her inner muscles tense. His voice was so sensual, so familiar. The tone evoked memories of their night aboard the ship and the sweet loving upon the cliff. She wanted to fight him, but her body would not. It hung by the branch, submissive yet yearning, as ripples of pleasure ran through her flesh.

His mouth abruptly left her neck and his hands dove deeper into the torn edge of her clothing, grasping each ragged piece. He waited, waited while her body flushed with tension. He used her own anticipation against her, knowing that her body both wanted and resisted him.

"I can feel you," he taunted her. He pulled the cloth apart one inch. The sound of the tearing seemed unusually loud. He leaned forward and kissed the area right below her breast that was now exposed. "You want me, even though you try to deny it." He ripped another inch and the ocean winds snuck around her sides and swirled into her belly button.

He licked the indentation, making Istabelle gasp with pleasure. Again he bit her, claiming her skin, marking her as his.

With agonizing slowness, he tore the blouse to the waistline, letting his thumbs trail over her exposed flesh. "Your skin is on fire," he told her. "It gleams in the firelight as the rising moon reflects off the ocean waves. You are part of the ocean, part of the flames and part of the wind. You are as nature created you." As his seductive words melted into her, he abruptly ripped the rest of her clothing, baring her completely to the elements.

"That is how I want you," he told her. "Like this. Ready for me. Tied to the tree. Wanting me. Wet for me. *For me and only me!*" He kneeled in front of her and nudged her legs apart.

She did not resist. She depended upon the strength of the branch to hold her upright. She felt warm and dizzy. "I'm going to faint," she cried.

"No, you won't," he answered. "You need to feel my touch." He lifted her legs over his shoulder and wrapped her knees on either side of his head. A delicate wind blew between her thighs, cooling her. He kissed her, just barely avoiding her most secret place. The breeze instantly chilled the wet spot, causing her thighs to become covered in tiny goose bumps.

She lifted her hips, unknowingly urging him forward. He ran his hands up her legs to her buttocks and spread them as he opened her nether lips. The cold wind and his hot breath excited her beyond reasoning, and she finally forgot where she was. She forgot what was happening to her and forgot to resist her passion. The firelight, the stars, the crashing waves all receded, replaced entirely by the sensations he evoked. Her helpless position only served to increase the excitement, allowing her to welcome his tender touch.

He kissed her, softly, insistently, lovingly and she cried out in rising pleasure. His tongue was buried between her legs, flicking back and forth as she moaned. His forefinger shifted from her buttocks to the hidden crevice between and he stroked her in a new, untouched area.

Istabelle quivered, arched, the sensation so different and yet so exciting. She opened her legs, trying mutely to grant him further access. He took it, sinking his tongue inside her moist channel while his finger slipped inside her from the back. A short scream erupted from Istabelle, a scream of pleasure. He moved his finger in and out, mimicking his mouth's movements while she flung her head back and forth in rising ecstasy. The dual sensations were far beyond her experience and her mind began to explode with tiny sparks.

He moved quicker, faster, more forcefully and she screamed louder. His tongue swirled around her, then shifted to the small nub, only to be replaced by his thumb. Suddenly three sensations welled inside her and she could not contain herself. She screamed and spread her legs as wide as she could. The sparks coalesced into huge flashes of white, bursting behind Istabelle's eyes as her inner muscles clamped down.

The orgasm shuddered through her, rippling from one site to the next, from his forefinger to his thumb to his mouth, and then back again. She pulled herself up with her bound arms and squeezed with her thighs, unable to control the physical reactions racing through her.

He stood up as she clenched, and before she could react, he slid his cock inside her. He grabbed her ankles and wrapped her legs around his waist as he pressed her back against the tree. Even as her own orgasm was still rushing through her, he ground his hips against her and forced her body to receive him. Her scream increased in pitch as she thrashed against the tree, unable to conceive that her body could reach higher, but it did. Her inner sanctum opened for him, became drenched with desire, became slick with recurring passion as another climactic wave overcame her.

He held her waist with punishing force, but she welcomed his strength as he pounded into her. He slammed in and out, faster, faster, his legs spread to increase the power of his motions. His face tightened, the cords of his neck stretched taut. He closed his eyes and groaned. Then he pulled her as close as he could and froze. Deep, deep within her he pulsed. His tumescence swelled, squeezed and poured his essence into her. He felt her folds surround him, pulling him deeper and he responded by lengthening. He reached her, he touched her . . . he claimed her.

They both gasped together, astounded by the emotions rocking them as their bodies pressed closer together. "Istabelle," he whispered.

I know this man, she thought. I know him better than I know any other. Only he could touch me like this. Only he could reach my heart and send it catapulting beyond the winds, far beyond the stars.

"Ruark," she answered with a sigh.

He supported her with one hand as he carefully cradled her head. His onyx eyes gazed into her silver ones as she blinked in the firelight. "If you know me, then you must know that I will not let anything happen to you again," he murmured to her.

She looked up. His words were so assured, so convincing. Hope swelled inside her. He had come for her. He wanted her. Perhaps—perhaps he loved her, too. She gazed at him as he carefully untied her and wrapped her in his own shirt since her clothing lay in tatters at their feet.

He enfolded her in his embrace. "Do you believe me now?"

Péril swooped down from her perch and landed on Ruark's bare shoulder, cocking her head to peer adoringly into Istabelle's eyes.

She smiled. "Yes. I believe you."

He nodded. "Good. Then I have one other thing to tell you."

She held her breath as emotion caused her throat to constrict. "What?" she whispered.

"Mangan is here, as well. He came to help rescue you by attempting to reason with Horik."

Istabelle frowned, surprised by his words. She didn't understand what he was talking about. Her blood was still pulsing through her body and she was light-headed from ecstasy. "Mangan?"

"Yes. I sailed to the monastery where I met up with him previously and told him about Horik and the Dunhavens. He spoke with a priest to annul the marriage and obtain your freedom, but I fear Horik has refused to listen."

Pain knifed through Istabelle's heart, but she struggled to hide her sorrow. She had hoped to hear words of love and devotion, but passion was not love. Just because he wanted her did not mean he loved her. He was not going to whisper sweet words. She sat up and cleared her throat, dragging her thoughts from the romantic to the strategic. Pulling the shirt closer around her body, she shook her head. "Horik will never listen to logic. If Mangan went to him, I would expect him to hold Mangan for ransom. I know the settlement. I know where they will keep him. I suggest we strike tonight, before they expect an attack."

Ruark nodded in agreement. "You are a brave woman," he told to her. "I . . . I admire you."

Istabelle glanced away, fighting tears. She did not want his admiration. She wanted his love.

Chapter 20

After finding some additional clothing in the supplies Boris had packed, Istabelle dressed herself in a pair of clean, leather breeches and located a sword and dagger. The weapons felt good in her hand and she grinned.

"Ready?" Ruark asked, smiling back at her.

"Ready. Here is a vest for you, but I could not find another shirt. Will it do?"

"Of course." He pulled on the fur-lined piece of clothing, welcoming the warmth. With a nod, he motioned for her to precede him.

They crept around the edge of the bay until they reached the settlement. Tendrils of night fog snaked from the ocean to dance along the shoreline, making the beach appear ghostly and surreal. Istabelle pointed to the main house. Keeping her voice low, she whispered in Ruark's ear. "That is the place where all meetings and discussions are held. I could see the building from Horik's cabin, where I was detained. I suspect they will keep Mangan and the others there."

"We cannot fight the entire village. I will go in and try to sneak them out quietly, but be prepared to defend us if the outlaws discover our intent."

Istabelle nodded as she unconsciously stroked her abdomen. For the first time in her life, she was not looking forward to a fight. The child she carried in her womb needed protection. If she was stabbed, the baby could die. "Be careful," Istabelle responded.

Surprised, Ruark took her proffered hand and kissed it. "Are you worried about me?"

"Yes—and about the others," Istabelle answered.

Ruark's heart flipped and he felt an odd tickling in his stomach. A silly grin stole across his face as he pulled her close. He slid his hands up her neck and buried them in her hair. As he tilted her head up to him, he dropped his gaze to her lips. They were wet, succulent and slightly parted. He lowered his head, not knowing if she would jerk away or let his mouth caress hers, but she remained pliant. Gently, as if she were a fragile blossom, he brushed his lips against hers.

She sighed, leaned forward and clasped him around the neck.

He closed his eyes, absorbing her surrender. He didn't want to let her go. He wanted to kiss her for an eternity.

The clash of swords at the doors of the main house startled them both. They broke apart and spun around.

"Who is that?" Istabelle asked as several men hurtled out of the doorway.

"That is your cousin Mangan," Ruark hissed under his breath.

They both gasped as Mangan whipped around and raised a sword to defend himself against Horik, while Taber and the Dunhaven sailors fought with upturned chairs and broken table legs in their hands. A dozen outlaws chased after them with drawn battle-axes and swords.

"Mangan and the men are escaping!" Istabelle cried. "We must help them!"

"This way!" Ruark shouted to Mangan and the sailors.

Mangan glanced over his shoulder, looking relieved to see Ruark running toward him.

"Help the others!" Mangan yelled. "They don't have swords!"

Ruark leapt forward and attacked an outlaw, drawing his attention away from Taber. The man swung his battle-axe at Ruark's head, but Ruark ducked and jumped forward, engaging the man in hand-to-hand combat. They fell to the ground and rolled over one another until Ruark managed to end up on top. He punched the man in the temple, knocking him unconscious.

Istabelle motioned for her crewmen to follow her, leading them to where the boat lay hidden. Ecstatic to see her alive, they raced toward her. "Come!" she shouted.

They ran out of the village as more outlaws poured from their homes, weapons drawn. Ruark, Taber and Mangan followed as quickly as they could while they defended their retreat from Horik and his comrades.

Horik's face was a mask of fury as he barreled down on Ruark. "You again!" he bellowed. "I should have killed you on the ship!"

"Try it now, and you will be the one drowning in your own blood," Ruark snarled as he lunged, engaging the man in a deadly fight. Horik stumbled backward, desperately parrying Ruark's thrusts.

Istabelle glanced back, terrified that Horik's men would soon outnumber them. "Push the boat out past the surf," she commanded the sailors as she spun around to join the fight. "We have only moments to spare!"

She swung her sword, rapidly disabling two of the eight men who had already reached them. As she plunged her sword into the chest of another, the thin blade cracked.

"No!" she screamed as thoughts of the baby ran through her mind. From the corner of her eye, she saw Mangan fighting two outlaws as Ruark battled Horik, leaving two other outlaws free to circle and attack the Dunhaven sailors.

She quickly looked around for a weapon, but all she could see was the flickering campfire. She dashed to it and plucked a flaming stick out of the ashes. She could hear one of the outlaws advancing behind her, so she whipped the stick around in an arc, slamming it against her attacker's chest. The man screamed as burning coals sizzled on his skin. Angered, he raised his sword, and with one decisive swing, splintered the branch into thousands of flaming pieces that flew around them like dangerous, shimmering stars.

Ruark glanced up when he heard Istabelle cry out. The cascade of sparks distracted him, and he briefly lowered his guard.

Horik barreled forward with a dagger and plunged it into Ruark's unprotected side, just below his rib cage.

Pain exploded in his body and Ruark fell back, clutching his side. The blade was roughly serrated and the wound was deep. Horik raised his battle-axe as Ruark attempted to locate his sword where he had dropped it, but his hands wouldn't obey his mind. He felt himself weave in place and he fell to his knees.

Suddenly Istabelle was standing in front of Ruark, protecting him. She held Ruark's own engraved sword high in the air. Powerful vibrations emanated from the blade, creating swirling air currents that danced around her russet hair. Her silver eyes gleamed as she opened her arms, imitating the spread wings of a massive falcon with metal-tipped talons, then swept her arms together, swishing the blade through the air.

A falcon's cry echoed across the beach, and Horik stumbled back in horror, unsure where the sound came from. Then suddenly, Péril screamed from the treetops and dove, talons outstretched.

Horik swung at the feathered attacker, then yowled as Péril's sharp talons raked his face. With Horik temporarily blinded, Istabelle plunged Ruark's sword into his shoulder. Horik's eyes sprang open in disbelief as he tumbled over and fell facefirst into the sand.

Péril flapped her wings over the man's head and pecked at his ear. When he did not move, she flew up and perched on Istabelle's shoulder.

"More are coming . . ." Ruark gasped.

Istabelle took a deep breath and blinked several times, calming the vibrant energy that flowed through her. She yanked the sword free, then turned and addressed the men. "Launch the boat and help me get Ruark onboard." She gripped Ruark's arm and helped him rise. "Hurry!"

"Over there . . . Mangan needs you . . ." Ruark panted, pointing to her cousin.

Nodding, Istabelle raced to help. Together, the cousins felled the final outlaws, then, as they spied others running toward them through the trees, they scrambled out to the boat. Within moments, the strong oarsmen pulled the fully loaded craft out over the breakers and into the deeper water, where they were hidden by the ocean fog.

Ruark tried to stay conscious. The pain along his side was burning hot, and he felt dizzy. "South," he managed to croak. "Head south to the village on the point. The ship is waiting for us there."

"Aye," Istabelle whispered. "That is a wise plan."

He stared up at her, his black eyes fathomless. "You saved me," he replied softly.

"You saved me, too," Istabelle answered.

"I might not make it. I think he nicked my gut." Ruark paused to cough.

"You will make it," Istabelle insisted. "I demand it."

Ruark tried to smile, but the effort was too great. He closed his eyes and let the darkness enfold him.

With Istabelle in command and Mangan and the sailors helping, they managed to raise a small sail while Ruark lay unconscious and bleeding on the floorboards. As soon as the little craft was stabilized, she turned to face Mangan.

"Cousin?" she asked.

Mangan nodded. "Yes, I am Mangan, your cousin. You must be Istabelle."

Smiling wryly, Istabelle motioned to Ruark. "You don't look anything like each other."

"No. Only someone who has not seen me since I was five years old would have made such a mistake. I am sorry he caused you such difficulty."

"It was not all his fault." Istabelle instantly defended Ruark. "I never gave him a chance to explain."

Mangan raised his brows but did not reply directly. "You have lived an unusual life, Istabelle. Your letters have always been full of amazing stories."

She shrugged. "I guess I wanted to prove that I was not like my mother, but somehow I forgot to find out what I wanted for me."

"Do you know now?"

Istabelle glanced down at Ruark. "I know what I want, but perhaps, for the first time in my life, I can't get it."

Mangan shook his head. "God works in strange and inexplicable ways. But Istabelle, you must be realistic if you find yourself wanting a man with no home and no family. Ruark is a paid warrior. He is not someone who will willingly give up a life of war and danger."

Istabelle grinned. "I would not ask him to do so, just as I could not change for him. We are each who we are and if we find that our paths unite, it will have to be because we understand each other."

Looking down at Ruark, Mangan frowned. "Injuries to the gut are not good, Cousin. If Horik's blade sliced his innards, he will die from the infection."

"I will not let Horik take him from me," she stated angrily. "He already tried to take so much. I draw the line at losing Ruark." She explored the wound. The bleeding had slowed, but she was afraid any movement would start it again.

Péril perched on the railing of the boat, acting as concerned about Ruark as the humans did. She hopped down and peered at his face, then emitted a loud shriek. For once, Istabelle ignored her friend.

She shivered as the sea wind blew through her hair while she rummaged through the supplies. She found an old blanket, along with various fishing, cooking and hunting equipment. A water skin was also wedged into the bow next to a package with flint and dried dung.

"You should wrap yourself in that blanket," Mangan called out. "You will do no one any good if you grow ill from the cold."

"He needs it more than I," Istabelle replied as she crawled back to Ruark and proceeded to cover his bare chest. She tore one strip from the blanket and dipped it into the salt water. Baring only his wound, she cleaned it, careful not to start the bleeding again.

He stirred and opened his eyes. "Istabelle?" he asked.

"Yes, I'm here."

"Where . . . how . . . are you all right?"

She smiled. "You should not be concerned about me. I have no injuries, whereas you have been stabbed. How do you feel?"

"Sick to my stomach."

"I doubt that has anything to do with your injury and everything to do with lying in the bottom of a rocking boat." She smiled. "Will you never get over your seasickness?"

He groaned and tried to sit up.

"Don't," Istabelle cautioned, sobering instantly. "If it starts bleeding again, you will lose more life force. You are already too pale."

"I'll not lie here and let you and Mangan do all the work. I have more experience sailing than he does"

"And I have enough experience for the two of y

Sit back and rest. Once we reach *The Adventuress*, the barber will tend you. Then you will have plenty of time to argue with me."

"Kiss me again," he commanded softly.

"Kiss you?"

"Kiss me. We were interrupted before."

She glanced briefly at Mangan and shook her head. "No, I don't think that is a good idea."

Ruark drew his brows together in a dark frown. "I may die and you are concerned about convention." He struggled to sit up.

"I told you not to move."

"And I told you to kiss me," he replied, completely exasperated.

"Oh, very well. If you insist." She leaned down and touched his lips with hers but before she could pull back he grasped her neck and held her close.

"I can see down your—my—shirt when you lean over like that," he whispered, then chuckled at her affronted look. "Don't worry, I like the view. Now kiss me like you mean it."

This time she pressed her lips to his, molding her mouth to meet his hard contours. Frissons of delight whispered up and down her spine and she suddenly became breathless.

"That is better." He sighed as they broke contact. His eyes fluttered closed and he sank into the bottom of the boat, semiconscious.

Istabelle sat back and stared at the gyrfalcon. "Who

found me?" she asked the bird. "You, like you always do? Or did he help you this time?"

Péril cocked her head and ruffled her feathers.

"They seem to work as a team," Mangan answered. He shifted positions uncomfortably, unsure how to respond to the sight of his unwed cousin kissing Ruark. Electing to ignore the relationship for now, he gestured to the falcon. "They act like they do not like each other, but I sense a bond between them."

Istabelle leaned forward and stared at her cousin. "And what about your role? What have you been doing?"

"I entered a monastery and spent a year meditating."

Istabelle almost laughed until she saw Mangan's serious expression. Struggling to understand, she asked, "You truly entered a monastery?"

"I feel a calling to do more than run Kirkcaldy's castle and lands. I feel that there is something else I must do, although I am not certain what it is."

"What does your father say?"

"He does not know."

"If you follow this path, who will inherit the earldom?"

"A distant relative. I am sure my father will choose someone wisely."

Shrugging, Istabelle bent down to stroke Ruark's face. "So, you left your monastery and came up north to rescue your impulsive cousin?"

"I knew you needed me. God told me."

Snorting in unladylike fashion, she settled next to him. "I needed you earlier, when I sent you that letter. You should have come then."

Mangan shook his head. "It wasn't time. Do you regret meeting him?"

Istabelle touched her abdomen and thought back over the last two months. "No," she answered slowly, "but I do fear the future. I do not know what I am going to do."

Mangan placed a comforting arm around her shoulders. "Only time will tell. Trust in God. But, Istabelle, please be careful."

Chapter 21

As the sun rose, Ruark tossed and turned feverishly and Istabelle and the crew battled the winds that sought to drive their boat out to sea. After spending a night trying to stay away from the shoreline, they now fought to stay close, for the danger of being too far out in the ocean was far worse than accidental beaching would be. She barked orders at Mangan and Taber, who obeyed her without question. "A storm is approaching," Istabelle yelled over the whistling winds. "We will never survive it in this craft."

"If we don't reach the ship soon, they may head farther south to avoid the weather," Taber replied.

Istabelle nodded her understanding. She would not have wanted it any other way. "The ship and her crew come first," she agreed. "At this rate, we will spend more time fighting the winds and tides than getting south. How much farther?"

Taber looked up at the angry clouds gathering on the horizon. "At least a day," he answered. "I don't like the look of this weather."

Istabelle tightened the sail and then kneeled down

next to Ruark to feel his head. Tears welled in her eyes. "He is so hot," she murmured. She lifted the blanket and examined the wound. It was swollen and discolored and the red rim around it had gotten more pronounced. "Ruark," she said. "Ruark, wake up."

He tried to turn toward her, but the boat rocked him away. He could not lift his eyes or push sound out of his mouth.

"He cannot hear us," Istabelle said. "His fever is worsening. I have to help him now. If I wait to reach the ship, it may be too late."

Ruark moaned. His swollen tongue would not obey his mind and no coherent words made it to his lips.

"I am not a healer, but I have learned some of the art at the monastery," Mangan replied. "I believe the wound is festering and needs to be opened to allow drainage, much like his brother Sven's injury. Can we create a flame on the boat? You will need to clean his wound and stitch it closed."

"Yes. Anything. I don't want him to die."

"Look at the green fluid that fills the boil. That must be released," Mangan said, pointing to the stab wound.

Istabelle cradled Ruark's head in her lap and nodded. She brushed his hair off his forehead. The strands were damp with sweat. "Stay with me," she whispered. "I survived imprisonment and torture at the settlement. You can survive one small wound," she pleaded. "Do it, if only to tell me what a fool I was to not tell you what I felt for you before I was kidnapped. You want to do that, don't you? Tell me that I was wrong and you were right?"

Ruark's breathing became shallower and Istabelle clutched him to her heart. "Fight!" she yelled as she shook him. "Fight like the warrior you are!"

Mangan struck the flint and lit some of the dried manure, which he then held underneath some wood he had broken off from one of the boat's benches. Once the wood caught fire, he placed it in a pot and allowed the small flame to smolder in the container. "Is he . . . ?"

"He is getting worse by the moment. We have no time to lose." She trembled with fear but struggled to remain calm. "I will heat some water to clean the site."

"Good. Let me burn the knife so it will cauterize as it cuts."

"It will hurt. I will do the cutting if you hold his shoulders down."

Mangan huddled next to them and grasped Ruark's shoulders firmly. He nodded.

Istabelle lifted the blanket that was wrapped around Ruark and exposed the festering wound.

"This is why Ruark was at the monastery when I received your letter. His brother was injured and needed help," Mangan remarked.

"Well, we don't have a monastery close by, so we had best be better barbers than he was," Istabelle replied as she placed the knife on the infected site. "Ready?"

"Aye."

She stabbed the boil and quickly sliced down. Ruark spasmed, jerking his body upward, but Mangan held him in place. Working rapidly, Istabelle squeezed the wound, forcing the purulent material out. Green and yellow infection mixed with red blood as Istabelle wiped and washed the site, then poured salt water over it.

"Hold him!" she instructed Mangan as Ruark twitched back and forth. "I need to cut some more." She cut the ragged tissue off, wincing as Ruark moaned.

"The wound doesn't appear to have penetrated all the way into his abdomen," she said gratefully. "It is just through the skin and muscle. Give me a splinter—a very sharp one. My stepmother told me once about how she sewed up a wound using hair and a splinter. I am going to try it."

Plucking several strands of hair from her scalp, she braided them to form a length of strong threadlike material. Then she wound the end around the splinter, and using the wood as a guide, she sewed the cleaned edges of the gash together. After she was done, she washed the site again.

"I will pray," Mangan said as Istabelle finished.

Istabelle stared at Mangan as tears ran down her face. "Please do," she whispered softly.

"Captain," Taber interrupted. "Look! A ship!"

Fear raced through Istabelle as she peered at the sail on the horizon. "It comes from the direction of Horik's settlement," she commented. "If it is a search party, we cannot risk being seen. Horik's ship could have fifty armored men aboard. We will be massacred."

Currents vibrated between her and the gyrfalcon until the massive gray bird lifted into the air and hovered above them. Then, with a fierce cry, Péril flew toward the ship.

"Péril will determine if they are foe or not, but until then, I think it is best we hide and let the ship and the storm pass. Drop the sail and row in to shore."

"Aye, Captain," Taber replied.

"Ruark," Istabelle murmured. "Ruark, you must wake. Enemies approach."

Struggling to rise, Ruark blinked and tried to sit up, but he collapsed back against the wooden slats.

Wrinkling her brow, Istabelle touched his head and stroked one finger down his cheek. "Don't worry. We will carry you. Rest and recover."

"Leave me in the boat," he managed to croak. "Don't let me slow you down. I don't want you to be caught again—"

"We will not be caught, but we will not leave you either."

"Istabelle," Ruark attempted to argue.

"Hush!" she commanded. "I am the captain and I have made my decision." Just then the crew bumped the boat onto the sand. Istabelle and Mangan each supported an arm to help Ruark out of the boat and dragged him onto shore as the crew members pulled the craft into the bushes.

Well before the ship got close enough to spot them,

Péril returned, acting agitated, and Istabelle nodded sagely. "It is his ship. I knew I wounded him, but apparently not well enough."

Ruark took several deep breaths and rested against the tree where the cousins had propped him. He watched Istabelle as she paced back and forth just behind the tree line. He shifted positions and looked down at his wound. The redness had receded and the awful pain had significantly diminished, although he still felt weak and disoriented. "Water," he whispered.

Istabelle instantly kneeled at his side and offered him the water skin. "Drink." She smiled.

"Thank you." He licked his lips and savored the refreshment as he stared at her. Her silver eyes never ceased to amaze him. They sparkled like fine jewelry framed by thick black lashes. A faint blush rose on her cheeks as he continued to contemplate her face.

"Is something wrong?" she asked, looking uncomfortable.

"Nothing, nothing at all. You are so beautiful, I can't help looking at you. There is a glow . . . a bloom to your cheeks that is so lovely. What is different about you?"

Istabelle looked away. "Nothing," she mumbled, unsure how to respond. The others were milling around and she felt uncomfortable with his openly appreciative regard. Trying to distract him, she pointed to the ship that was sailing past. "Horik is very persistent," she said. "I wish he would simply give up and let me go on my way."

Ruark shook his head. "He wants money and land, and through you he can obtain both. It is a powerful incentive to keep fighting. I know. I used to think that wealth and property were all that mattered. I spent every moment searching for them and every day trying to obtain them."

"I think I know where Horik is going," Mangan interrupted. "He is not just chasing us, or he would be sailing more slowly, searching for our boat. I think he is going to the monastery."

Istabelle and Ruark both looked at Mangan questioningly.

"I told him that a priest at St. Ignacio had signed papers in support of an annulment. I suspect Horik will go after the priest to stop the petition."

Istabelle shook her head in dread. "Even Horik would not consider murdering a priest!"

Mangan gazed across the breaking waves to the ship as it passed them without slowing. His eyes hardened. "Unfortunately, there are those in this world who do not respect God's blessings, and they do not differentiate between men of war and men of God. Horik is one such man." He turned and stared at Istabelle. Raising an eyebrow, he questioned, "You were with him. Do you truly doubt that he could be planning something as dastardly as killing a priest?"

Istabelle shrank against Ruark's chest, seeking his comfort. She shook her head. "We must reach the monastery as soon as possible," she said fiercely. "I will not be the cause of a priest's death!"

* * *

By the next afternoon, they reached the southern port and held their breath in anticipation, hoping that *The Adventuress* still awaited their arrival. The squall had been short but furious, and they were not sure if the ship would have stayed or sailed to safer shores. As they rounded the peninsula that sheltered the port, the crew cheered.

"There she is!"

Istabelle smiled, tears in her eyes. "There were times at the outlaw settlement when I was not sure I would ever see my ship again," she murmured.

Ruark leaned closer. "She means a lot to you," he stated.

Nodding, Istabelle replied, "Yes. She is my home. This ocean, those winds, that far horizon—it is as if there are endless possibilities waiting for me to explore."

"Yet you have not explored them. You have stayed close to home and protected your people."

Istabelle shrugged. "There is still time," she replied. "Someday, I will sail farther and longer than anyone else has ever done before. And I will do it on that ship."

"Will you take anyone with you?" Ruark asked.

Istabelle flushed as she touched her abdomen surreptitiously. "Perhaps," she answered.

"Péril?"

"Yes, Péril will fly with me."

"Anyone else?"

Istabelle dropped her gaze. "Perhaps," she repeated.

Ruark took her hand. "I want to talk to you to-night, alone."

She slanted a look up at him through her lashes, granting him a flash of silver before she glanced down again. "I would like that. I have something to tell you, too."

Within the hour, Istabelle, Mangan and Taber climbed aboard the ship, and with the crew's assistance, helped Ruark make his own way up the rope ladder to the deck. Although he moved slowly, he insisted on climbing by himself.

"The best way to recover," he stated, "is to keep active."

Istabelle grumbled about ruining stitches and opening wounds, but she smiled nonetheless, pleased to see his recovery. "Active or not," she said, "I'd like you to rest while we set sail. Go down to my cabin and sleep."

Ruark nodded, too tired to argue. He made his way down the hatchway and fell into Istabelle's bed. As he drifted to sleep, he smiled. He could smell her essence on the sheets and it enfolded him in security.

When she came down to join him, he thought to himself, he was going to tell her what he felt about her. He wanted only honesty between them.

"You don't need to wake up," she whispered several hours later when Ruark rolled to the side of the bunk to face her. She was sitting in a chair, staring at him with only the moonlight to brighten the dark room.

"I knew you came in."

Sighing, Istabelle leaned back and smiled wryly. "I thought I was very quiet."

"You were. But I felt you. I felt your gaze."

"Would you like me to leave?" she asked.

"No. I'd like you to come and sit next to me on the bed."

"I'll light a candle."

"No. Leave the cabin dark. I have made many mistakes by not talking to you about . . . things . . . and I don't want to make that mistake anymore. In the dark, I can talk from my heart and not from my mind."

"If this is about your deception, I understand. You did try to warn me, and in truth, I think I suspected it all along."

"Nonetheless, I apologize. I should not have misled you, for it started our relationship on lies."

"As long as we never lie to each other again," Istabelle murmured.

"Agreed." He reached out and cradled her face in his hands. "Tell me what happened there. I feel so guilty. I know that Horik hurt you. Did he rape you?"

"No. He was impotent. An injury to his groin made him ineffective. Mangan would say that it was God's protection."

"I want you to know that it would not matter to me. I would still care for you and I would understand."

Istabelle leaned down and kissed his cheek. "Thank

you. You are good and kind, but he did not hurt me that way. He did beat me, whip me and kick me. He starved me and humiliated me. I cannot tell you that I did not suffer at his hands."

Ruark sat up and pulled her close. "Again, I am sorry. I never want you to be hurt again. I should never have left you!"

Cuddling into his powerful arms, Istabelle started crying. "I was not certain I would survive. I started to give up. Does that make me weak?"

"No! It makes you human. You are so strong, but even you can break if forced to endure too much. Very few would have survived and still had the will to attempt escape."

"I did not run away for me. I did it for someone else I needed to protect."

Shaking his head, Ruark rocked her and kissed her bent head. "Who?" he asked.

"My baby," she answered softly. "Our baby."

Ruark clutched her so tightly, she had to hold her breath. "Our baby?" he repeated. "Are you sure?"

She pushed back and looked into his stunned eyes. "Yes. I didn't know at first. I kept dreaming about you, wishing you were coming for me, and then . . . then I realized that I had not had a monthly course since we . . ."

"Oh my God," he whispered, pulling her close again and rocking. "A child."

"If I cannot get the annulment Mangan speaks of, our child will be under Horik's control and will carry his name."

"No. The child will bear my name, as will you. I will never let either of you go again."

Istabelle gasped. "What are you saying?"

"I am saying that I love you, and I want to be with you. I want to raise a family with you. It is possible? Could you accept me? You are so talented and wild and free, and you come from a highborn family. Could you ever accept a man like me? A man with nothing to offer?"

"Ruark! You have everything to offer! You have your strength, your wisdom and your support. I do not need wealth. I need love. If you also have love to offer me, then you are giving me the world."

"I do. I love you."

"And I love you."

Grasping her head in his hands, he kissed her deeply as their souls merged in the moonlit cabin. They each surrendered. They each conquered. They each devoured each other, their mutual passion spiraling upward in a towering flame of need.

He swept her underneath him, gently removing her clothing until her body was bare to his gaze. He kissed her abdomen, then sank lower, kissing her thighs and her delicate toes. Then he moved upward and suckled her breasts, wanting every inch of her body in his mouth, his own wound forgotten.

She gasped, gripping his shoulders with her hands, and let his need direct hers. She arched her back, giving and taking. She wrapped her legs around his waist, wanting and loving him, accepting and welcoming all of him. Then, when he began to shake with the overwhelming emotion of the moment, she rolled him on his back and sat on top of him, kissing him and whispering soft love words to him.

She braced her hands against his chest and kneaded his pectoral muscles as she swished her hair over his face, draping him in a curtain of protection. Then she shifted lower and shook the tendrils over his abdomen. The strands slipped over his rod, which twitched with need. As if she could understand his body, she moved her hips and brushed her wet center over his hardened shaft. "I don't want to wait," she whispered.

He groaned and held on to her waist, moving her into position. "I want to be inside you forever," he told her. "I want to fill you with love."

She slid along his shaft, moistening it with her essence. "I want you, too," she whispered. "Forever." Then she reached between her legs and grasped his manhood. It quivered in her hand, swelling larger. She rocked forward and angled her hips so the tip brushed her nub. They both gasped at the sensation. Moisture coated them, a mixture of sweat and love's ambrosia, joining them.

She flung her head back and sank down, wrapping around his steel. She gasped as he groaned, and then suddenly they were both rocking furiously. Her breasts bounced with the force of his thrusts and her thighs quivered with erupting passion.

He shifted her so her nubbin rubbed against him with each movement, and she cried out with the new sensation. Faster he rocked her, rubbing her as he plunged inside, searching for the pinnacle that beckoned them forward.

She reached it. She cried out, screamed, tossed her head back and forth, but he wouldn't let her stop. He forced her body to keep moving, forced her first climax to spread into another and another as he exhilarated in the contractions deep inside her core that told him she had accepted him completely.

Then it came to him. At first it tickled at his testes, then it surged up his shaft until suddenly it exploded from deep within his soul. He shouted aloud as he ground her hips into his, twitching and pulsing as he filled her with every drop of his heart.

Afterward, they could not speak. The emotions between them were too intense. He lifted her satiated body from his and tucked her against his curled body. They did not need to say the words again. They both understood.

Chapter 22

Within two days they reached the village port of Canna and docked *The Adventuress*. Péril hopped back and forth along the railing, clearly disturbed. She could not stay still. She fluttered, squawked and cried, until she flew in quick circles around the ship and perched again.

Istabelle bit her lip, becoming more and more nervous.

Ruark placed a comforting hand on her shoulder, but he, too, gazed toward the hills of the monastery with concern. His side ached, but the effects of the fever were gone.

"Perhaps the priest has already left," Mangan offered.

Istabelle shook her head. "No. I am certain that he is still there and is in danger, or Péril would not be so agitated. If anything happens to him or your house of worship because of me, I will be devastated."

Mangan took her hand and forced her to look him. "Istabelle, nothing that man does is your fa He is who he is, and his actions are his own.

cannot take responsibility for the world upon your shoulders."

Taber leaned against the railing next to them. "The same is true about Dunhaven. You cannot fix everything, Captain. We all know how much you care, but you cannot change an entire legacy of selfishness by yourself."

"But I must!" Istabelle said fiercely. "I do not want to see others suffer when I can help. If I have to do that by myself, I will!"

Ruark pulled her up against his chest and kissed her head. "No, you don't. I have spent a lifetime pursuing the very things you have thrown away in your quest to help those in need. I was the one who sought a dream that would never grant happiness, yet I did not know it. You will not be alone again, Istabelle. I will be with you and I will pledge my heart and soul to helping you set the wrongs of this world right."

"Which is my mission as well," Mangan agreed. "Together, we can assist many people, but today we will help one person. When we disembark, we will gather the horses and ride to the monastery. If we reach it before Horik does, we will provide an envoy for the priest's safe passage to the court. If not—"

"There is no other possibility," Istabelle replied firmly. "We will save the priest."

The villagers produced Ruark's horse, Mangan's and Istabelle's mare. All had been well fed and . After packing some supplies, the threesome rode off, with Péril flying in the lead. Although several members of the crew wanted to accompany them, Istabelle insisted they stay behind and guard the ship.

"Horik is wily," she replied firmly when Boris tried to convince her. "I want the ship fully protected. We will approach the monastery cautiously and decipher Horik's whereabouts. Then we will enter and protect the people."

Boris shook his head as he reboarded the ship after waving them off, fearing that it was in the captain's nature to be reckless and that despite her soothing words, she was capable of rash action.

By that evening, Mangan, Ruark and Istabelle had covered over half the distance to the monastery. They stopped to camp only when darkness obscured their path and their mounts lagged with exhaustion. Ruark chose a site and lit a small, smokeless fire while Mangan and Istabelle worked together to prepare a simple meal.

After eating, Mangan leaned back against a tree and closed his eyes, drifting halfway between sleep and wakefulness. He was pleased about Istabelle and Ruark, although he knew their union would be cause for talk. Her unconventional past and virtual isolation from society would protect her, and with strong sponsorship, they should be granted the king's blessing. He, however, faced a much more difficult path Leaving the earldom would throw the powerful fam lies of Scotland in turmoil, for anyone with a famil connection to the O'Bannons would fight to claim title. Although his calling to serve God was strong, he had to balance his desires against the needs of his people and the nation. Was God's work more important than earthly responsibilities?

He sighed and shifted to a more comfortable position. For over a year he had meditated upon that very question, but no answer had come to him yet; thus it was unlikely he would solve his problems tonight. He smiled to himself, listening to the lovers talk softly on the other side of the campfire. Tomorrow would be busy. He should get some sleep. Peeking through his half-closed eyes, he saw Ruark and Istabelle holding hands, their love for each other glowingly beautiful.

He was pleased. God does help those who need his hand. These two people were so right for each other, but without God's intervention, their paths would never have crossed. Mangan hoped that God would help guide his own path, too. He closed his eyes and fell asleep, his faith comforting him.

Ruark gathered Istabelle onto his lap and placed a protective hand on her abdomen. Opening to her as he had never done with anyone, Ruark told her about his early years as an orphan. He spoke haltingly about the pain of loneliness, the pangs of hunger and the risks of sleeping too soundly in the overcrowded streets of his village. He spoke about Sven, and how he had rescued him and how they had developed a nd so close that they called each other brother.

n turn, Istabelle explained how her early years formed her when she had lived at Kirkcaldy after her father had abandoned her. After she reunited with her father, they had become extraordinarily close and he taught her to sail. She had even built several small sailing vessels by hand. But the rebelliousness developed during her first five years had never left her and that, combined with life on an island, had set her toward a life as a sea captain. Somewhere along the years, with her stepmother Alannah as a guiding and steadying presence, she had channeled her restlessness into a need to help others.

Istabelle lay down and placed her head in his lap. "Are you concerned about Sven?" she asked as the coals gleamed red and Ruark stroked her hair.

He nodded. "I hope he is healed."

"I do, too. I look forward to meeting him."

Ruark chuckled. "It will be interesting. I am not sure what Sven will think of you."

She twisted and playfully slapped his chest. "What do you mean by that?"

"I mean, he is used to me bedding big, blond, peasant girls. You are the last person he would ever expect me to shackle up with."

She placed her hand on his chest. She could feel the steady beating of his heart. "Do you regret meeting me?" she asked somberly. "I am not an easy person to love."

"No, you aren't. You are unpredictable, impulsive and rash—the complete opposite of me—but I don't regret falling in love with you. Not at all. What about you? Does it make you nervous to love me?"

"No," she whispered as she snuggled closer. "Not at all. But I do hope that Sven will accept me as fully as you have."

"Of course he will. No one could be near you without falling in love with your spirit."

As he talked, Ruark watched her face soften. Her hand strayed to stroke her abdomen and he intertwined their fingers together. Their child was beginning life very differently than its parents had. Whereas they had been born and raised in turmoil, unsure of whom to trust or love, this child would be born to two loving, caring people who would protect its little life with gentle persistence. The baby would not be an innocent caught in the wheels of fate. It would be loved, just as its parents loved each other.

As they finally lay down to sleep together, he noted the increased swell of her breasts, the glow in her cheeks and the softness in her eyes that signaled her budding pregnancy. It was beautiful. She was beautiful.

She frowned. "Smoke," she said. "I smell smoke." They had risen at dawn and ridden hard to reach the monastery, which was now less than a mile away.

"I smell it, too," Mangan agreed. "Look, over the hill. Smoke tendrils."

"Do the monks burn weeds?" Ruark asked.

"Not in winter," Mangan replied. "Something must be wrong. Horik has already been here."

Dread filled all of them as they kicked their steeds into a gallop and bridged the final slope before seeing the gray walls of the monastery. As they drew closer, they heard the crackling of burning wood and the shouting of many men. Ruark looked over at Istabelle with concern. She glanced back, her face ashen.

"Horik," she breathed. "I pray to God he has not been successful." Flames engulfed the wooden outbuildings and livestock were scattered everywhere. "We must hurry!"

"Wait!" Ruark cautioned. "This is not a time to race in without a plan, Istabelle. There could be outlaws hidden anywhere. We must proceed with caution."

As Mangan nodded in agreement, Istabelle shook her head. "No! We attack now, with the element of surprise. Horik will not think we could follow him so rapidly. We do not have a moment to spare!" She brought the reins down upon the mare's rump and sent her crashing down the slope, toward the monastery.

"Stop!" Ruark yelled. "Don't do this! Use your head. This is not a time to act impulsively and recklessly!"

"No, Istabelle!" Mangan shouted.

But she ignored them, flogging her mare even harder and maintained the lead. Istabelle would not let Horik kill the innocent priest! It was time she ended this fight between Horik and herself. If she could kill him before he caused any more harm, not only would she be free, she would be saving hundreds of other Dunhaven people as well as the monks and the priest.

The slope turned abruptly uphill and she leaned forward, urging her horse to greater effort. The terrain gave her the advantage, and she intended to reach Horik well before Mangan and Ruark reached her.

Ruark kicked his steed mercilessly, but he could not go any faster. His tactical mind raced, and fear spread through him with devastating force. The outlying area looked too unprotected. It appeared as if Horik had set some sort of trap. Suddenly he felt Péril flying alongside him. "Stop her!" he shouted. "Please! I can't lose her! Not now, when I have finally found her!"

The gyrfalcon surged forward, flapping her massive wings with immense power until she passed Istabelle's horse. She shrieked but Istabelle pressed forward. Péril did not hesitate. Striking talons first, she plunged at Istabelle's horse just as the pair reached the cleared area around the monastery.

The mare reared up, whinnying in fear. She twisted on her hind legs and tossed her head, trying to dislodge the attacking bird. Istabelle screamed and clung to the horse's neck, but the mare started to fall sideways.

"Istabelle!" Ruark cried as he saw her slip from her horse and land heavily on the ground. The mare was falling as well. In seconds Istabelle would be crushed. "Please God!" he screamed. "Save her!"

A flash of blinding light burst from deep inside the monastery walls. Stones were flung far afield and burning timbers were tossed about like kindling. The terrified mare twisted in midair, the force of the explosion sending her backward. She fell on her back, only inches from Istabelle's still form. The awful crunching of the horse's spine echoed down the valley. After one dreadful shudder, the mare was still.

Ruark and Mangan reached Istabelle and leapt from their steeds. Ruark rushed to Istabelle's side and checked for a pulse. "Wake up!" he pleaded. "Don't leave me!"

She stirred and blinked up at him. "It hurts," she whimpered. "My baby . . ."

"It's all right. You are all right."

"My baby!"

Ruark glanced down and saw blood staining the ground. "Oh no," he whispered. "I—Istabelle—"

"Am I losing my baby?"

Ruark clenched his hands. He felt so helpless. The horror in Istabelle's face was too much to bear. "No," he promised without thinking. "You won't lose it. Stay here. Don't move." He held her shoulders tightly and stared into her frightened eyes. "Tell me you will listen to me and will stay here! For once, do what is sensible and stay here!"

"The monks—the priest—"

"I will do what I do best. I will kill Horik. I haven't lived the life of a hired warrior for nothing. Let me help you this time. You are not alone. Trust me?"

"Be careful," she whispered.

He kissed her briefly, then surged to his feet. Several strides ahead he saw a crude trench dug into the earth with sharpened spikes lining the depths. "Death traps," he said as he pointed to them.

Mangan swung up on his mule. "She would have been impaled instantly had her mare continued forward." His normally kind face was tight with fury. "This man is evil."

Ruark jumped on his horse. "I am going to murder him."

Péril landed next to Istabelle when she struggled to sit up. "Go," Istabelle said to the men, sinking back into the grass. "Péril will stay with me. Hurry!"

The men carefully guided their steeds around the death traps, then set them racing up the hill. Screams drove them forward. The doorway of the monastery was wide open, its wooden frame burnt to the ground. Still mounted, Mangan led the way, with Ruark close behind. They ducked inside and their horses clattered through the stone hallways until they reached the main room, where the religious artifacts were stored. Several outlaws were stuffing items into satchels, but turned to face the mounted men in surprise.

Mangan roared with fury and charged forward, his sword swinging. Catching one off guard, he felled him with a powerful stroke, then turned to attack another. Ruark joined him and together they slaughtered the marauders. As blood splattered over the golden chalices, tears filled Mangan's eyes. "You will be punished for your greed," he hissed as he chopped off the hand of one outlaw. "For your desecration. Your destruction." He sliced the men unmercifully. "May your souls rot in hell!"

"Mangan!" Ruark shouted. "Come on! Leave them. They can do nothing more. We must find the monks and the priest!"

With a final blow that beheaded his last foe, Mangan yanked his horse around and followed Ruark through the hall toward the courtyard. Smoke billowed down the enclosed areas and the horses balked.

"It is coming from the kitchens," Mangan yelled. "The ovens must have exploded from the heat."

"Aye," Ruark agreed, wondering if the explosion that had saved Istabelle had truly been a moment of chance or divine intervention. He covered his mouth with his bent arm and kicked his horse. The steed whinnied in terror, but finally leapt forward. They clattered through the hall and burst into the courtyard, where the smoke swirled up and darkened the sky.

"Over there!" Mangan hollered, pointing to the small church where the monks held matins.

On the steps leading to the doorway, Sven swung his sword, desperately guarding the men that huddled inside. He fell to one knee as the force of a blocked attack shuddered up his arm. "No!" he shouted. "I will not let you inside. The men of God are not your enemies. Plunder the halls, but leave these men alone!"

"You fool," one of the outlaws bellowed. "It is the priest we have come for. Send him out and we will spare the others."

Sven staggered to his feet. "I have battled in many useless wars, and I have hated every moment of it, but today I praise the fates that taught me to fight. I will never let you kill the priest!"

"Then we will kill you first," the man replied and lunged at Sven.

"Stop!" Ruark shouted as he and Mangan galloped forward. The outlaws turned in surprise.

Taking advantage of their lapse, Sven sprang to plunge his blade into the outlaw. He glanced at Ruark in gratitude. "Once again you have come to save me," he yelled.

"No, Sven. If you have protected the priest, you have saved me!"

The remaining outlaws roared as Ruark and Mangan flanked them, pinning them between Sven's sword and their own. "You have fought your last battle," Ruark shouted. "Be prepared to die, for today your blood will flow!"

Mangan and Ruark were relentless, and Sven fought with more determination than he had ever shown on a battlefield. With merciless fury, the three men felled the marauders one by one until only two remained standing. Ruark pointed his bloody sword one of them.

'Where is Horik?" he demanded. "I have not seen ody."

outlaw shook his head. "He is not within the

monastery walls. He is waiting in the woods. He left the priest to us."

"Where?" Ruark asked frantically, thinking of Istabelle lying helpless and undefended. "Where is he hiding?"

The man shook his head. Without thinking, Ruark swung his broadsword and plowed a six-inch furrow into the man's side. With a stunned gasp, the man toppled over. Ruark swayed in the saddle. He closed his eyes, trying to stop himself from fainting with fear. How could he have been as reckless as Istabelle? He had done just what she had done—leapt into battle without thinking! He may have saved the priest, but his love was now at Horik's mercy!

The final outlaw stared at the swords and the three furious men. Glancing at his felled comrades, he raised his chin. "I will tell you nothing," he screamed. Raising his sword, he raced toward Ruark.

Ruark's eyes sprang open but his mind was moving sluggishly. Thoughts of Istabelle clouded his brain and he could not react quickly. As if his hand were filled with granite, he could not lift it to defend himself in time. The outlaw's sword swung unimpeded through the air, directly at his head.

Mangan shouted and lunged forward to protec Ruark, but he was too far away. He could not par the outlaw's thrust.

In the instant before the man's sword reached Ruark saw his life flicker in front of him. He flash of his mother's face, the hole where he hidden before she was killed, the streets had managed to survive . . . he saw Istabelle's glittering skin when he pulled her from the loch, and the sparkle in her silver eyes when she smiled. As if the world had slowed down, he leaned back, but the outlaw's blade rushed forward. It would sever his neck. He would die. The knowledge of his own death did not worry him, but he screamed for Istabelle, for the child she carried, for the love he knew he would not be able to give her.

He lifted his eyes and saw the church spire as the outlaw's sword swept down upon his head.

Chapter 23

Sven met the outlaw's sword thrust. The two blades clashed and sparks fell from the swords where they slid across each other, giving Ruark the split second he needed. His uncharacteristic sluggishness evaporated as he lifted his broadsword and plunged it into the attacker's gut. The outlaw dropped his weapon and clutched his abdomen, then fell forward, his face twisting with pain.

Ruark yanked his blade free and stared at Sven in amazement. "You did it," he whispered. "You battled like a true warrior."

"It's about time I did what you have been trying to teach me," Sven said with a smile.

Mangan laughed aloud. "That I lived to see the day that Ruark Haagen needed to be saved in battle! It is a miracle!"

"No, *that* is a miracle," Sven said as he gestured to the monks inside. They all kneeled in front of the altar, their heads bent in prayer while the priest stood in front of them, intoning verses.

"No one was killed?" Mangan asked incredulously.

Sven shook his head. "I'm sorry, but there was one death. Brother Francis was slain as he rang the warning bell. He managed to sound the alarm so the rest could seek sanctuary and I could defend them. He sacrificed himself for the others."

"God bless him," Mangan murmured.

Ruark spun around and headed for the courtyard entrance. "Istabelle is still out there, and Horik will find her. Our duty is not done."

Mangan handed his mule to Sven. "I will stay with the priest. You follow your brother."

"Aye." Sven jumped on the animal and followed Ruark through the hall and back out to the hilltop.

Horik stood above Istabelle, his eyes blazing with madness. "With you dead, I will inherit everything!"

"You can't kill me," she gasped as she tried to shuffle backward. "The Dunhavens made you promise not to hurt me!"

"It no longer matters. I know you tried to get the priest to annul the marriage, and my comrades are murdering that bastard as we speak, but there is no way to ensure that neither you nor your friends will not try with another priest, or the king himself. As of this moment, you are legally my wife, and upon your death all your possessions become mine. Thus, ⸱ is in my best interest to kill you before you find a ⸱y to escape me again."

Istabelle struggled to sit upright, but the pain in her abdomen was excruciating. "No! Don't do this!"

"Why not? It is just revenge for what you have done to me." He raised his battle-axe and shook it above her head. "You humiliated me, you thwarted me and then you maimed me in an unmentionable way. You deserve to die, but even more, you deserve to die knowing that I will destroy everything you ever cared about. I will rape your land and starve your people."

"Then you are a fool! In wreaking petty revenge upon the innocent, you will only hurt yourself."

Infuriated that she continued to argue with him, Horik kicked her, making her scream in agony.

"Something wrong?" Horik taunted her. "You look like you are in pain. Does your belly ache? Is there something you forgot to tell your husband?"

She cried out and scuttled backward.

He squatted down and peered at her. "You look rounder than I remember. Could you be carrying a babe? Did that man, Haagen, trespass upon my wife?"

"I don't know what you are talking about," Istabelle whimpered.

"I think you do, and I think I will enjoy your death all the more, knowing that you are helpless to protect your child from my blade. What irony! You made me unable to father children, so I will take yours from you."

"There is no honor in killing the weak and help

less! Let me live and bear the child, then murder me. I will give you everything you want, just let the babe live!"

He narrowed his gaze and pulled a spear out of his pack. Taking careful aim, he threw it at her. It thudded into her thigh.

Istabelle bloodied her lip trying desperately not to scream. He was evil beyond all reason. She was not going to plead for her life, for he would not listen. Instead, she would die as she had lived, strong, wild and free.

"I am going to kill you piece by piece. I want to see you suffer as you have made me suffer." He lifted another spear. "This one is going into your hand."

"Not unless you can throw it from the grave," Ruark growled from behind him.

Horik spun around in shock. "You!" he gasped. "Will you always haunt me?"

Ruark advanced ahead of Sven, his sword glinting in the light. "Guard her as you would guard me," he told his brother. "I will fight this monster—alone."

Horik flung his remaining spear, but Ruark darted nimbly to the right. The weapon shuddered harmlessly into the ground as Ruark laughed. The sound was dark and menacing, and Horik's eyes widened.

"You don't have any more spears," Ruark informed him. "There is no coward's way out. Raise ur blade and fight like a man. Fight me, not a unded woman lying helpless at your feet."

"No, Ruark! Your side! Your wound will open!"

Istabelle struggled to regain her feet, but Sven gripped her arm and held her still.

Ignoring her warning, Ruark lunged forward, slicing Horik's arm before the other man had time to react.

Horik scrambled backward and parried the next thrust using the handle of his battle-axe.

"You dare to threaten my woman and my child," Ruark warned as he pressed forward. "You will rue every strike against her." He stabbed with his sword, and the first several inches of his blade sank into Horik's chest.

Horik howled in pain and yanked away, clutching his bleeding muscles. In a rage he swung his axe in a circle above his head and flung it at Ruark.

Ruark braced himself and chopped the air with his massive broadsword. The intricate scrollwork on the blade that had originally captured Istabelle's attention glinted in the sunlight for an instant, then the crash of the metal against the head of the axe reverberated over the hillside. The axe head splintered off, spinning harmlessly to the ground.

Stunned, Horik froze as Ruark pointed his sword.

"Prepare," Ruark snarled. "Make your peace with God or die without absolution."

Horik turned and ran. In fury, Ruark took after him, intending to tackle him, but Istabelle flung off Sven's restraint and leapt to her feet. As Ruark raced past her, she grabbed his arm. "No!" she screamed. "Remember the pits!"

Ruark stumbled with Istabelle's weight hanging or

to him. Then they heard Horik scream, his body impaled upon the sharpened ends of the spears that pointed up from the bottom of the death traps. His eyes bulged and his arms and legs waved helplessly in the air. With each movement, he sank deeper onto the spears. His screams echoed louder, then descended into pitiful wails.

Sven peered down at the bottom of the pit. "He will die an agonizingly slow death," he said.

"So be it," Ruark answered as he held Istabelle in his arms.

She trembled as she touched his face. "Are you all right?"

"Yes, now that I know you are safe."

Istabelle nodded gratefully, then went limp.

"What is wrong?" Ruark cried out as he held her up. She was deathly pale and blood soaked the ground around her feet.

"The baby—" she whispered.

"No!" he shouted. "Not now! Not like this!" He gathered her into his arms and frantically kissed her face. "Promise me, Istabelle. Promise me you will not die. I need you!"

"I love you," she answered him and then her head lolled.

For the second time, Ruark asked the monks to mend someone he cared about. This time, however, he would not leave her side. Even after the bleeding slowed, he clutched her hand and would not budge. She fluttered in and out of awareness, alternately asking about the baby or Ruark. Each time he told her they were both fine, but she didn't seem to hear him.

By the second day, she woke enough to touch Ruark's face. "Did I lose the baby?" she asked again.

"The monks say that the child still grows within you."

"Where is Péril? She flew away from me right before Horik arrived. She has never left my side before."

Ruark grinned. "She found me and led me to you."

She smiled and touched her abdomen. She still suffered intermittent pains. "Are you certain the babe is safe?"

His gaze slid away from hers. The monks had said only that they did not know yet, but he couldn't bear to tell her something so terrible. She needed support. He would carry the burden of uncertainty and let her spend her energy healing. "Is anything certain?" he finally replied.

"I am certain that I love you," she answered softly.

"And I love you." He smiled. "I hope the child thrives. Do you realize that I can marry you now that Horik is dead?"

"I want to get married on the beach."

"Whatever you want, sweetling."

They stood side by side, facing the ocean. A dramatic change in weather had brought a warm, southern breeze that skated across the water and teased their hair. Istabelle and Ruark held hands as they faced the priest. Istabelle's white dress fluttered around her ankles and pressed against her flat abdomen with a gentle caress. She had lost the baby, and even several months later, she still ached for the child that would never be born.

Ruark had held her, comforting her through terrible nights and guilt-ridden days, but together they had weathered the pain. Their loss had drawn them closer together, and they both knew how deeply they could depend upon the other for love and support.

. Today, they gazed into each other's eyes and looked to the future. Behind them, Mangan nodded his approval. He stood shoulder to shoulder with his father, the Earl of Kirkcaldy, and his mother, the infamous Countess Matalia. Tomorrow he would tell his parents of his intention to travel far from Scotland in God's name. His restlessness was unlike Istabelle's. He did not need to battle the evil in the world with reckless abandon, but he did feel an unfulfilled calling to find the one thing his life was still missing. Perhaps it was God; perhaps it was not. Perhaps he would take his vows after he completed his journey. But whatever he chose to do, he would find it far away from these shores.

Istabelle's parents also stood behind the couple. Xanthier, the displaced son of the former Earl of Kirkcaldy, braced his feet apart as if the beach sand were the deck of a ship. His powerful gaze stared intently at Ruark as he debated whether the warrior was good enough for his only daughter. He shifted positions, becoming agitated, until his blind wife, Alannah, placed a soothing hand on his arm.

"It is no longer your duty to protect her," she murmured. "She is a grown woman with her own needs and desires. We have done what we can to teach her about what is important in this world. Trust her and trust her choices."

Xanthier grunted and patted his wife's hand, knowing that, as always, she was right.

Other guests filled the area, many dressed in elaborate clothing as befitted their elevated stations, and many dressed in simple clothing as befitted theirs. Sailors, aristocrats and peasants alike smiled as Istabelle spoke words of love and obedience and laughed aloud as the priest asked Ruark to repeat the same words back. All those present, however, bowed their heads in awe at the glowing emotion surrounding the couple. Their love was as powerful as they were. It was physical, dynamic and all-encompassing. It was as strong as the earth beneath their feet and as delicate as the wind against their faces.

The Adventuress bobbed in the ocean behind them, ready to set sail, but now she sported an official flag of Scotland, which fluttered proudly from the mast. The king had granted the couple leave to visit Scotland's outlying areas in order to ensure the people's safety and security. Now that Istabelle's dower Dunhaven lands were flourishing under fair management, Istabelle and Ruark could concentrate on helping others. With her fierce ideals, his strong backing and their unending love, they were invincible.

Sven leaned against a rock, his leg still giving him intermittent pain. He would always have a limp, but he felt it was a fair trade for the blessings God had granted his brother. He grinned as Ruark and Istabelle kissed under the raised hands of the priest, announcing their eternal union. Although such bliss was beautiful to see, he was confident that he would never be snared in love's web.

He walked forward and congratulated the newly married couple, but they barely heard his words, due to their mutual self-absorption.

"I have a wedding gift to give to you," Istabelle whispered as she stared into Ruark's onyx eyes. Her healed nose listed slightly to the right, giving her beautiful face just enough imperfection to make Ruark love her even more.

"I have no need of gifts from you," Ruark answered. "You are present enough."

"Nevertheless, I have one for you. Do you want to know what it is?"

He laughed. "Of course. What surprise have you been harboring?"

She smiled, took his hand and placed it on her newly rounding belly.

All your favorite romance writers
in one place

SIGNET ECLIPSE